To Yvonne,
Hope to see you
guys &

Shan Davis

Nothing Like Friends

Nothing Like Friends

Shannon N. Davis

To order copies of this book, book club meeting and signings contact:

DeLoach-Davis Publishing
P.O. Box 1858
Brick, NJ 08723
www.DeLoach-DavisPublishing.com

Email: SELFPUBLISHED04@AOL.COM

Dedicated to the memory of
Dorothy DeLoach
Richard DeLoach
Robin Campbell
Charles Campbell
Lettie Parham
Connie Crudup
Mary Reed

Acknowledgements

First, I would like to thank the Creator for giving me the insight and power to write. My beautiful children for giving me the drive to go for it. Zarah, my princess, you have been there since I typed my first word. I was blessed to have you. You were a great baby during nursing school and I only pray that you don't remember that I went back to school when you were just six days old. Thank god you slept all night. And to my sweet Elijah, it's funny how your name is all throughout the book before you were even thought of. Your birth gave me the inspiration to take my book out of the computer and put it on paper. Mommy loves you both dearly.

To my husband for letting me get crazy. To me, part of being a good husband is letting the wife get nuts sometimes. My male characters were partly based on you. I love you, honey. I'm glad that I was your first novel that you have ever read.

To my mother, Princess, for always being my biggest fan. I wish all mothers and daughters have our bond. I'm glad that you loved the book so much that you gave it to two of your friends against my wishes. But I'm truly glad they loved it.

To my first reader and dear friend, Annemarie Perry, thank you for the feedback while I was putting this together chapter by chapter. Can you believe I am finally here?

To Aunt Hope and Aunt Carol, no, I did not base any of the characters on people we know.

To Candy, thanks for enjoying it and telling me what you thought and not holding back.

To Venita, my nutty friend, thanks for saying that you are proud of me. You truly are the dark side of me.

To Crystal, Tesha, Arlene, Samarah, Lawaun and Sahr I love you dearly.

To Lichelle, thanks for being the best big sister in the world.

To my neices, Dionna, Amira, Arielle, Brittnay, Auntie Shannon loves you. Remember to follow your dreams!

To my brother, Chris, keep your head. This could be our big "break".

To my nephews Raynard Jr, Myshon, Jaden, Tyjuan and Shon, may you grow up to be responsible and respectable young men.

To the ones that I speak to on a regular basis and to the ones that—God forgive me—I don't, thanks for the support. There're so many of you that I could not name all; nonetheless, you are and always will be thought of.

I would also like to thank Dr. Flannigan, my seventh-grade creative writing teacher, for telling me that I had a knack for writing.

To C&B Books, Brenda and Carol, thanks for having a good thing going and the fair made me want to branch out and start my own business. I met some positive people there. Sonya Harris and Erica Martin, our names will be in lights one day. Keep doing and inspiring like you are.

To Ujima-Nia, thanks for being the first book club to have me. I'm glad I joined.

Crystal, Tesha and Candy, thanks girls for helping me at the fairs and knowing that you will continue to be there is a blessing. The first cover holds special meaning for me.

To Eli, thanks for taking a chances with me and for a nice cover.

To romance, thanks for reminding me that there are still men out there that can be romantic—just when I had given up hope.

And to all the readers who purchased the book, I hope you enjoy reading it just as much as I enjoyed writing it. Look out for book two.

Shannon N. Davis

Chapter 1
Alexis

Today is the day I have waited my whole life for: my wedding day. I am sitting here awaiting my horse and carriage. People told me to take out the horse and carriage, but I know this will be the only time I will ever get married and I want the day to be right out of a fairytale.

Everything is going smoothly. I have an immaculate wedding dress. No one would ever know that I got the dress for ninety-nine dollars at David's Bridal. When I saw it I said it was plain, but it was the exact style I wanted. Even the saleswoman had been shocked that I walked out of the store with such a plain wedding gown. I tried on the designer brands, and I admit they were beautiful, but a coworker of mine once told me that you would know what dress is for you because any other dress you saw after that would not make an impression. I wanted this dress and I bought it. I loved the way it accented my breasts and showed off my tiny waist. Off the shoulder with a bell skirt, it was the purest white satin material I had ever seen—no designs, and nothing extravagant. I knew it would be plain only until my mother got hold of it. I knew she would turn it into a dress that Cinderella would kill to have. And she did just that.

She designed a sheer overcoat to go with the dress and then embroidered it with a rose design and a diamond in each of the roses. And she did the same with my veil and the bell of the dress. She had even somehow managed to put the same design on my shoes.

My three bridesmaids, who had been my very best friends for over thirty years, wore slim, form-fitting, spaghetti-strapped lavender gowns. Since I am close to all of them and had not wanted to choose among them for the maid of honor, all of them became my bridesmaids or maids of honor. To match my dress in a slightly noticeable way, my mother had made them all sheer stoles with the same rose and diamond design. They looked beautiful. I made sure everyone's hair was in an upswept hairdo. The one thing I hate is when a wedding party does not look uniform—when it looks unorganized and quickly put together. And this day had to be perfect for it would be one of the best days of my life.

I sit in my horse and carriage feeling like a real princess. People on the streets look and wave at me as if they knew me. I smile and wave back like I am the newest winner of the Miss America pageant. After all, I am about to marry the man of my dreams, Mr. Aaron McKnight. Aaron and I have been together for four years, and from the first time I met him, I had known that I would be his lifelong soul mate.

How could I not be? This man makes sure my every need is taken care of. He hates to see a frown on my face. And the truth of the matter is, I do not ask for much. He just gives just as I give to him. This is the finest man I have ever met. Physically perfect in every way: six feet three inches tall, has the purest dark chocolate skin that could make a diabetic go straight into a coma, the strongest facial structure, and to top it off, the prettiest straight white teeth and the sharpest connected goatee. And if you want to talk about the body, he has the broadest shoulders—my entire wedding party could lay their heads on his shoulders. He dresses to impress, and he does not even need to wear name brands to look fine and expensive. My future husband has the ability to smell good without using cologne.

I am in love with this man—mind, body, and soul. I have never and will never love another. We have made love numerous times, and every time we do, it feels like he is touching me for the first time. I mean, this man can give me an orgasm that could make me change religions. With the seductive look in his eyes and the moisture from licking his full lips, I am a crack fiend. And he knows it. He enjoys making me devour all the love that he gives me.

I just cannot wait for the honeymoon. We have tickets for the Atlantis in the Bahamas for a week and after that we will go to our new home. We closed on our house last week and decided that neither of us would move in until after the honeymoon. So we cut our two-week vacation in half so we could use the week to get things moved in.

My home is a three-bedroom bi-level house. It has two bathrooms, a finished basement, laundry room, and a huge yard. My house's best feature is the pool in the backyard. I love it! It had been a total steal. I fell in love with it at first sight. I have everything planned for it. I know how I would fill that house with children and love. Two to three kids are what we talked about, and tonight is when we will start trying. And to know that today is the day we will start the life that every decent man and woman would want, I could just die today. Today is the day that I realized life is good. A dream wedding, a wonderful husband, a great family, and friends— I know for a fact that life is good.

I'm here at the church and the lot is full of cars and people are inside waiting to see me. I must admit that I am nervous, but I am ready for this. I was greeted by one of my maids of honor, Sidney. She looked wonderful. I love Sidney. She had always been the one of all my friends that kept a straight head. She always had her life together. She has been married to Marcus for seventeen years. Since high school, these two have looked at each other like it is the first time they've met. And now they share a home, a restaurant, and three beautiful children.

She greeted me with a tight hug and a kiss. "Girl, you look so beautiful! I am so happy for you!" She quickly took me to where the other girls were. In a silly tone she said, "Here comes the bride all dressed in . . ." She stopped suddenly and put her pointer finger on her head. "Now, should we be wearing white or black?"

We all let out a laugh. Simone, who for some reason had a chip on her shoulder, did not laugh. She said she was a bit down because her date had given her an excuse for not being with her today. She looked me over and said, "I think black. But no one would have to know how you get down, girl!" Then she laughed and gave me a hug and a kiss. Simone is Sidney's fraternal twin sister. They came from the same womb but you would never know they were sisters. Not only do they not look alike, they also act and handle situations in totally different ways.

Simone is brown sugar of the set, while Sidney is caramel coated. Simone acted like she was from the streets whereas Sidney acted like she had been raised in the Valley. She always has the right thing to say, and has kept the same man for seventeen years and never had another. She had meant what she said when we were kids that the first man she slept with would be the only one she has for life. Meanwhile, Simone seems to enjoy everyone else's man but her own. Sad to say she has never had a meaningful relationship even for a little while.

Tracy came to me, straightened me up, and gave me the motherly once-over. "Now we have about fifteen minutes until show time. We all look perfect. Right out of a wedding magazine. I think you need a touch up on your makeup." She signaled for Simone to get her makeup bag. "I think this will do. Alexis, you are so beautiful." I saw tears build up in her eyes. She must be remembering when she and her late husband Malcolm had gotten married. They married thirteen years ago and had a son. Malcolm died in a car accident before his son turned two. She never recovered from that. Nor did she ever have a man again, not even a one-night stand. She spent her life raising her son and building her advertising firm. To this day she still wears her wedding ring and the only way that ring would come off is if her feelings for the next man she meets overpowers what she had felt for Malcolm. She believes no other man in the world could take the place of Malcolm. And that she could never love another like she had loved him.

"We don't have time for the tears of the past, Tracy," Simone said with a smile. "We must look toward the future for Alexis and Aaron."

"I know that's right!" my mother said as she made sure her designs were true to form. She went over each of us to make sure we wore her creations the way she saw fit. "I am so thankful to God that I am here to see this day."

"Oh, Mommy, please do not get mushy. Tracy just fixed my makeup," I said holding back the tears.

"Well, you are my only baby girl, and if I want to make a fuss, then I will." She wiped away her tears. "Aaron looks so handsome out there. He seems nervous but he is holding on fine. As a matter of fact, all the groomsmen look so fine. Humph . . . if I were younger I may have to make a move on one of those fine black men out there myself." She walked to the door, turned around, and put her hands on her hips. "'Cause I still have it you know. You young girls are not the only ones who could still land a man. But for now, I am going to send your father in for you. I hope you're ready, girls, because it is show time."

As I bent down on my knees to pray, my girls prayed with me in silence. I stood up. "I'm as ready as I will ever be, girls." And then we reached for a group hug.

As we were huddled together my father walked in. "Is this a private moment or can the father of the bride take his beautiful daughter and give her to a man that better not disappoint me?" His suit fit him perfectly. Its white color and his bronze tone went well together. I can see why my mother married him and would not let him go. For a man close to his sixties he could still make Billy Dee weak in the knees. He looked at me as if he were about to lose me forever. "You know, I knew this day would come, but I did not know it would come this soon."

"Daddy . . ."

"No, let me finish. I like Aaron and I have had my talk with him already and I told him that under no circumstances would I sit back and allow him to hurt my baby girl." He gave me the most tender hug. "When I walk you down that aisle and give you to him, he has to take on the same responsibility I had with you. I never let you down." He grabbed my face and looked me straight in the eyes. "Have I ever let you down?"

Like the little girl in me, I gave him the puppy face and sad eyes. "No, Daddy. You have never let me down and I know Aaron will not either. I love him, Daddy. And he loves me. Watch, you will see just the man he is and why I have to marry him." And I kissed him on the cheek like I always do.

"He better! Because I have not put a young buck's head to bed in years and I will be glad to show him that this old man still has it." He entangled my arms in his and we stood outside the sliding doors to the altar. My father was so happy but heartbroken and having a difficult time with this whole wedding nonsense. He never said why but for some reason he had a sadness about him, but kept the reason for it to himself to keep me from being unhappy. He paid for 85 percent of the wedding expenses. He said he would have paid for the whole thing, but he wanted to see what kind of stock Aaron was made from.

My heart is pounding as our cue came on. The wedding march. All of the maids of honor were there and the rose petals from the flower girls were on the red carpet waiting for me. My first sight was of Aaron. He looked at me as if it were the first time he had ever seen me. I could not believe how handsome and sexy he looked. He gave me that crooked smile that always made my juices run. The closer we got, the tighter my father held me. I gently massaged his hand to let him know that I am going to be all right.

Standing next to Aaron was his best friend since infancy, Elijah or EJ. EJ is just about the same height as Aaron, about six feet and one inch, and had Hershey-brown skin. EJ has the ladies in all kinds of traps when he wines and dines them. He loves that sort of thing. I think it makes him feel like the king or something. But he always says, "A man is supposed to love the woman that he is with. Give her all that she deserves, but when she is no longer worthy, cut her ass off!" He is currently single because his ex-girlfriend, Shelley, decided she wanted to see other people. I know he will have no problem meeting a woman here at this wedding.

Reverend Collin Davis was giving the sermon and smiled at the upcoming union of the young couple in front of him. "Ladies and gentlemen, we are gathered here today . . ."

I could hear what the reverend was saying, but I was more focused on the look on Aaron's face. He looked troubled. I know that face but I figured it was the cold feet that everyone experienced.

Reverend Davis asked, "Do you, Alexis, take Aaron to be your lawfully wedded husband?"

I looked at Aaron and my eyes showed him all the love that a woman could give a man. "I do."

"And do you, Aaron, take Alexis to be your beautiful and lawfully wedded bride?"

Sweat beads dripped from his head. "Uh . . . Uh . . ." He took a gulp of his own saliva. "Uh . . . Lex, can I talk to you in the chambers a minute?"

From the crowd came a gasp of disbelief.

"Aaron, what is wrong?" I said, trying my damndest not to sound worried. "Is everything OK?"

"Please, just come with me." He grabbed me and we walked to the chambers. I could tell this was not going to be good. He began to pace the floor and then looked at me like this was the last thing he wanted to do. "Lex, I just want to get something off my chest or I can't go through with this."

"Aaron, you are scaring me. We have a church full of family and friends and this is not in the damn script." I took a deep breath and prepared myself for what could be next. "Whatever this is, it must be big for you to stop the wedding."

He looked me straight in the eyes. "You know I would never want to hurt you . . ." He shook his head. "I had an affair."

My heart dropped to the floor. I knew I was dreaming at this point. "Please, God, tell me you did not say what I thought you said."

"You heard correctly. I did not want to tell you like this but . . ."

"But hell! You cheated on me? You stupid son of a—"

Just then I heard my parents outside the door banging on it and yelling for us to open up. I couldn't deal with my parents right now. I just couldn't. There is no way I could look them in the eye and tell them that the man I told them would love and cherish me forever was a fraud. It was too much to bear at this time.

But my father was insistent. "Alexis, open the door, sweetheart. Now!"

"Daddy, just a moment. Everything is OK!" I turned to Aaron. "How could you? I thought I meant the world to you." I could not stop the tears from flowing. He had shattered my whole world in just a second. I could see he was having a hard time getting this out and I was not going to make it easy for him. "Who? When?"

He turned away from me. "It was a while ago and at first it was nothing but harmless flirting but then . . ."

"But then? You had to fuck her and see what the pussy was like, huh? Is that what you were going to say?"

"No, not really. There was more to it than that. We better open the door before your parents bust it down." He went to the door and opened it. "I guess you want to know what is going on in here."

My father had a murderous look on his face. "Son, you better have a damn good explanation for this. You are humiliating my daughter!"

"I know, Mr. Blackmon, you must be confused but I have made a terrible mistake." He took a deep breath and took a step back. "I had an affair on Alexis. And I'm sorry but I can't go through with this."

The whole church audience gasped for air. "Aah!"

My parents turned beet red. I cried hearing the truth again.

My father balled up Aaron's tuxedo in his hands. "I know you must have fallen and bumped your head! Are you crazy? Boy, I could kill you with my bare hands right now! Is this a joke?"

My mother tried to calm down the situation. "Richard, please! Don't do this! Richard!"

I could not say one word. All I could do was cry and try not to go out of my mind, but I was slipping from reality. "Aaron, why in the hell did you wait 'til now? Whatever happened to just telling me when it happened? Or is it still going on?"

When he said nothing, I got my answer. This affair was current as we spoke. That right there sealed my coffin. That also made Daddy lose his mind. He began smacking Aaron like he would a rag doll. Aaron seemed to just let him smack him up as if Daddy were his pimp. Once Daddy got him on the floor, Reverend Davis came busting in to see what all the commotion was about. "What is going on in here? This is the house of the Lord and whatever is the problem can be solved with patience and prayer."

"We can do all the praying for his health 'cause I'm about to kill this fool!" my father said.

Just then, Simone came rushing through the crowd. "Please stop! Stop! This is the father of my child! Please stop!" She ran to Aaron's side and tried to shield him from Daddy.

Again the audience gasped in disbelief. "Aah!"

The whole room stopped and I think my jaw fell to the ground. My best friend of thirty-plus years just said she was carrying my fiancé's baby. When did this happen? Where had I been when it took place? How could they be so tasteless? Why had they let me plan this wedding when they were creeping behind my back?

I looked at them both. "Simone, you were my friend, what were you thinking?"

She stood up and looked me dead in the eye. "It just happened, Alexis. I hate that I hurt you but I love him."

I could not believe what I just heard. "You what? How could you love him?"

"I just do. And I am going to have this baby." She turned to help Aaron off the floor. "Baby, are you OK?"

At that point my father charged toward him and gave him an upper cut that Tyson could not have withstood. "And then you have the nerve to talk sweet to your mistress! Man, I outta—" My father's brother, Roger, grabbed his arm and took him off Aaron. My father kept a tight grip on Aaron's neck, "You coward! You hurt my daughter and I told you I would see to it that you would physically hurt the way my daughter is hurting, didn't I?"

EJ stepped in to try and break it up. "Aaron! C'mon, man!" He continued to struggle to separate the two men.

My Uncle Roger got hold of my father. "Come on, Rich! Let him go! I think he has the point by now!" He was able to loosen my father's grip. "This poor excuse of a man needs the ass whoopin' but your daughter is hurting and needs your attention more right now. Now, we have a church full of people who now know what is going on. We have to do damage control. Rich, take your eyes off him for a minute and listen to me. Come on. We are in a church."

EJ helped Aaron up and tried to make sense of what was going on. "Yo, A, man, you did this? Are you nuts? Alexis was your woman that you pondered over and this is how you treat her?"

"E, man, I messed up but I have to deal with what I have with Simone right now. Therefore, I could not marry Alexis." He looked up and stepped back.

My father walked toward Aaron. "I had a small doubt about you and I was hoping that it was just that I didn't want my daughter to marry, but I never thought the man she is so in love with would destroy her on her wedding day. How can she recover?"

Aaron caught his breath. "Mr. Blackmon, I deserve what just happened here. I am sorry but I made a mistake and this baby changes everything." He looked at me. "Lex . . ."

"Alexis," I said.

"Alexis, I am so sorry. I know I can't begin to make this up. But she is carrying my child. I have to take responsibility for that."

My mother held me and looked at him and Simone. "Girl, you dressed up and pretended to be a friend and all the while you were sleeping with your best friend's man. Is that why you had an attitude all day?"

"Yes, ma'am." She put her head down. Then she looked up and noticed her mother.

Simone's mother and my mother are best friends. Mrs. Campbell is a plump woman that was just as down to earth as my mother is. When she saw what was going on in here she was ashamed to speak but had to say something, "Oh, my dear daughter. Monie, why? This is so wrong. Look at what you created!"

"Momma, I'm sorry but I can't help who I have fallen in love with. Why doesn't anyone understand?" She wiped the blood from Aaron's mouth.

"That is because you crossed the friendship line. I know I raised you better than that. Sidney would never do such a thing." She turned and walked toward Sidney who was in tears alongside my mother and trying to hold me. "This is your best friend, Simone. Or should I say, *was* your best friend."

I couldn't take much more of this. I had to get away from this whole scene. I picked up my dress and was very unsuccessful in holding back the tears. "Well, there isn't going to be a wedding." I walked to Aaron and spit in his face. "That is for all the dreams you shot to hell. Don't ever call or bother me again." And I walked to the door. "And as far as the house is concerned, consider yourself homeless!" And I walked to the front door of the church. But I had to say one last thing to Simone before I left. So I stormed back to the chambers and everyone was clearing out and she was the last one I saw. "Oh, and, Simone, I want you to hold something for me for you to remember our friendship by." And I punched the hell out of her and she fell to the floor and only her new man, my ex-fiancé, went to her rescue.

I let my parents address my guests because I will have to face them sooner or later. I tracked down the limo driver and told him to drive as far as he could. I had no destination, but I knew that I wanted to get away from everyone and be alone. The best and worst days of my life all in the same day. That is enough to make you want to throw in the towel. All I could say was, "Congratulations to me!" And I let the driver drive and the tears flow.

Chapter 2
Simone

Aaron took me home and I knew he was going to try and find Alexis. I was really upset over it 'cause I feel like his place is now with me. He was changing out of his tuxedo and I could not help but inquire, "Are you going to find Alexis?"

He made a sigh of annoyance. "No, I'm going to send EJ to find her."

"For what? You know she wants to be alone. Besides she most likely does not want to see you or Elijah." I walked to the closet where he was changing. "Are you sorry that you told her?"

"Well, Monie, I hurt her and I chose the wrong day to tell her. How would you feel if I did it to you?" He walked away from me and started putting on his shoes. "We had a past and I ended it like a jackass. The least I can do is make sure she is all right."

"Alexis will not kill herself, Aaron."

"Please do not tell me you are jealous, because that would really be hypocritical." He stood up. "We knew this day would come and now it is here. Only this time there is a baby in the equation."

I immediately got on the defensive. "Are you trying to say that I planned it this way? 'Cause I didn't get pregnant by myself. I can recall you being there every time we made love."

"You know I didn't want you to get pregnant, Simone. But since you are, I have to do what I have to do, don't I?" He put on his jean jacket that Alexis had bought for him. "Get some rest. I will be back as soon as I get in touch with EJ."

I had to run behind him. "Aaron, I love you. You know that, don't you?" I grabbed his face and looked him straight in the eyes. "I love you, Aaron. I know today was rough for you and all of us but it was going to happen sooner or later. This baby had nothing to do with it."

The look in his eyes became cold, like I had said something drastically wrong. "You just do not get it! I was going to marry Alexis today! The one real thing that stopped me was this baby that you are carrying."

I backed up from him and was in total disbelief. "You would have married Alexis if I weren't pregnant? You were never going to tell her, were you?"

His patented silent treatment was always his answer when he could not speak the truth.

"Aaron, do you love me?" I asked as the tears flowed from my eyes. He opened the door. "I have to go."

"Answer me!" I yelled.

"Not now. Please, not now. I will talk with you when I return. Is that OK with you?"

"If you did not already get eight black eyes from Richard Blackmon, I would give you one. But for now the ones you have are enough." And I walked away from the door. And felt like a fool when he just walked out.

We had never planned to have an affair or to get pregnant. That part I did all myself. I knew he would have married her if I were not pregnant. And when I told him last week, I thought he would have called it off then, but he didn't. I know I should have said something, but how could I tell my best friend of thirty-plus years that I had been sleeping with her fiancé for four months? I had helped her plan and organize her wedding. I had listened to her complain when things were not going right and watched her hug and kiss the man I had fallen in love with.

So you could imagine what I was going through when she walked down the aisle and she said "I do." And when he did not say the same, I wanted to scream "Yes!" But I kept my composure. I know Aaron loves me and right now he is just confused and hurt for hurting the woman he had *once* loved. But it is my turn to shine. My sister Sidney is married, and I want to be. I have watched people fall in love and I want it to be me now. I want children and to own a home. He is the right man for the job. I know Alexis will fight him on the house, so I guess we will be on the hunt for our own little house of love. This was my turn to have a man that loves me. He shut his wedding down to be with me and that should count for something. We have some issues to work out and we will work them out.

xoxoxoxoxoxo

I can't believe that one of my dearest friends has gone through something as devastating as this. She is the last person who should have had this done to. She loved Aaron with all her heart, and well, we thought he felt the same. Though I felt sorry for Alexis, I could not help but be grateful to God for giving me a husband that I am still married to. Marcus is the man for me and has always been since high school.

As I am here at my vanity in a wrap brushing my hair, I could see him looking at me with love in his eyes. I sometimes act like I do not see him doing this just so I could see how long he would watch me. But tonight I couldn't go on with the charade. I walked to my side of the bed and lay next to him. "What a day, huh?"

"You can say that again. Oh man, how could Aaron do that? He messed up a good thing with Alexis for Simone?"

I got a bit offended. "And what is wrong with my sister?"

He backed off me. "I am not dogging your sis, but Simone is a little bit out there. Alexis devoted her time to Aaron and loved him like no other." He stroked my hair like he always does. "I mean cheating is one thing, but doing it with your girl's best friend and telling her at the altar is something altogether different."

I had to agree with him. They could have chosen someone else to have an affair with but instead they had wanted to make a Jerry Springer episode. I must admit that Alexis had handled it better than some of these other women out here would have. Simone is lucky that Alexis had not mopped the floor with her ass. So I turned toward Marcus. "Marcus, I love you. And you are so right about this. Simone and Aaron have messed up terribly. It just made me think of how blessed we are to have each other and our children."

"Speaking of children, you are finally going to be an auntie." He gave a chuckle. "She tightened her claws in him with that. If you want to know the truth, I think he would have just slept with her and never said a word if she were not pregnant. How much do you want to bet that that little bit of info will come out later?"

"I never gave that a thought! Oh, Simone, what were you thinking? Don't these women out here know that a baby will just make them

thirty pounds heavier and alone? When will they learn?"
He started touching me with a naughty look in his eyes. His hand caressed between my thighs and up to my love triangle. He knows how to use his hands and lips and he has a thing where he softly kisses my neck and face. I've never turned this man down and I do not think I ever will. I gave into his love gestures and lay down next to him. I wrapped my arms around his neck and let the love begin.

xoxoxoxoxoxo

I have so many deadlines before Monday—it is ridiculous. Coming home from the wedding that never happened was exhausting. I wonder if I would have been this tired if the wedding had gone through and I had danced all night with my date, Jerome. He is my assistant at my advertising firm. He is a nice man that has been a huge asset to my firm. That man can get us out of a tight situation and can land the most difficult accounts that have made our fiscal year immaculate. There are times when I wonder what his problem is because he is single and has been for the last two years.

My thing is that I have a twelve-year-old son, Malcolm Jr., who is my main concern. I want to be a good mother to him. With the way men run around here cheating and beating on their women, I'd rather be alone. Then you have these men that want you to take care of them. Don't let them find out you have some cash and a home. They will do their laundry and never leave. I will not have that mess in my home and around my son. I will only have a man that has some morals and respect for himself and everyone around him. That is about something. One who knows what he wants in life and that is not all scatterbrained. That is the kind of man I want Malcolm to become. That is the man his father was. Oh, how I miss that man.

He would have been really proud of his son. Malcolm Jr. is medium height like him. He keeps those fuzzy eyebrows and that wide smile like his. He even walks like him. He would definitely be proud of the grades Malcolm gets in school. He always maintains an A-B average and stays on the honor roll. I only scold him for the normal things that boys do— not cleaning the room and saving his homework until he has played at least fifty games on the Playstation. Other than that, he is an all-around good kid. I could not have asked for a better son.

As I get into bed, my son comes in my room. "I thought you were asleep."

He climbed into bed with me. "Mom, how do you think Aunt Lexi is doing now?"

I put my arms around him. "I think she is hurting now but I know she will come back OK."

"That is messed up, what happened. I thought I was watching *All My Children*, or something. I could have punched Aaron myself but Mr. Blackmon is the man!"

"All right now, that is not nice." I kissed him on the forehead.

"Mom, you have to admit that he kicked Aaron's butt!" He jumped up and started boxing like Rich Blackmon. "Seriously, Mom, can I ask a question?"

"Can I stop you?"

"No. Are you ever going to get married again?"

I was shocked that he asked me this. It had never bothered him before that I was not married. I sat up. "Why do you ask, Malcolm?"

"Well, I think you should have a husband or at least a boyfriend. I want you to be happy."

"I am happy and me not having a man is not going to change that. If I find someone suitable then I will make sure you are the first to know." I pinched his nose.

"Mom, c'mon, I will be thirteen soon and I won't have time to be around. I am going to start liking girls this year. Get my basketball to perfection. I'm going to be the next Jordan, you know. And I don't want to worry about you."

"Well, we will see what the future holds for me in the relationship department, Mr. Jordan. Until then, Malcolm, be a child and worry about child things. I will be fine with or without a man." I turned off the light.

I felt him lean over me to kiss me goodnight. "I think Jerome is a good guy. He is always helping me when I need it. He even said that he would help me with my jump shots. I think he is a really nice man. Do you?"

"Goodnight, Malcolm."

How could I answer him? The funny thing was that I felt like he was breaking up with me. He wants me to be happy. I thought I was. How did I just let a twelve-year-old tell me what I needed to hear? I never gave Jerome a thought like that. I mean, I thought he would be a good catch, but for someone else.

Most importantly, there was the matter of my late husband, Malcolm. I treasured that man something fierce and now our son wants me to love another. I wish so much that he had gotten a chance to remember him. When his father died, Malcolm was not even two years old. I only have pictures and memories for him to cherish. Maybe my baby is right and I do need to live life like I have womanly needs.

xoxoxoxoxoxo

"Aaron, man, you can't have me go and see if Alexis is OK. I am quite sure she does not want to see you or anything that would remind her of you."

Aaron looked like a man who's about to lose everything he desperately needed. He knew from the start that what he had been doing was wrong but now he just wanted to see if she was all right. As he paced the floor, he pleaded with EJ, "Please, man, I know you care for Alexis like a sister and I know she will talk to you. I just need to know if she is going to be all right."

"Aaron, you are my boy and all but I am not the one who needs to make amends here. That is *your* job. And right now the best thing for you to do is leave her alone and let her get some space to sort things out and swallow the bomb you and Simone dropped on her." EJ hoped that Aaron would listen to him and change his mind but Aaron had the look in his eye that meant business. So EJ just gave in. "If she wants to talk to me, what am I supposed to say?"

As Aaron sat in silence and thought of something to say, he tried to figure out what would be appropriate. "Just see if she is all right, that is all. If she wants to talk to me, then tell her I'm here. I will give her the space that she needs." He looked at the watch she had given him for his birthday. "She engraved her love on this and said that we will stand the test of time. And I fucked this shit up. Damn!"

"Would you go back to her if she would let you?"

Aaron shook his head knowing that there would be no way that could ever happen. "Man, she wouldn't do that especially now that Simone is pregnant." He smacked himself in the head. "What was I thinking? I don't love Simone. She asked me that tonight and I didn't give her an answer. I mean, what does she want from me? It was supposed to be sex and that is all. I mean, I care for her but I would not marry her and now I feel like I am obligated to stay because she wants to have this baby."

Elijah sat on his sofa and asked, "You blew the love of your life for someone that you don't even love? Oh man, if you were going to ruin the best thing that could happen to you or any other man, at least let it be worth it."

"I know." Looking pitiful, he sat next to EJ. "Elijah, man, would you please go? I know she is at the house. She has no apartment 'cause when we were to come back from the Bahamas we were going straight there. All her things are there. I don't expect her to take me back. I would not even ask. I would be a damn fool to try. For me, please go to her."

"I will but I do not feel sorry for you in the least. Alexis is the finest woman that you ever went out with. I would testify on her behalf if she killed you." He stood up. "I just hope she does not take her frustrations out on me. I know she is going to ask me if I knew and I'm going to have to tell her the truth. And I'm not going to lie to her; she has been lied to enough already."

Aaron stood up and gave EJ a brotherly hug. "Just tell her that I love her."

"I don't think that I will tell her that. I am just going to make sure that she is all right. If she wants to talk then I will listen, but if she wants me to go I am gone. I am not taking responsibility for anything that goes down when I walk in or out of those doors." He opened the door and walked out.

Shannon N. Davis

Chapter 3
Alexis

Well, I'm here sitting on my bed in what was supposed to be our new love nest on the day we were to start our new life. All the furniture we have in here is our brand-new bedroom set. We figured we might as well start our life in the bedroom since we wanted to start with children right away. There goes that plan. He is the one having the baby without me. I just can't believe this is my new life.

I do know this is *my* new home. I make enough to make the mortgage payments and then some. I know it would be a struggle. I thought we were going to be on easy street. With him and Elijah partners in their own law firm and me just getting my master's and being nurse manager and director of the women's health clinic, finances were to be a breeze. I just wish he had told me that the plans had changed and I would have made plans accordingly.

Sitting here in my wedding dress, makeup ruined and hair a mess, I feel like an ugly rejected duckling. I took off my wedding dress and threw it on the floor, which left me in my slip. I guess somewhere along the way I had not been enough for him. I wish he had told me that too. Why can't I stop the tears from flowing? He screwed up; I didn't! I know

I wanted to be alone but I wish I had someone here.

The doorbell rang.

"Who is it?" I said apprehensively. I thought, *It better not be Aaron!*

"Alexis, it's Elijah."

As I opened the door, I said, "Elijah, what in the hell are you doing here? How did you know . . . ?" I blocked him from coming in. "He sent you over here, right?"

"Yes. Can I come in?"

I gave the gesture to come in. "I have no where for you to sit. I'm sorry but due to recent events I had to come in here a bit early. Come to the bedroom, you can sit on the chair in there."

He followed me there. "I just wanted to know if you are OK, not just for his sake but for mine as well. You were the last person I would want this to happen to."

Lord knows I tried to hold back the tears but I did want some company and Elijah is one of the sweetest men I know. I sobbed uncontrollably and he came and sat next to me on the bed. "How? Why? What did I do to deserve this? What, Elijah?"

"I don't know why. What I do know is that it is not your fault. It was not some lack of doing on your part. He made a huge mistake and now he knows that he has to pay for it." He continued to rub my back. "You are a beautiful woman, Alexis Blackmon. You have all the qualities that a man, a decent man, would want. You're smart, you have business sense; you handle your own without the help of a man, and you carry yourself in a mature and womanly fashion. Not to mention that you're fine as hell! I can't tell you why, I really can't! Shit, I wouldn't."

I wiped my face. "You knew, didn't you?" I knew asking him that would put him in the middle of our situation. "It's OK, I know you did. You guys tell one another everything."

He took his hands off my back and folded them between his legs then took a deep breath. "Yes, I did. I did tell him that I was not on his side with this. However, I didnt know that she was pregnant."

I jumped from the bed and began to rant and rave. "How in the hell do you do that to a person that you supposedly loved! Don't I deserve an inch of respect? Now I am here in a home that we purchased together but I'm alone. My goddamn wedding dress is on the floor! And I am supposed to be grateful that he told me *before* we got married! No! No! No!" I paced back and forth. "Somehow I just want to get back there and kill him! Cut off his mother fucking balls and shove them down his tired-ass throat!"

Elijah stood up holding himself. "Calm down, Alexis."

"Calm down! How would you feel if he did that to you? Would you be calm?" I walked toward him and punched him in the chest. "Would you . . . would you . . . would you?"

He just grabbed me to him and held me so tight that my arms were curled between us. He stood there holding me while I sobbed and sobbed. He began caressing my hair. "Go ahead and cry. I'm OK with it. My chest hurts but I will be fine."

I looked up and began to laugh. "I'm so sorry, EJ. It is just that . . ."

And he kissed me on the lips so soft, tender, and friendly that I wanted to cry all over again. He grabbed my chin and kissed me again. "You are beautiful, Alexis. Don't let this take away your self-esteem. No one is worth that."

I have no idea what came over me but I got lost in what he was saying, so I kissed him in a not-so-friendly kiss. I put my arms around him and put my all in this kiss. I'm not sure if I wanted revenge or if I just wanted to be held and caressed or if we just got caught in the moment. What I do know is that I liked it. I liked whatever this was. I needed to feel this right now and I hoped that this was the right thing to do. I felt his masculine but tender hands wrap around my waist and his mouth take my lips and tongue. I guess he is feeling something as well.

He suddenly stopped and backed off. "Oh shit. Alexis, I have to go. This is not what was supposed to happen here." He turned and faced the wall. "I just wanted to make sure you were all right."

"And you have. I'm sorry too." I sat on the bed and could not help but feel lonely again. My tears returned. "Just lock the door on your way out." I lay across my bed and cried harder than I had ever cried before. I'm not sure if I made him feel obligated to stay but he came toward the bed.

He stood there and then touched my feet. I could tell he was at a loss and so was I. He sat at the foot of the bed and rubbed my feet. "What can I do? I just can't leave you like this. I know that you're hurting and will be for a long time. But right now, what can I do?" He slid behind me and wrapped his arms around me and did not say a word. I just needed to be comforted and that is what he did.

xoxoxoxoxoxo

I woke up and noticed that two hours had gone by. Elijah was asleep and still holding me. When I felt him and realized that I had not been dreaming, I began to cry. I tried to do it silently so he would not wake but that failed. I felt him massaging my arms and he kissed the back of my head. His tender gestures made me more emotional. I could not believe what was happening to me. It is 2:30 a.m. and I am crying on my wedding night, and not from tears of joy.

I turned around to face him and looked at that handsome face and gave him a not-so-friendly kiss. Only this time he did not reject me. As he kissed me, he stroked my hair and my thighs. Never once feeling apprehensive about what he was doing. In fact, he began to take over the kiss as if he felt more than pity for me. And I devoured every minute of it. Taking charge of this intimate moment, I felt his hand on my breasts, massaging them ever so gently.

I couldn't help but become excited over this. I began to moan and groan to let him know that I was feeling him. I'm still not sure what is going on at this point but I won't take the time to investigate it. I need to feel needed and wanted. I need to know that I am a woman that a man desires. I need to know that I can go on after being humiliated at the altar. I definitely needed to see how far this make-out session would go—how good it would be and if I would want more.

Elijah pulled down my slip and began to suck on one of my breasts and massaged the other teasingly with his fingers. I began running my finger through his curly hair and letting this man consume my breast. My pelvic area began to throb and moisten and I wanted this man. When he put his hand down there to feel how much love he was withdrawing out of me, I felt his nature rise. I felt that he wanted me just as I did him. His hips began to gyrate against my body and his erection became more and more intense.

He then went down and pulled my panties off and began to lick in and out of me. I can tell that he watched me as I lost control of my senses. How my pelvis rocked up and down in total pleasure. How my vagina got wetter and hotter with each stroke of his tongue. I could not help but to grab his head between my hands, massaging the top of his head and holding on to his ears. I felt him taking off his pants and un-wrapping a condom and I let out the sweet moans of ecstasy in antici-pation of what was about to become. "Please don't stop, Elijah," I cried.

He came up and kissed me. "Damn, I want you. I have always wanted you. Alexis, you are even more beautiful than I imagined."

My heart began to beat out of my chest. I knew I felt more than sex from him and I love it. I became more eager to have him inside me. "I want to feel you. Please let me feel you."

He slid himself inside me and we both lost control. Our bodies moved in sequence and the love that we shared somehow became more than me needing to be held and him just obliging. It became special as if we had wanted this for some time now. I watched him as he licked and bit his lip to keep from losing ground. He continued to caress and stroke my body at the same time he pulled himself in and out of me.

When he gently flipped me over to love me from behind, he lost all composure. "Lex, damn you feel so good, baby. Oh my god . . . you feel soooo good." He leaned down and ran his tongue down my back and I almost convulsed. "Are you feeling me, Alexis? Are you? I'm damn sure feeling you."

Being swept away in Elijah's love, I couldn't help but to rock to his beat. "Yes . . . yes . . . Elijah . . . umm." I lay on my stomach and he followed me down and turned me over to my back. I grabbed his face and kissed him so endearingly and sensually that he changed rhythm and I felt my body begin to quiver and he made me look him in the eye when my love came pulsating out. I held him so tight with my thighs and clenched the sheets with my fist. I lost my breath and I begged, "Hold me. Don't let me go."

He rested his arms under my head and kissed me all over and when I lifted my legs up and wrapped them around his waist, we both began to tense and hold each other tighter. He began pushing himself deeper inside me and I went absolutely crazy. I quivered and shook all over again, letting more of my love greet him at the same time his love greeted mine.

He lay on me, kissing and loving me still. He then turned me to lie on my side so his chest could rest on my back. He continued to kiss and stroke the back of my neck and head. I have never felt so comfortable and at ease before in my life. We never said a word and I noticed the clock and I closed my eyes. Elijah was still up because I could feel him rubbing the curve of my body. He then reached over and kissed me on the cheek. "Get some rest. I will be here when you wake up."

xoxoxoxoxoxo

The sun was hot on my face and woke me instantly. Again, I realized that I was still in my nightmare. Elijah was sound asleep and I quietly slid out of bed, making sure not to wake him. I walked to the bathroom in my master bedroom. I wanted a hot shower to relax my mind. I had made love to the best friend of the man I love. Even though Aaron had hurt me, I'm not able to say that I am no longer in love with him; it would be a cold day in hell though if I took him back. My motto is that if a woman let her man come back after cheating the first time, then she just gave him a free pass to do it again. And there will be no free passes here. No matter how much I love him, he had destroyed our bond forever.

As I let the water beat down on my face, I wondered what Elijah was going to say to me after the night we had shared. I'm still taken aback at the night of passion we had spent together. It had actually been wonderful. I couldn't help but to love every minute of it. It had been so sensual and passionate. My shower came to an end and I got out and went into the bedroom.

Elijah was awake by this time. He sat up. "Good morning. Are you OK?"

"Yes, I am. What about you?"

He leaned on one arm. "I'm good. My concerns are with you. I mean, look what happened between us last night."

I sat down on the bed. "Well, nothing happened that I did not want to happen. We are both consenting adults."

"Yes, I know, but what do you want to do? Do you want to leave it alone or do you want to let it ride out? I'm not putting pressure on you."

I lay against the headboard and turned to him. "I liked last night. I care for you deeply but I can't deal with relationships right now. I did just get dumped at the altar." The tears began to blur my sight.

"I know what you've just been through. I understand completely. So you want to keep what happened between us?"

"Well, yes. I don't think Aaron needs to know this. You two have the firm and it is doing well and this will most likely end it. As if he should be upset."

"But he will be. He loves you, Alexis. I know you can't tell this right now but he does."

I hated that he said that. I closed my eyes and just let the tears flow. He gave me a moment of silence, and when I had gathered myself together, I said, "His love killed me yesterday. I'm not too sure that I can love like that again. Just the thought of risking my heart again is just as painful as yesterday. So you tell me, what do you think about last night?"

"I think it was absolutely wonderful! I mean, I gave and received total pleasure. But once we walk through those bedroom doors, the honeymoon is over." He gave me that sexy smile. "I fell in love with you that first night I saw you in the Shadows nightclub."

"What?" I said, surprised.

"I saw you first but Aaron got to you first. He didn't know I spotted you first but I wanted you for myself. I mean, just looking at you, I saw sophistication. Your satin brown skin, bright eyes, and real hair." We both laughed. "Your body was looking tight in that strapless black dress with the knee-high boots. Girl!"

"You remember all that? That was years ago. Does Aaron know?"

"Yes. He also knew that I wouldn't press up on you. Though he wouldn't be too thrilled with me lying next to you all night long. Let alone making love to you."

"Well, he won't ever know. I'm not going to tell him or anyone. Last night was an intimate and private, not to mention much-needed, night."

He grabbed his chest as if he were heartbroken. "Oh my god! You used me?" He smiled. "I know. I didn't know what else to do. Even crying with swollen eyes, you were so beautiful. I feel bad because I think I took advantage of your vulnerability. You were feeling mighty low last night. Doubting your womanhood and losing sight of who you are. I hated to see that. Don't get me wrong, I have imagined what it would be like if we ever got together in that way."

"You did?" I touched his face. "Elijah, I am so sorry. I had no idea that you felt that way."

"Oh no, I'm cool. We will take last night and put it in with other fond memories of the heart. I made love to you last night and don't regret one single minute. Hell, I wouldn't mind if you wanted more." He started laughing. "I am cool with this, though. Let us keep what happened within these walls and eliminate the drama. You're not ready and I damn sure don't want you on the rebound. The woman I want in my life has to be drama free."

"And I do have drama." I gave a fake chuckle. "Plus, you would eventually have to deal with Aaron and the business may suffer. I do not want that. Black people need to keep their own businesses nowadays. You men have been friends since infancy and I don't want to come between that."

"Yeah, well that is true. Alexis, I do care for you, and if somewhere down the line you gave me the green light, I will damn sure drive through it. Especially now that I know what can transpire between us." He stroked my arm. "I think you felt it too. Am I right?"

"Oh yeah! Elijah, I am so messed up right now. I have to start putting my life together. Since plan A did not work out, plan B must be put in action." I got up from the bed.

"How about us just being friends? There is nothing like friends. Do you think we can do that?"

He put his pants on and walked next to me. "Yes, I can be your friend. I've been your friend. You are so right, there is nothing like being friends." He pulled me close to him with one arm. "Don't worry, I will be on my best behavior. The last thing I want to do is loose you completely. I will always be there for you no matter what. Whatever you need I am here. Even just to talk."

"You are a wonderful man. How Shelley wanted to date other people is beyond me. I would want you all to myself. You better get dressed. I know my cell phone has many messages on it. I know my parents are going stir crazy." I walked away just to avoid looking in his eyes. "We are cool, Elijah. Maybe we can do lunch sometime when my life gets back to normal. I have two weeks off and a brand-new home that needs everything!"

"Well, you will have the time." He put on his sweater. "You can do a lot in here. I like it a lot. What are you going to do in this house all by yourself?"

I looked around the room and noticed that the furniture in here was the only furniture I had. "Well, we know the bed works!"

We started laughing and gave each other a tight embrace and kiss. Part of me didn't want him to leave but the other part felt like I was treading on thin ice. I let go of the embrace first. "You better go. I have a lot to do."

We walked to the door together. Elijah turned to me. "Everything is cool, Lexi. Let's just chill until things are a little less strained. I'm not going anywhere." He opened the door and stepped out halfway. "I have more respect and admiration for you now than I ever did. You are an incredible woman. Don't forget it."

I gave him the little-girl smile. "Thank you and I won't forget it. Thanks to you for not letting me slip. You are too kind. Let's give it some time. I know you will call and check on me. And tell that two-timing bastard friend of yours that my well-being is no longer his concern. He can now worry about his trifling girlfriend and their unborn child!"

He put his hands up to surrender. "On that note, I'm gone! Love ya, girl."

"Love you too."

Shannon N. Davis

Chapter 4
Sidney
(Seven months later)

Marcus and the kids are gone for the day. He took the kids to Great Adventures Hurricane Harbor. I was glad to have the day to myself and clean and do any other little thing around the house. Even though my children are fifteen, eleven, and seven, it still seems like I have babies. I remember when I used to say I can't wait until these kids get old enough to clean up their own mess. But now it is a different mess. For instance, my eldest, Nickia, immediately comes home from school, takes her shoes off, and drops her coat and book bag where she stands, never once thinking of picking them all up. Then there is Marquis, my son, who has to leave his football, basketball, or baseball supplies where he drops them. Not to mention those damn Gameboy games and things. Last but not least is my baby, Sasha. She is just going to be a plain slob if I do not correct her behavior quick. This child will leave her little panties on the bathroom floor or in her room or wherever. And those nerve-wracking Barbie shoes that trip your feet up. She never realizes that every time I see them I throw them out. And for Christmas she wants more Barbie!

Later today, I am meeting with Alexis and Tracy. We have not had lunch in a while. We usually do that sort of thing once a week. That was before the wedding from hell had taken place. Poor Simone, she is about to drop that load in one month and has not seen any parts of a ring. She more or less keeps to herself now; I guess because of the shame. At her own baby shower she had cried. We were not sure if she cried because not even half the people she invited showed or because Aaron was only there out of obligation and she had ruined a friendship over that.

I attended and that was because my mother demanded that I did. I gave her a stroller and other baby items but she did not make out like a bandit like women usually do on their first child. She and Aaron have a lot of things to buy before that baby gets here.

I hate the fact that Alexis was so heartbroken. She is doing her thing, though. She has made that home into a palace. I am almost jealous.

I have always had the nice home and things and people would always compliment me and tell me how nice I keep this place up. How I should love Marcus to death because every few years I get new furniture and all its components. I do like that and I love Marcus. That man has kept drama out of our home for seventeen years and I love it. The stuff that these other women go through I can not relate to—cheating, beating, alcohol and drugs, even baby-mama drama. I've had none of that and I thank God every day.

I finished cleaning and was getting ready for my luncheon with the best girls of the world when the doorbell rang. There was the postman holding what looked like a certified letter. "Hello, is that for me?"

The mailman was an older white gentleman with the worst haircut I have ever seen. "I have a certified letter here for Marcus Grant. Will you sign here, please?"

"Sure." I signed it and took the other mail that came with it. I am about to have a heart attack. I can't believe the past is coming back to haunt us. How had she found us? What does she have to say? The letter is from Taniesha Holder, a woman Marcus had slept with before we got married, while we were still dating. We had a horrible fight over some dumb teenage issue that I can't even remember, and he slept with her out of anger toward me. So he says. He said it only happened once and he was so sorry and guilty about it that he told me the next day.

Oh we had drama! I hated that bitch. She had wanted him so bad in school; and the fact that the plain girl Sidney had gotten him was too much for her. She was dealing with some older man at the time and she slept with Marcus just to get me. I was so hurt and devastated over it that I began to cut school just to avoid the two of them—him looking like the sorry dog that he was, and her snickering and gloating to her friends about it as I passed them in the hallway. Her older man at the time did not go to school. He was then twenty-five and she was sixteen I think. So it was easy for her to flirt and fool around inside school but every day after school he would be out there in his car waiting for her. She would then act like he was the light of her life.

So one day, when I decided not to cut school anymore, I beat the other kids out of school early so I could have a chat with this older man she was seeing. And yes, I told him everything—what a tramp he had and how she had slept with my man and all the other boys in school. Rumor has it that he beat her up in the car but she denied it the next day in school. Then to top it off I took Marcus back to make her even madder. Needless to say I wanted to take him back. I knew that Marcus and I would be together forever. So what in the hell does this slut have to say?

Before I opened the letter I noticed that the return address was local. She lived in Red Bank, New Jersey. We didn't live too far from her; we live in Neptune City. All these years we were that close, or maybe she had just moved in. I sat on the living room sofa and noticed that Tracy would be here in an hour to get me and I am not close to being ready. And will I be after reading this letter? I took a deep breath and started to read. I could not believe my eyes.

Dear Marcus,

I know it has been a long time and this is probably the strangest thing that I have ever done . I know you and I had no contact after we graduated from high school and the one night we shared but things have changed in my life since then.

I know you married Sidney and I hear that the two of you are still together after all these years and believe it or not I am happy for you. I too have gotten married since then. Well, maybe about five years after you. I married Michael Stone. I know you remember the man that used to pick me up from school everyday. Well we are married and are getting a divorce.

You must be wondering why I am telling you this. Well, I had a daughter named Robin and he wants custody of her. Well, there is no better way to tell you this. Robin is your daughter. I named her Robin because of your middle name Robert. Weeks after our night together I found out that I was pregnant. I was scared at first because I was not sure if

*it were Mike's or yours. I told Mike it was his be-
cause I knew that you and I were never going to be
an item. I knew how much you loved Sidney. And
when I wanted to tell you, I heard that you two were
getting married. Even though there was a huge part
of me that wanted to just stick it to Sidney, I had to
play my cards right.*

*When I first saw her after she was born I knew
she was your daughter and that is why I gave her
your name. And yet I continued with this lie and
lived with it. Now that Mike and I are separating
and he wants my baby, I figured it was time to put
out the secret. I am not asking for back money or
anything but for you to know what is happening
and for you to step in on the fate of our child.*

*When I told Mike, of course he did not believe
me and I had no problem getting them tested.
Marcus, she looks just like you. People say she looks
like me but I know she looks like you. I mean it is so
weird. She is shaped like you and has that crooked
smile like yours. She even snores like you do. I kept
this a secret to keep my world from being hectic.
There was no way that I was going to raise her without a father. I am quite sure that you would have
been there but not with me, strictly for her. There
was no way that I could go to bed alone and know
that you were getting on with your life, loving Sidney
and most likely having kids with her. So to keep my
daughter and me from being the estranged family, I
did what I had to.*

*Marcus ,please help me on this. I am not asking
for you to do anything but refuse the custody and
adoption. Now that he knows she is not his, he wants
to adopt her as well. She has not been told yet. I
wanted to see what you were going to say first. I
got her hair sample and had that tested instead of*

telling her the truth. She loves Michael and would be devastated at this whole mess. I am sure that she will come around to the idea.

I would like for the two of you to get to know each other. I am not trying to stir things up with you and Sidney and your other kids but I do not want to have my daughter—our daughter taken away from both of us. Every time I look at her I want to tell her who you are and I wish that I could have told her that she was conceived out of a healthy relationship instead of a one-nightstand. But I could never do it. I wanted to maintain a secure world for us both. And with Michael, that was possible. You need to know that she lives in a good home. He took great care of her. She is on the track team. Funny you were the track king in high school. When I watch her at her meets, she reminds me of the way you used to fly around the track.

I would never have told you the truth if it were not for this. She is our daughter and I feel you need to step in and at least stop the custody battle. He can't get custody of something that is not his. I will set up an arrangement for the two of you to meet whenever you get back to me.

Either way, you have to contact me because you will be getting a court order to come to court some-day soon. Just in case you do not believe that she is yours and not Mike's, here is a copy of the DNA results proving Mike is 99.9% not her father. You know you were the only one I was with. Regardless of what people said about me. Once I had a boy-friend ,I had a boyfriend. Of course except for the night we shared. So if you want to get tested I am OK with that.

Please forgive me about this. I know it will be a test on your marriage and I am beyond trying to

break the two of you up like I did in high school.
Please get back to me. My number and address are
listed at the bottom of the page.
    I wanted to send a picture of her but I thought
it would be too much at this time. Marcus, when
you see her ,you are going to be so proud. Again,
please forgive me for springing this up on you and
your family now. Taniesha Holder-Stone

"Oh my god!" I screamed. "What the fuck is she trying to pull? This is some sick high school joke!" I'm pacing back and forth like a mad woman. Not my husband! My whole life is crashing right before my eyes. She has to be lying. She has to be.

I never told anyone about the affair he had on me. I let what happened between us stay between us. I knew he was sorry and we were kids and I have forgiven him since then. We got married right away after. He wanted to show me how much he loved me. And that was a day I will never regret. But never in a million years did I think that I would have to rehash this whole nightmare again. Not after I worked so hard to beat the odds. People usually do not get married and have the relationship that I have with Marcus. I can't stop these tears from flowing.

If this is the truth, eventually everyone will know we do not have the perfect marriage. We will end up like everyone else. This is such bullshit! What is he going to do? Will he want to meet this girl that he had or might not have had with Taniesha? I can't believe it! Taniesha! Anyone but her. She had his first baby and I had his second. My husband can very well have four kids and I have three. Maybe if I throw the letter away this will not happen.

I have to get ready. Tracy will be here in less than an hour. I have to compose myself or Tracy will pick up on my tension. Then she will want me to explain and I have not even discussed this with Marcus yet. Marcus, my husband of seventeen years—my soul mate, the man that has loved me uncontrollably half of my life and given me three wonderful kids and a fabulous home. He maintains the restaurant so I do not have to lift a finger. I love my life. It is the life that every woman wants.

We do not have drama except for him leaving the toilet seat up and clipping his toenails in the bed. He knows I hate that. I will not let this bastard child get in the way of my family and the perfect life I've created. I am going to get ready for my lunch with my best friends. This is not an option. And that is my final answer.

Shannon N. Davis

Chapter 5
Tracy

I have to hurry up before Sidney kills me for being late. That is one woman of punctuality. She needs everything to flow smoothly at all times. I wonder how she would act if something life pressing would come into her perfect world. I know we would have to resuscitate her behind. My little Malcolm is at school and will be home right after. He has a date with Jerome for the basketball practice before he goes to the tryouts in three weeks. My son really likes Jerome and Jerome seems to like him.

Now do I like him? Jerome is very nice, business minded and organized—not to mention handsome. He is of medium height; I would say about five feet nine. A bit stocky but made of muscles and not fat. He has a great sense of humor and is a great dancer. I asked him to escort me to a banquet once and we were on the dance floor like it was nobody's business. I loved the way he led the dance and gracefully whisked me across the dance floor. I even loved being dipped and God only knows that I have not been dipped in years—and I do mean years.

Jerome sometimes seems to be interested. Last year he even asked me to go out with him as a couple. I used the excuse of being his boss and that it would not be a good idea. The truth is, I'm not sure on having a relationship with another man. I mean it has been over ten years, about twelve to be exact. He seemed hurt by it but never let it come between us professionally. When I turned him down he never changed his attitude toward me. He remained my business partner and confidant.

He had even dated a few women and I gave him opinions on them. Now that I think about it. Every woman he had introduced me to, I told him, was not for him. I am thinking, was she for him or was she just not me? I have to smile at that thought. Subconsciously I had been sabotaging his relationships. But for what? I do not think that I was jealous. Or was I?

I finished getting dressed and this damn phone is ringing. "Hello."

"Hey, Trace, it's me Jerome."

"Oh hello. I was just thinking of you."

"Oh really? Missing me, huh?" he said sounding pleased that I was thinking of him.

So I changed the tone of where this could go. "Don't get all teary eyed. Malcolm told me that you were coming to help with his basketball today after school. Are you still coming?"

His tone changed and he sounded a bit disappointed. "Uh . . . Yes. Tell him I will be there but I wanted to ask you if you would like to come with me to a Broadway show. I wanted to see *Rent* and I thought you would like to come."

I had to hold my enthusiasm back. "When?"

"Tomorrow night. Can you make it? Or do I have to take my mom out again?" he joked.

"Well, since you are desperate, I'll go. I heard it is a pretty good show."

"Good. I will see you later when Malc gets home."

"OK . . . I will be back a little late because the girls and I are having lunch and you know that can take a while."

"No problem, I will wait until you come home. I mean, that is to be with Malcolm until you come home."

"Oh yes, of course."

"Bye, Tracy."

"Goodbye, Jerome." I hung up the phone and could not help but smile. He is kind of cute.

He is starting to ask me out again. I guess his little relationship with Debbie, the secretary in the office across from ours, has ended. She is nice and everything but she is about six cans short of a six-pack. And that is bad. I don't think they even looked right together. She was a bit overweight but it did not look sloppy. She always wore this ponytail covered with cheap gel to hold down that brown hair that needed an ultra perm. Plus, she already had three children with two daddies and didn't want to have more. I knew Jerome was not going to have that hang around too long. What he wants is a wife that wants to bond and grow with him. He does not have children but wants them desperately. I guess that's why he has been so good with Malcolm. Plus, it seems like Malcolm wants a man around. My baby is tired of my womanly advice.

When I see him later this evening, I will play it cool like I always have. For some reason it felt like it would be a bit harder than usual, but no matter what, it will be business as usual.

xoxoxoxoxoxo

Alexis

I am starving and I can't wait to eat. Sears seems to be a little more crowded than usual. I'm still buying things for the house. I'm actually done, but you can never have enough sheets and towels, my mother would always say.

I'm glad that I am finally at a point where I don't feel hurt when I get a little reminder of Aaron. I don't wake up and feel like my world is coming to an end. I am finally getting over being dumped at the altar. Maybe being caught up in decorating my home and being the director at the women's health clinic kept me busy.

Aaron has tried to contact me but I never took his phone calls. The last time he called I did return it on his voice mail. "Aaron, why in the hell don't you stop calling me? Haven't you got the picture yet? I meant what I said; I do not *ever* want to speak to you again. Ever! So save your breath for that little brat that you are going to have. Do not let me get a restraining order or better yet tell my father! There is nothing that you can say that will make me want to listen. You said enough on our wedding day. Have a nice life."

After that, he never bothered again. I heard that he and the mistress, Simone, are not in Pleasantville. And I can only laugh. What? Did they think that they could do what they did to me and live happily ever after? I think not. God has given me a new power in life and I am basking in it right now.

Elijah, on the other hand, has contacted me. He calls every so often just to check on me. I like when he calls. Not in that way. I like the fact that we have remained friends after the night we spent together, that secret passionate night. I liked the way that he still respected my space and never spoke a word of what we had shared, a true gentleman. We actually never spoke on the subject when we did speak. We carry on as if it never happened. And I am glad of that.

I'm ready for a date, though. Not with Elijah but with a man that I don't know and that it will be new to us both. There is no past between us. I have not dated nor had sex since my wedding night. The sex I had with a man other than the groom, that is. I want a man that will love me to no end. Make sure my hopes and dreams come true and not send me some pipe dream. Or blow it on a piece of ass. Why do men disgrace a lifetime good thing for a moment of passion? It took a while but I got over it just like everyone said I would. And I have never heard of a more accurate prediction. Look out, world, I am back and ready to fly!

Chapter 6
Simone

It's one in the afternoon and I am bored to death. I have gained thirty pounds and feel like a blimp. When I spoke to Sidney she said that she, Tracy, and Alexis were going to have lunch together. I sort of miss having lunch with my best friends. I think my sister just tolerates me because she is my sister. I think after the wedding she barely spoke to me, just like Tracy. And Alexis and I have not spoken since that day. There have been times I wanted to call her and just talk and get things off my chest and to let her get things off her chest. But knowing Lex, she will never speak to me again. And as a woman and a friend, I wouldn't speak to me either.

What is worst is that I blew a friendship I'd had over thirty years for a man that I *thought loved* me. I know Aaron does not love me and I just act like our situation does not exist. I know he stays around because of the child I am carrying but doesn't and never will love me. We had a four-month sexual fling. You know I don't even know why and how we got that way. I guess I was lonely and thought that a good man like him would take me and love and marry me like no other. Only thing is that he loved Alexis like no other. And I knew that as well. I guess that is why I am eight months pregnant, thirty pounds heavier, and alone. Yes, he is here physically but I am alone.

We don't argue all the time but we are not all peaches and cream either. Right now he is in the living room and I am here in the baby's room organizing. He sometimes acts like he lives alone. We hardly ever talk and when we do it is about nothing that either one of us wants to talk about. He never rubs my feet or asks me if I am OK when I am cleaning the tub. So I don't ask either. He went with me to do the baby registry but would have rather been elsewhere. When I asked him about this he simply denies it and says it is my hormones talking.

There is a part of me that wants to tell him to go to hell and that my baby and I will be fine. But then that would mean that I ruined my friendship for nothing and the joke would really be on me. Then there is that part that feels like I would rather be alone than be ignored by the father of my child. I'm scared to death of what the future holds for me. I mean to be a single parent and live without the father. I have seen Sidney over the years being adored by Marcus and raising their family as a functional unit. That is what I want for my child. I want his or her daddy to be there when he or she wakes up. I fell in love with Aaron before I got pregnant and I love this baby but I know I have some decisions to make if I am going to be happy. If I'm not happy, my baby will not be either.

It is not like I need him for his money. I make a comfortable living for myself. I am the best CPA at my office and I have saved tons of money. Not to mention the fact that when I go back to work after I have the baby I will be making more money because of my promotion. And believe me, I will not let him miss a payment on child support. He makes a better living than I do and I will not take him to court unless he drives me there. I know I won't have that problem though. But with these men, you never know. So I am not with him for financial gain. I just want a man in my life and it seems like I got one, no matter what the cost. And I am paying a lot.

I'm staring at him watching TV on the sofa peacefully and do not want to disturb him but I have to talk things out with him. So I had to gather my energy for what was about to come. "Aaron, we need to talk."

He looked up as though he was annoyed to hear my voice. "Yes, Simone."

"Well, I have been thinking and I wanted to know if we're going to get married."

"I told you I am not ready for marriage now." He turned the TV off. "Where is this going, Simone?"

I sat next to him on the couch. "It is just that I'm pregnant and I want to know if we are going to try and make this work or not. Or if we are not going to work it out, we will have to make other arrangements."

"Well, Simone, I want to take part in my child's life. This is definitely not the situation that I would have wanted. And I know you know that. I want to be with the mother of my child if it can work out that way."

I took a deep breath. "Well, I don't want to be a charity case either. You can be in the baby's life as much as you want but I want and need to be taken care of as a woman as well. And you were doing that at first and now I feel neglected."

"I have a lot on my mind and I just wanted to keep my distance. You knew the situation when you first told me. So I called off my wedding because of it. If that is not trying to make it work and make sacrifices, I do not know what is."

"You just answered my question. You don't even care about me, Aaron. Damn."

"Now wait a minute. I do care for you and you should know that. How do I have to prove it? We are living together. I am supportive of you with this pregnancy. I have gone to appointments with you. I sat in the ER when you were having those cramp things and I try not to cause you any stress. What more do you want?"

My heart is aching. "I want a husband. I want a man. I want security. I want a family. Isn't that what you want?"

"Yes."

"Oh, just not with me."

"You are putting words in my mouth, Simone. I can't marry you. I never sold you a pipe dream and you know that. When all was said and done, I told you I would be there for the baby."

"Just not for me?"

He stood up. "I did not say that!"

"Well, you might as well have!" I went and stood next to him by the window. "Aaron, do you love me?" He walked away from me and I grabbed his arm. "Don't walk away from me! Do you love me? Do you want to try to function as a man and woman? Possibly husband and wife? Do you?"

He sat back on the sofa and I sat next to him. He looked me straight in the eyes. "I am not in love with you, Simone. I care about you but I am not in love. I care enough to try and be supportive to you and the baby but I can't say that I want to marry you."

I don't know why I am upset but I am. I am hurt and I want to stop from crying but I can't. "Well, you will have to move. I can't have you here if we are not together. We did this to ourselves and we will have to deal with it. I know the bulk of the blame will be on me."

"What are you talking about? You want me to move? And then

what?" He threw his hands in the air as though he were the *only* one annoyed.

"Then you live your life and I will live mine. Except I'm with a child. I refuse to live with a man that will not treat me like the woman I am. I am grateful that you wanted to try and be supportive but I don't like the support you give. It is not enough. I deserve more and I want more and if you cannot give me that . . ."

"Look, do not get yourself all upset. Let's just see what we can do. You may not think so but I am looking forward to this baby. I am going to be a father for the first time and I want to be around for all aspects of it. Now we did this and you are right, we have to deal with it and I am dealing with it. I am not in love with you but I have known you for years and I do care about you a lot, but marriage I can't give. If you want me to move then I will have to see my baby when you say."

I had to stand up for this. "You can't have it both ways! I am not making you make a choice. I am making the choice. Since you don't love me and not even considering marriage, I want you to move out and get your own place. This is how we are going to deal with it. If you stay, there will be a point when you will meet another woman and want to be with her and then what?" I felt the baby kicking harder than ever and began rubbing my stomach. "Then I may meet someone who will want to treat me like a woman should be treated and I don't want any odds and ends to clean up. Aaron, I *am* in love with you and it hurts me deeply when we lie in bed and you barely hold me. And when we have sex you do it as if it were a job, something to do just to keep me quiet."

"What? Simone, that is not true. I can't wait 'til you have this baby 'cause you are tripping with these hormones. I sex you like I always have."

"If that were true, I would not have any complaints! When we were creeping around it was a lot better than this. I feel like shit afterward now. And I have to have to use mental visualization to have an orgasm! I'm not going to be one of those low self-esteem bitches that want the daddy around no matter what! You have to go!"

He followed me to the bedroom. "Who in the hell do you think you are? First, you have no problems sitting on my dick, wanted me to leave my girl then wanted to have a baby. Now you want me to marry you! Simone, please!"

"Oh, so now I'm the cause of all of this?" I went into my walk-in closet and started grabbing his clothes. "And just so you don't think that I am pulling a stunt, I am not! Can't you see what this arrangement is doing to me?"

He took the clothes from me and put them back in the closet. "Simone, please calm down. I know you are not pulling a stunt. However, I do want you to calm your butt down. I will leave but I don't want you upset. Let's sit down and talk about this."

I let him guide me to the bed and I just let the tears flow. "I miss my friends and my sister. I am pregnant with a baby by a man that does not care whether I live or die. My hormones are not out of control, my life is!" I leaned on his shoulder and continued to sob.

He began stroking my hair. "Simone, I do care whether you live or die. Don't be like that. I have much respect for you. You do have control over your life. Shit, you are putting me out right?" He began to chuckle. "As for your sister and friends, well, that will take some doing. We both know that. What we did devastated Alexis and all other surrounding parties. How do you think she feels? If you ask me, we are both going to hell. We just have to make the best of what we have. For us, life as we know it has changed. I am prepared to go forward with it. Are you?"

I looked him straight in the eye. "I'm scared. I thought I will be happy but I am so not happy. Not happy at all. I have no one to talk to about what I am feeling. You never talk to me. I have lost my best friend. My mom thinks I am pond scum. All I have is this baby. Nothing else. When this baby comes I know I will have to deal with motherhood and being a single parent. I am scared to death. I know I have never backed down from a fight and this is one fight that I will have to deal with. And I will win." I got up and stood in front of him. "Aaron, you have to leave and let me start my new life now. You do not fit in the equation."

"I will go stay with Elijah for a few weeks or so until I get my own place. I won't have a problem doing that. I want to make sure you are OK though. Right now you are very vulnerable and it is my job to take care of you the best way I know how, though you say it is not enough."

"I am glad that you are here, Aaron. And you don't have to leave today. Just let Elijah know you are coming. Just don't show up."

I started wiping my eyes and I noticed how handsome he is. "You can stay the night."

He grabbed me next to him. "Simone, you are a beautiful woman. I wish nothing but the best for you. I always liked you and you know that. You have the dangerous sex appeal that a man loves. Maybe that is why men that are involved seem to flock to you."

"What the hell are you talking about?"

He started laughing. "I'm not trying to diss you. It is just that you are very exotic and that is attractive to most men. I want you to find a man that will love you completely. Baby, I can't do that. I am glad that I am honest enough to tell you that. I have no energy to lead you or any woman on. I will not stand in your way. Now we have a baby coming, and from the looks of your belly, he might come out here tonight!"

"He? This could be a girl, you know."

"He or she. I want to be there when he or she comes to this world. You are not going to be alone. I'm here for you. I promise you this, I am here and no other woman is going to come first. Baby and Simone come first. If you ain't right, then the baby ain't right either. Isn't that how it works?"

"Yes. And I promise to take care of this baby and not slash your tires or your throat when you get another chick." We started laughing.

"Can I get that in writing please?" He grabbed me and kissed me so gently and it reminded me of what attracted me to him in the first place. He wrapped his arms around my waist and dove deeper in his wet kiss and I followed his lead.

We lay on the bed and returned each other's sultry kisses and let nature flow. Never had he been so tender and loving and I could not let this go. I just let my love for him flow. He kissed me from head to toe and massaged me from front to back. Rubbing my belly and running his fingers through my hair, I could not help but to let out sweet moans of ecstasy. Taking in all that he owed me and more. Aaron and I are always going to be bonded with the life of our child but that does not mean I will be his doormat. Yes, he is making me feel so good right now and I need it. Lord knows I need it. But this will be the last time. Hell, there is nothing wrong with having one for the road. And a long road it shall be.

Chapter 7
Alexis

"Hey, Lex!" Tracy said as we gave each other a tight embrace. "Damn, you look good! The milkman is hitting off lovely, huh?"

We sat down. "I wish somebody was. I don't drink that much milk. But maybe I should start." We started laughing and looked around for Sidney. "Where is Miss Always-on-Time? This is not like her."

"I know. She didn't call me on my cell to tell me something came up. So I guess she is on her way. Tell me, what have you been doing? I know we talk on the phone but I have not eaten lunch with you guys in so long. I know Red Lobster was wondering where we were."

Just then the waitress came to the table just as jolly as she wanted to be. She must have been fresh out of high school or something because she just had a childish glow. She had her hair in a ponytail with pretty blonde bouncy curls. When she walked, the hair flowed and bounced with every stride. "Hi, I'm Sandy, can I get you some drinks while you decide what to order?"

We ordered our usual drinks: Tracy's Bahama Mama and my Strawberry Daiquiri. And I took the liberty of ordering a virgin daiquiri for Sidney. We told Sandy that we need some more time because we were waiting for one more person. She happily walked away with her bouncy blond curls.

Just then Sidney came in like the wind. She's completely preoccupied. I figured that one of the kids had done something to get her this upset. So I inquired, "Geesh, Sid, are you OK?"

She draped her jacket over the chair. "I'm fine. Why?"

Tracy and I had eye contact and were in total agreement that this was not good. "Well, for starters, you came in like some mad woman. You barely spoke. You know we know you. So what's up?" Tracy said.

"Did you guys order drinks yet? I am parched." She patted her throat.

I said, "I got your usual. Here comes our waitress now."

Sandy came and dispensed the drinks. She retrieved her pad and pen ready to take our order. "Are you ladies ready to order or do you need a few minutes?"

"Sidney, you ready or want more time?"

Sidney closed the menu. "Yes, I will have the Ultimate Feast. I want baked potato and Caesar salad. Oh, and could you bring me a *strong* Strawberry Daiquiri?"

Tracy and I looked at each other in amazement. Sidney never drinks. I mean never. Not even a sip of champagne on New Year's. So that was the icing on the cake. I know something is wrong and it must be big for her to want to drink and stressed the word "*strong.*" We gave our order and tried to figure the deal with Sid.

Tracy went first with the questions. "All right, Sidney, just spill it!"

"Spill what?"

"You are drinking so tell us what's up. That's what," Tracy said.

Sidney took a deep breath. "My crazy son may get left back in school if he does not get a high grade on this next test and final. Can you believe that shit?"

"So you drink because of that?" I said. "Sidney, are you sure you are OK?"

"Yes! And for the life of me, would you please give this up? Marcus and I spent money on a tutor just for him to be failing. And to top it all off, he has never told us that he was having trouble in three, not one but three, of his classes. The school counselor called to see if there were problems in the home. Do you know how humiliated I was when I found out that he was forging his grades? Y'all know how I am when I am made a fool of! And my son did it."

"What? Has Marquis lost his mind?" Tracy said. "Does he know how important school is? What's wrong with him?"

"He knows you and Marcus are big on schooling. Why would he do such a thing? Most of all he knows what a perfectionist you are."

"Well, I have trouble in my paradise," Sidney said, annoyed. "Enough about me, what's new with you two?"

Tracy began, "Well, I have this huge account I am trying to land in Vegas. The biggest account I have ever taken on. Jerome and I have to fly over there in a few weeks. I am so excited. Shit, if I land it, lunch is on me!"

"All right now!" I said. "So you and Jerome, huh?" I said slyly, tracing the rim of the glass with my finger.

"Among other people. It will not be *just us*, Alexis," Tracy said defensively. "You just worry about when your next milk shipment will come in."

"What shipment?" Sidney said.

"Don't listen to this nut! She said that I had a glow and that she thinks the milkman is hitting me off."

"Well, is he?" She started laughing. "We all know it has been a while for you. If you can get some and some milk, go for it." She and Tracy gave each other a high five.

"Oh, Tracy, I know you are not talking! You have not had sex in over a decade! Who got cobwebs where?" I said.

"Hell yeah! You know, Tracy, you do not even count. You are a born-again virgin. Here is my *virgin* daiquiri," Sidney said trying to hold back the tears. We all started laughing and did not care how loud we were.

All the while we were laughing, it was so obvious that something was wrong with Sidney and she was trying really hard to hide it. When Sandy brought the food over and made a mistake with Sidney's order, the truth came out. Sidney waited for her food to return the way she had ordered it by tapping her fingers on the table. Tracy and I remained silent; knowing that this was her cue to let us know that there is something going on. The one thing about Sidney is that if she does not want it known, it would not be known. I have always admired her for that. She keeps the family business in the family. Not to mention if you tell her a secret, there will be no way someone will find out.

Sandy anxiously put her food down. "Sorry about that. I hope this is better for you."

"Yes, it looks like it and I am sorry for being rude earlier. Look for my apology in your tip," Sidney replied and smiled. She then looked at her food and never looked up. She stopped suddenly and looked at us with such pain in her eyes. "Marcus may have a daughter."

"What?" we said simultaneously.

"You heard correct. I got a letter today from a woman that said that Marcus was the father of her daughter and she wanted him to know that and come forward."

Tracy and I were amazed. To think that Marcus had cheated on Sidney was just something unheard of. "Are you sure? This can be some woman that is just being a bitch. You know women can be scandalous."

"What did Marcus say?" asked Tracy.

Sidney could no longer hold back her tears and she wiped her eyes with her napkin. "Well, he did sleep with her. I knew that. He told me that himself."

"What?" Tracy and I said again

"I can't believe this shit! I devoted my life to my marriage and family and now some tramp bitch could possibly destroy it!"

"Dear god, when did this happen? How old is the girl? Most importantly, what is Marcus saying?" Tracy examined her like an attorney would.

"When we were in high school. She will be seventeen. And Marcus had no idea."

I had to step in. "You mean to tell me that he cheated on you in high school and you are just now finding out about this child? I know you are not talking about that no-good Taniesha!"

Sidney looked surprised that I knew. "How do you know about that? But yes."

Tracy became lost. "Taniesha who? Where was I when this took place?"

Sidney explained, "Back in high school senior year we had a fight and broke up . . ."

"But you got married senior year," Tracy interrupted.

"Well, it was before that. It just happened once and he felt so bad that he told me and proposed. But *now* she claims to have gotten pregnant that night and had wanted to tell him but refused when she heard we got married. I can't eat this food. I have no desire to eat."

"When is Marcus going to find out?"

"When he and the kids come home from Hurricane Harbor. This is bullshit!" She slammed the fork down and buried her head in her hands.

"This girl is older than my daughter. I thought I was the *first and only* woman to have his baby. I have loved this man for as long as I can remember. Now all of that has changed."

"Look here, Sid, so what if this woman may have had his baby before you. Marcus has only loved you. Please do not take this out on him. What you have to do is talk this out with him," I said rubbing her back.

"Yeah, Sidney, this is not his fault. Sleeping with her is one thing but not knowing about this alleged kid is a whole new ball game," Tracy said.

"I'm not too sure about that. I don't think that I can deal with a teenage stepdaughter. What are *my* kids going to say? I was never unfaithful. Marcus was the only man that I have ever slept with. I know nothing else. What if Marcus wants to be around this girl?"

I knew I was skating on thin ice when I said, "Well . . . uh . . . Sidney, if he is the father then he should get to know her."

"She was never a part of my family and now I have to play Mommy Dearest. I don't know this girl—don't want to know her either. She has a father and he wants to remain in her life but that tramp Taniesha figured she would drop a bomb on him and tell the man that the kid is not his just so he would not try and take her away!"

I shook my head in disbelief. "Taniesha will never change. So she held that skeleton all these years until it became necessary ammunition. And you wonder why men dog women?"

"I just lost my appetite. I say we need to go home and get dressed and hit the Shadow tonight!" Tracy said. She started dancing in her seat and then paused. "Naw, I have so much to do with work. Malcolm has basketball practice with Jerome."

"I can't go no where, girl. I have to talk this over with Marcus and quick. The court date will be here soon and I have to know where he's going to stand, with them or with us."

"Don't make him choose, Sidney," I said. "You just may end up with results that are not in your favor."

"And if that happens he will never step foot in my house again! We will be finished for real. He slept with that bitch and I'm supposed to be the forgiving one? I don't think so. He better choose right!"

"That's not good. Just hear him out tonight," I said motioning for the waitress. I asked for the check and paid the bill for all of us. We gathered our belongings and headed for the parking lot. I no longer wanted to reason with her. Her mind was pretty much made up that she was going to make him choose. I feel it would be the wrong thing to do. There is one thing that I can agree with and that is going out tonight to the Shadows nightclub. I have not been dancing in quite sometime and I am overdue. Maybe I should go. I will have to see.

Chapter 8

The mothers of the four girls were doing their usual out having lunch. They had been friends for over forty-five years. They had been friends since they were young adults and had never broken the bond. This had made their daughters grow up to be friends. At one point, Tracy's mother, Leslie, had moved to LA to be with Tracy's father. He took a job out there and wanted his family with him. She had kept in touch but it was nothing like being there with her very best friends. When she found her husband to be unfaithful, she packed herself and Tracy up and moved back east, never trying to see if she can piece her marriage back together. Her thinking was that if he cheated once then he would do it again if she condones it this time. She did not care about being a single parent and the financial woes that came with it. Her husband, Albert, made plenty of money and she never even divorced him. She just left, and he was man enough to just send enough money so that she did not have to work; and he paid for babysitting expenses.

She always made jokes of the fact that they are still married and he still sends her money even though Tracy is long grown. She calls it "lifelong alimony." Truth is, there were times when he came to town and stayed in the house he had bought and paid for. Leslie denies playing house when he comes, but the other ladies seemed to think differently. She had dated since then but her current gentleman caller is ten years older than her and looks ten years younger and was named Charlie Goody. He was a personal trainer and kept in good shape and treated Leslie like a queen. He even knew that she never divorced Albert. He wanted to marry her and she had been about to divorce Albert to do it, but when one of Charlie's trainees left a love note with lipstick in his bag, she figured why bother with divorce. So to her, being married to Albert was like a safety net. And she had never really stopped loving Albert.

Leslie was a woman of medium build. She kept her shape and looked as though she would be going on a runway. She never worked at it; it just comes naturally for her. She ate all she wanted and never gained a pound. She had shoulder-length jet-black hair with a strip of

61

gray on the right side. She never dyed it. She let nature take its course and it is actually attractive on her especially with her hair always in the fullest state it can ever be in. She had that type of hair that, no matter what happens to it, would not break off. She's a pecan-colored woman that always claimed to be the model of the group. She never made scenes in public, always remained ladylike and a joy to be around. She always had the right thing to say. Her one regret in life was that she'd never had another child. Her marriage ended and she never met anyone that sparked enough interest for her to want to take it that far. Charlie was the one that had come close, but by the time she met him they were simply too old to do it.

Simone and Sidney's mother, Sharon, had always been the most down-to-earth woman anyone could ever be a friend to. She did not care that she had been overweight almost all her life. She liked to eat the good food that she cooks. Sharon is an excellent cook. And despite being overweight, she made a size 18 look like a 13 or 14. She kept her appearance up and never paid attention to what thin people said. She tried to diet and starve herself after giving birth to her twin girls but had no success. She finally gave up when she landed herself in the hospital diagnosed with malnutrition. She could not believe you could be overweight but be malnourished. Her blood work was so abnormal that she was in the hospital for over a week. After that, she ate in moderation anything she wanted. No diet in the world could convince her otherwise.

Being overweight never stopped her from having a man though. After her girls' father left and never returned, she met men that were decent and, most importantly, adored her. Her girls' father had said he could not deal with a family and wanted out and that is just what he did. It had been devastating at first. She always thought it was because of the seventy-five pounds she put on after having the girls; but two years after he left, she found out that it had been another woman that was behind it all along and he was too much of a coward to say so. He left Sharon and their two daughters to be with a high school dropout and her four kids. He was too ashamed to say that. It just so happens that he was spotted at the McDonald's playing daddy to these other kids.

When Sharon found out, she was so hurt and did not tell Simone and Sidney about it until they were much older. She finally caught up with him and was able to receive support for them. He was such a slime ball that he tried to convince a judge that he had four other children and could not afford the $110 a week to give to Sharon. Well, Judge Sheila Watson had not been convinced. She told him that those four other children had a father and that was not him. He would have to take care of his blood first and then what was left will go to his stepchildren and for him to get another job if need be. So Sharon received a check until the girls were eighteen and she never spoke a word to him. He stayed true to his new family, leaving Simone and Sidney in the wind.

For six years now Sharon had been married to William Gebre. William was an architect that had never married or had children. So when he met Sharon, her kids were obviously already older and he adored her grandchildren like they were his own. Sharon and William were like high school kids. They went on vacation twice a year and went stepping three times a month, and had even won a stepping contest. When they went out at night they were the finest couple in the house. When they danced people watched and cheered them on when they did their thing out on the dance floor. The one thing with them was that they knew where the other stood on issues. She did not overstep her boundaries, and neither did he. When these two were together, their connection lit up a room.

Alexis's mother, Dorothy or Dottie for short, had always been timid but also down-to-earth. She had always been the at-home wife of the group. Richard had seen to that and she was content with that. Raising her only daughter was her life along with making her husband happy. Before Dottie had Alexis, she had given birth to a little boy named Alex. He had died shortly after delivery. He was in such fetal distress during labor that he had been too far gone to be saved. He lived for a short ten minutes after. That was a traumatic experience for both Dottie and Richard. For the two of them to go a whole nine months preparing for this blessed event and then come home empty-handed was too much for Dottie. She stayed in bed for two months. Richard did all he could to make her feel better and deal with her loss. He had a terrible time dealing with losing his first-born son and trying to make sure he did not lose his wife in the process, not to mention trying to keep his chain of clothing stores together.

Leslie and Sharon were also there for Dottie and were the ones who had actually pulled her out of that bed and demanded that she stop this and get on with life. Leslie had actually dumped a bucket of soapy water on her and said, "If you don't go to the shower then the shower will come to you!" Broken-hearted Dottie had no choice but to get out of the soaking wet bed. They had laughed and cried, laughed and cried. But Dottie had taken that shower and they went to lunch.

Though Dottie lost a lot of weight she still looked good. The funny thing was that she only lost the thirty pounds she had put on. Her short-ness and small frame had always looked good on her. Richard kept her pressed and dressed. She had never gotten a relaxer in her life. To this day, she still used a pressing comb and looked just as good as a *Dark n' Lovely*. Richard was so pleased when one day he came home and his precious wife was there waiting for him at the dining room table dressed in the prettiest sheer peach nightgown he had ever seen. She had even cooked his favorite meal: barbeque chicken, collard greens, baked macaroni and cheese, rice, corn bread, and peach cobbler for dessert.

Three years later she had gotten pregnant with Alexis. She had named her Alexis in honor of her older brother Alex. The whole time she was pregnant she was so cautious. Even though what had hap-pened to her son was not her fault, she just had to be cautious for her sanity. Richard had made sure she did not lift a finger the whole preg-nancy. He hired a housekeeper, but told Dottie that she had to cook—he wanted only her cooking. But he had even gotten over on that. He decided even her cooking meals was too much for her. Dottie's mother, Lettie, cooked all meals for them. With all that pampering, and catering too, it was no wonder they'd had the baby they had. Alexis came out healthy and more beautiful than Dottie could have ever imagined. She had not a wrinkle. She came out and looked as though she'd been here for a month. She did not have a newborn feature in sight. No flaky skin, no wrinkles, and not even a cone-shaped head. Leslie and Sharon said it was because she had not had a care in the world while she was pregnant. She had not needed to cook or clean. She just slept all day long and so Alexis was the product of pampering. Dottie did not care. She had a daughter that was alive and well. Richard and Dottie had only wanted one child and Alexis was it.

Sitting and having lunch at Main Street U.S.A in Ocean, New Jersey, they were having their famous talks. This was their ritual, to have lunch and discuss the good and the bad. This tradition had been instilled in their daughters as well. They had always hoped that their daughters would grow up to be just as close as they were. To them there was nothing like having true girlfriends. They had never really traveled outside of their circle of friendship.

The women ordered their desired lunches and became quite giggly from the three rounds of chardonnay they'd had before even ordering. Leslie wanted to get down to business. "What are we going to do with our girls? I mean, Tracy told me that there is a strain between them. I feel so bad about that. They were just as close as were are."

Sharon took a big gulp of her wine and finished it. "I know all of this is because of my daughter. That Simone, I swear. What in the hell was she thinking?"

Dottie finished her wine and motioned for the waiter to bring them another round. "Well she obviously was not thinking. I mean, Sharon, she slept with her best friend's man and decided to drop the bomb on her on her wedding day."

"We don't need to rehash it, Dottie," Leslie said.

"Oh yeah we do," said Sharon. "I could not get through to Simone after it happened. She was so gung ho about being with this man. Now look at her, alone, 'bout to give birth for a man that told her he does not love her."

"What? He said that to her?" Leslie and Dottie said at the same time.

"Oh yes he did. That man is a trip. He was there out of pity. He didn't want to upset her during her pregnancy. The nerve. His looks are good but his personality sucks." She drank some more of her fourth glass of wine. "He will be around for the baby but does not want to be with Simone."

"Did you think that he would stay with her? He called Alexis for months after that whole disaster wedding he gave her, begging Alexis to at least hear him out. Acting like he was just calling to say hello. Oh that man has more than nerve. He has huge elephant balls!" Dottie and the women began laughing.

Leslie tried to contain her laughter. "Do you think they will ever speak again?"

Sharon and Dottie stopped laughing and said simultaneously, "Who?"

"Damn, ladies, it was just a question. Simone and Alexis. Who cares if anyone speaks to Aaron's ass? Tracy told me that they go out and talk but minus Simone," Leslie said.

Sharon's tone changed. "Simone cannot be included with affairs that Alexis is part of. I told her time and time again to call Alexis and try and talk to her. She thinks Alexis would not hear of it."

"Well, I know for a fact that she does not want to deal with Simone. Could care less about the two of them. It is sad to say, but can you blame her?" Dottie said.

"I know if it were either of you two to do that to me, that would be the end of our friendship. But then again, I would want to maybe try," Sharon added.

"Try what?" Leslie said with an attitude. "You know good and damn well that you would kick our ass and leave us to die. You are just saying that because it is your daughter that is the trollop in this story."

"Trollop? Let's not call out names, OK? I would rather function in life than to end up a lonely old broad like Tracy. Her husband has been dead for years and she has not even touched a man! What is she waiting for, huh? Reincarnation?" Sharon said on the defensive.

"It's better to not have a man than to have someone else's! These young people want what they want no matter who gets hurt. C'mon Sharon, she was wrong and you know it. What does she want, sympathy? Well, she won't get any from Alexis."

"Ladies, let's not bite each other's heads off because of our girls. We all know Simone and Aaron were wrong. Calling them names will only strain our relationship. Alexis is doing fine. She is at the height of her nursing career and owns her own home and has a lot to offer a real man that can handle her. If she wants to patch things up with Simone then she will do that on her own time. I'm not too sure if she can handle being an auntie to her ex-fiancé's child. I mean, at the kid's birthday parties he will be there and she will be there. She would have to look at him with his family. It would be a constant reminder of what a raw deal she got handed."

"I am sorry for calling Simone a trollop. It is sad to say that this whole ordeal has put a strain on all of us. I only hope that they can possibly put something back together." Leslie took a bite of her steak. "I know Tracy has little to do with her as well."

"I know my Simone did wrong. Believe me she is paying for it. She lost her best friend, the one she said she loves, and now will end up a single parent. Sure, Aaron will be there in between his womanizing. I know she wants to talk to Alexis. To say what, I don't know. Maybe they should talk. They never spoke after the wedding. You see my daughter has never had a man of her own. She has always dealt with a man that was either married, dating, or just flat out told her that he sees other women, and she dealt with that just to have someone in her life. It is time for her to realize that she deserves better than that. And now that she is going to have a baby without a husband, it will be even harder to find a man with a child in the middle."

"There are men out there that are man enough for the job, Sharon," Dottie said.

"Yes, I know. Do you think Alexis will be open to having an open forum with the rest of the girls? I mean, they need to talk it out even if they are not going to be friends any longer. I want them to at least talk it over," Sharon said.

"Well, let's set it up! Put them girls in a room and let them hash it out. They all have some sort of issue going on. Simone and Alexis. Simone and Sidney. Tracy and Simone . . ."

Sharon interrupted Leslie. "It seems like my Simone is a little disgruntled. I think I made her feel bad when I always gave Sid so much praise—how well she was in school; how she kept her home life in order for many years. Maybe that put Simone in an awkward position. Shit, I need another drink! Waiter, refill these wine glasses please." She drank the last of her wine. "Simone wants to be loved by a man and I only pray that she will find one. She's a beautiful girl and I want her to realize that she can wait until one comes along."

Dottie finished her wine and asked the waiter for the bill. "Well, how about some time this week? That way it can be over and done with. This is what we will do. We will have them meet over at your house, Leslie, that way no one will be too suspicious and then we tell them to talk it out or die. And with a miracle, they could come out in one piece. Now let us get out of here before we are unable to drive home."

Sharon grabbed all of their hands together and looked each one in the eyes. "You know there is nothing like friends. You girls have been like a vital organ to me and I would not know what to do if for some reason we can't maintain this friendship." She had some tears flow from her eyes. "I love you, girls!"

"I love you too, Sharon," Dottie said wiping her eyes.

"Me too, you old geezers. Give me a hug." And the women hugged to embrace their seasoned friendship. The intensity of their hug let them and everyone in the room know that they had a bond that cannot be broken.

Chapter 9

Elijah was wrapping up last-minute projects at the office. With the secretary on a family medical leave, things were a little more hectic in the office. Neither he nor Aaron had any office skills. He was looking in his drawer for a file he needed when he came across Aaron and Alexis's wedding invitation. Looking at it gave him an overwhelming feeling of sadness and at the same time a warm and sensual sensation. Yes, that was the day that he watched his friends go through the hardest day of their lives but that was also the night he had made sweet love to a woman he had longed for as long as he could remember.

He had never told another human being what happened between the two of them. That was a night that meant more to him than Alexis could ever imagine. He never felt that she understood the love he had given her that night. How when he touched her his heart and soul poured out to her. His heart ached because he knew that she had been so torn apart that night and just needed to be held and needed. Not ever realizing that his heart was strong and true. How he had felt so good sharing this intimacy and thinking of how if Aaron ever found out it would risk the friendship they had had since the day they were born.

Aaron and Elijah had been born on the same day. Their mothers had shared a room after they had their sons and became good friends since. They lived in the same area and have known each other since the very beginning. They were more like brothers than friends. People sometimes suspected that they were brothers. Aaron being the only child had always looked toward Elijah as his brother; to the point where when Aaron got in trouble with other kids at school, he always had Elijah on the scene.

Elijah quickly put the invite back in the drawer when he heard Aaron walk through the door. "What's up, man?"

Aaron sat on the chair in front of Elijah's desk. "I need to get us a temp from an agency. This is a mess. I can't type and I have no idea how Linda filed anything."

"Well, I am down for a temp that's for sure. What are you getting into tonight?"

"Oh man, I don't know. This chick wants to take me out tonight. I don't think I want to go though."

Elijah snickered. "Damn, man, you got chicks taking you out and one pregnant and is letting you stay there until you find another place. No telling what else you got going! Yo, whatever happened to Nicole?"

Aaron put his arms up and behind his head and took a deep breath. "She is still around with her crazy ass! Calling me all the time on my cell. I told her that there might be something more than just casual meetings and she is running with it." He started laughing. "She is about to be cut the hell off! I mean, I told her that I was expecting a child and she thinks it is great! Most women would have stepped off but this one is relentless!"

"Well, it's you telling these women that they are the apple of your eye. One day it will catch up with you. Why in the hell do you think Simone risked it all to be with your ass? You know you told her all the buttery shit a woman wants to hear. Not to mention chewing on that kitty cat all so well."

Aaron laughed even harder. "Stop it, man! It ain't like that at all. Simone knew what was the deal but she ran with it. I can't help it if she lost it all. I care about Simone but I can't be what she wanted me to be. I have been with women and none of them came close . ."

Elijah interrupted, "To Alexis?"

Aaron put his head down. "Yeah, man. I really fucked that up. She never gave me another chance. Won't even return my phone calls! Can you believe her?"

Elijah could not believe what he was hearing. How could this man be so dumb? He had no remorse about what he did to the woman of both of their dreams. "Aaron, you are sick. You met your match, huh? Lex is not one of those broads that you can run any old game on. You fucked up, now enjoy it!"

"Hey, when you talk to her, does she ask about me?"

Elijah shook his head no. Then got up from the chair and went to the filing cabinet. "She never ever ask about you."

"Do you bring my name up?" Aaron inquired.

"Nope. Not at all. What am I supposed to tell her?" he said, still digging in the filing cabinet.

"EJ, you know that out of all the women I came across Alexis was the one for me. I mean, she is everything that a man would want. I wonder if she is dating someone." He stood up and walked toward Elijah. "I want to be with her. I really do. If she has not seen anyone since our breakup then I may still have a chance."

"At what?" Elijah said in disgust.

"A chance with her again. I still love her. I've never stopped thinking of her. Never! Elijah, I made a mistake. I'm changed in a big way."

"Since when?" Elijah slammed the cabinet shut. "You just got finished saying that you were going out with this chick tonight and that you have Nicole to think about and not to mention Simone home pregnant with your first child! Where does Alexis fit in? Aaron, we are in our thirties and you still want to play around. You had a great woman but you fucked it up completely! You have a baby on the way. Grow up, man! This is big. A baby is a big deal!"

Aaron threw himself on the couch in the office. "I know. Don't you think I know? I love kids and I am glad that I have this chance but you don't understand. It is not under the circumstances I would have wanted it to be. I would have loved it with Alexis. I think I am going to give it one more shot."

"You're kidding, right? Do you think she will go for it?"

"No. Not at all. I have to deal with this mess. Elijah, it is just that she is so beautiful. She has all that I have ever wanted. I was going on five years with her. Not one, but five! I cheated only twice."

"Only?" he said raising his eyebrows.

"I know but they were just flings that did not last a week. I took a month to pick out Lexi's ring. We bought a house and I never stayed in the mother fucker! Do you know how much I regret screwing her over like that? Now this baby! Oh my god, Simone is having a baby. Don't I get some credit for trying to hang in there with her? I commend her for just telling me to leave but she knew that Alexis Blackmon has been and will always be my one true love." He lay down on the couch like he was taking his last breath. "Girl! Girls! Girls! They are going to be the death of me. That night of the wedding, did she ever calm down?"

Elijah had hoped that he would never ask each detail of that night. He replayed in his mind how he had straddled her, kissing her tender lips ever so softly—the look on her face when he touched her where she loved to be touched. Now Aaron wanted to know if she had become calm or if she was upset all night. Elijah tried to figure a way to do so without leading on to what had really happened that night. He sat back in his chair and wiped his forehead. "Yeah, she eventually calmed down."

"In your arms I suppose?"

"Yes, in my arms. She was completely devastated. I just couldn't sit and watch her without consoling her. Don't you know you put me in a tight spot that night?" Elijah leaned back in the chair. "Why don't you just take some time to yourself? I mean, leave these women alone. Reevaluate what is important to you and for you. These women will be here. As for Alexis, well, just give it up. If it were meant to be for the two of you then it will be. But for now, think about this kid you got coming and the nutcase you have following you around."

Still lying on the couch, Aaron said, "I wonder if I was the last one she slept with. We held out on each other before the wedding and I know she is not seeing anyone. I also know that she will not sleep with someone and not be involved with him. It has been a long time. Eight months to be exact."

"Why would you care if she slept with someone?" Elijah had to ask.

"I know one day she will be dating someone but I do not want to see it. It would kill me. To know that another man has touched what I touched, wondering if he gave her orgasms the way I made her have orgasm after orgasm, loved what I still love." Aaron took a deep breath and rubbed his temples. "This is going to send me to an early grave. I just know it."

All the while Aaron was talking to his best friend, Elijah continued to visualize the night that was shared between Alexis and himself, the smell of her skin and the sounds of ecstasy that escaped from her tender sweet lips. Elijah can't believe how much that night meant to him. It meant the world to him. He would never let on to anyone of the night that was shared. He felt too much for her to let her down and go against her wishes. "Well, I just want you to be prepared for when she does."

Aaron jumped up quickly. "I am going to need you in my defense because whoever he is will be dead! But for real, though, I know she deserves what I can't give her. I want her to have what I could not give.

And this man better have his shit together. Or else I am going to have to beat his ass down!"

"Man, please!" Elijah threw his pen on the notepad on his desk. "You fucked up so don't get mad when another man steps up to the plate. The best thing you said was that she deserves better. Leave Alexis alone. Now go and get yourself some diapers and formula, Daddy! I love you, my brother, but you are too much for me."

"Oh, man, please! You act like an old man! You've played a few chicks in your day too now. Look at you and Shell. She told you she wanted to see other people and you went for it. You barely date anymore. What's up, man? You ain't going soft on me, are you?"

Elijah gave that soft chuckle that drives women wild. "No, I am not going soft. It is just that I am tired of dealing with women that want to drag me through the mud. Shelley had taken me through so much. I see her when I see her and that is that. I have dated other women but nothing too serious. Like this woman named Nadia. She is mad cool but she does not want to get married or have children. So why bother with her and get all serious when I know it will not go any farther than a Broadway show or her bedroom? Fine as hell and smart too, but not a maternal bone in her body. She hates kids and does not want any. So we keep it real and deal with one another just the way it is."

"Well, you still sleep around," Aaron said trying to put him in his boat.

"I don't sleep around. I have Nadia and Shelley when it is convenient. I have no commitments to anyone. I would want to, just not with either of them. What I want is for keeps. Signed and sealed."

"That is what I want too. Just not right now. I will just tell these women that I am only going to go so far," Aaron said raising his hands as though he had proven a point.

Elijah got up to put on his jacket and turned off the light as he and Aaron walked out of the office. "Just so you know, Counselor, your cock will cost you more than you can spend one day!"

"You don't worry about my cock! Just get yourself some and you won't feel so tight at the collar."

"Whatever, homeboy! Just don't get yourself tangled up to the point where some hoochie will get half of our business!" Elijah said patting Aaron on the back.

"Never that, Counselor. I'm straight. Let me go and check on Simone and then go give Nicole what she has been craving."

I am so glad to be getting out of the house tonight. Not to mention that Tracy offered to drive tonight. It never fails; when all of us get out, I seem to be the driver. I think Tracy is floating on something that none of us know about. "So Tracy, Malcolm is staying with Jerome at his house tonight?" I said jokingly.

Tracy sighed with annoyance. "Yes, and where is this heading? No, as a matter of fact, don't take this anywhere. Malcolm wanted to stay with him and it was OK with me. End of story, Alexis."

"Yeah, yeah, we heard it all before. Why don't you see yourself with this man?" I said poking her in the shoulder.

"You know you want to," Sidney added from the backseat.

"Jerome and I are friends! Stevie Wonder can see that! Why can't the two of you?" Tracy said as she paid the toll to the Lincoln Tunnel. "I mean, I have a great friendship with him and if things change it will be ruined and that is not a chance I am willing to take."

"Girl, go for it. Shit, that's what's wrong with us women. We are always putting up a front and trying to be politically correct. Trying to stay true to the no-good men that we deal with. Now you have someone in your life that wants to be with you and we *all* know it and you are acting stinky. You know what? You better get some. Don't be like me and keep true to one man. You see what happened to me. I have never ever slept with another soul. I thought about it and visualized it, but I never did it. I wanted to be with my one and only husband. And look at the thanks I get. I have three kids and my husband has four!" Sidney leaned up to the front seat between Tracy and me. "Newsflash, ladies, I was only pregnant three times. Will someone do the math around here?"

Oh god, I hope for the rest of the night we are not going to hear about Sidney and Marcus. I turned to Sidney. "Sid, you have what most women can only dream of and write books on. You have something that I would love to have. Don't you think that Tracy and I want that too? We want to be with one man instead of the ones we were with."

"Excuse me, Dr. Ruth, I was only with two men. Ronnie and Malcolm. And I can't count Ronnie 'cause we only did it once and I couldn't cum because I didn't know how. So technically I only had one," Tracy said in her defense.

"No, dear, you had two. Once the weenie penetrated, you had sex. Therefore, you had not one but two men," I said throwing two fingers in her face. "And that is a name that you have not mentioned since you met Malcolm. I wonder how he is doing."

"You ain't lying," Sidney joined in.

Throwing her hand in my face. "Whatever! Malcolm has and always will be my true love. I don't know of any man that can take his place," Tracy said, parking the car in the lot next to the Shadow. "Now, since you got so much to say, say that you have some money to park."

"We got your money, you loner," I said.

xoxoxoxoxoxoxox

Sidney

Oh this is my jam. I got to get on the dance floor and dance to Ja Rule's "Always on Time." It feels so good to dance and think only of staying in rhythm than to think of the fact that my husband's affair had had an end product. I just wanted to dance until the owner put me out.

Look at this fine-ass man dancing alone and it looked like he was coming my way. There is nothing better than a man that can dress. His chest was looking mighty good in that white button-down shirt with that nice gold chain around that strong neck. Those long but built legs and that honey-golden skin and tight hairline. Oh shit, here he comes! Let me just keep dancing like I do not even see him. Maybe he would keep going. I think not because here he comes with a nice-ass smile. He looked even better close up. This man was gorgeous!

"Excuse me, would you like to dance?" he said, holding his hand out. "And don't say no, please."

I did not want to dance with this man. Lord knows I didn't. "Yes, come on." I guess the Lord knew I was lying because not only did I want to dance with him, I wanted to take him to a hotel. Whew, the way his body just flowed with the bass of the music. His height was just perfect, he had to be six feet two. His chest was wider than Victoria Lake. He looked at me with deep large eyes. What a seductive smile he had. I am not complaining at all. I am no slouch on the dance floor and the music is moving me to a whole new beat right now. I don't know what's going on but I need to get close to smell the scent of his cologne. And he is wearing Paul Sebastian. Man, do I love that. Look at me getting it on with this man, rubbing my body next to this fine-ass total stranger.

Now that the DJ is jamming I am having a better time than ever. Jon B's "Don't Talk" sounded so good. I think I like rubbing up against this man feeling the width of his masculinity. He looked and smelled so good. Lord, have mercy! Marcus who? He was a great dancer. He seemed to like grinding against my body as well. Look at him wrapping his hands around my waist. And I like it. Yes I do. "What's your name?"

He smiled at me. "Maleek, and what's yours?"

I could not help but blush. "Sidney is my name. I like the way you dance. Are you here often?" I said while turning my back to him.

"No, this is my first time. I'm here with my cousins. I just moved here from Massachusetts," he said in my ear while stroking me from top to bottom.

"Oh I see," I said in a trance. Oh my god, he feels so good. I wonder what he is thinking. "Do you like New York?"

"It has its moments. But now that I met you I love it," he said with a sincere look on his handsome face. "Do you want a drink or do you want to continue to dance?"

I want to take you to a hotel. I wish I were bold enough to say that. "No, we can drink. Let's go." I let him lead me off the dance floor. I liked that in a man. I wondered what Alexis and Tracy would say if they saw this. But you know what? I am just dancing with him, nothing more.

He got us to the bar and waited patiently for the bartender. "What would you like?"

"A Sprite, thanks."

"A Sprite? You look like a lady that would like something like a *sex on the beach* or something like that, not a Sprite," he said with that fine-ass, gorgeous smile.

"Sorry, I don't drink." I guess I couldn't say I was flirting because I was drunk. I was so sober it wasn't funny.

We got our drinks. He sipped on a glass of Hennessey. He took me by the hand and guided me upstairs where we could talk I guess. "Do you mind us going upstairs? I want to take a break from the dance floor."

"No, not at all. I can use the break. I had an exhausting day." I was glad he asked. I would like to know all about him especially why he had come here all the way from Massachusetts. I was highly curious. I couldn't believe I was talking to a man other than my husband. And it actually felt nice. Marcus would get over it. He has to, just like I had to get over his affair. After all, I was only having a drink, nothing else.

xoxoxoxoxoxo

Alexis

Lord, look at Sidney with that handsome man. Life is so strange. Here she is married with a man that will walk through fire for her and she got another man that looks like God's greatest creation. And I am here dancing alone. I keep rejecting these big-head men with an abundance of cologne on. Not to mention that I had gotten dumped at the altar. Some women have all the men or none of them. Brandy's song "What about Us" sounds good as hell in here. I had not been out in so long. I know one thing, it felt good to be able to dance and let my body flow to the music.

My groove was quickly interrupted when someone's hands came from behind me. I swiftly turned. "What the hell—"

"Whoa, don't hit!"

It's Elijah. "Boy, I could have killed you! Don't do that! You were about to get decked dead in the eye!" I said, lightly punching him in the chest. And what a nice chest it was.

He backed up in surrender. "I didn't mean to scare you. It is just that you look so beautiful dancing like you do not have a care in the world," he said eyeing me up and down. "How have you been? I have not seen you since . . . well, you know."

"Yeah, I know. I'm doing fine. What about you?" I can't believe how attractive he is. That burgundy suit is hot. I loved the way his three-quarter jacket swayed off of his toned body. The one thing about Aaron and Elijah was that they could dress their asses off. I knew other men must be jealous when the two of them walked into a room.

"I'm OK. I was bored and I wanted to get my party on. Business is one hectic day after another. Who are you here with?" he said, guiding me to the center of the floor.

Accepting his lead, I spoke over Jay Z's lyrics, "Sid and Tracy. I hope to God you are not here with Aaron!"

He turned to me and held me by the waist. "I have no clue where that fool is. I never even called to ask if he wanted to hang. You know with him about to have a bambino any day now."

I had to be reminded of that. "Yeah, I know. You look good to-night. I have not spoken to you in so long. It is good to see you," I said, letting him caress my body. I had almost forgotten how endearing his touch was. It's a shame that he has no real woman to touch all the time.

"Thanks. I don't have to tell you that you are the finest woman in here. I'm glad that you moved on with your life. I knew you would be fine." He continued to graze my body with his, bending down low and letting me rub his head, all while he was following Jay Z's lyrics: "*It's about to go down.*"

I can't believe how attracted I am to him. I mean, I had always thought he was handsome but I would have never acted on it. He was more brotherly than anything. Now, I just see him in a totally different light. I guess it was from that night. I will never forget how sincere he had been that night. I know he basically confessed to me that he felt more for me than he should but I had not really heard him at the time. I let my hands sashay across his chest as he came up to my eye level. "I didn't know you could dance like this, Mr. Faison."

"There is a lot about me you do not know. You did have your chance to find out. Now you will have to just wonder," he said being unpretentious. "I'm no punk on the dance floor. You are not too bad yourself, Ms. Blackmon." He smiled so sweetly. He reeled me into his arms and held me tight as though he had not seen me in such a long time.

"Wow, that was a tight hug. Are you OK?"

"Yes, I just wanted to hug you, that's all. Did that make you feel uncomfortable?" He backed off a little but continued to dance with me.

"No, not at all. It just caught me off guard. Come on, let's go to the bar. I am parched. I think you danced the life right out of me," I said tapping my throat.

"I thought you could hang. I'm so disappointed in you, Alexis." He followed me off the dance floor and we walked to the bar. "What can I get you, my lady?"

"Rum and coke."

He aggressively turned around. "You should venture out and change your drink. You have been drinking that since I met you." He tipped the bartender and gave me my drink. "But then again, I am glad to see that you have not changed."

I leaned in closer to hear him better. At least that is what I told myself. "What is that supposed to mean?"

He smiled and wrapped his arm around my waist. "That is definitely a good thing. I think you are perfect just the way you are. Where are Sidney and Tracy?"

I looked around to see if they were in sight. "Well, Sidney went upstairs with some man and Tracy was over there dancing with someone. She doesn't seem happy though."

"Has she met a man yet? Or is she still pondering over her deceased husband?"

I wanted to laugh but I didn't. He was so right. She was never happy in the company of any man. I wish that she would realize that Malcolm is dead and he was not off to war or something. "Well, I won't touch that. Why are you here alone?"

"Well, I wanted to come out and hear some music. Men have troubles too you know," he said with his hands over his heart like he was so emotional.

"I know the troubles men have. Lisa, Angela, Pamela, Simone!" I said, imitating LL Cool J's "Around the Way Girl." "You know it does not even matter why you are here. I am glad I bumped into you," I said getting closer to him. I wanted so badly to fight the urge I had to just kiss his tender full lips. I have not been with a man in so long, not since we had gotten together on my wedding night, and he was so attractive. How do I say that? What would he say?

"You're being funny. Not all of us are like that. Some of us men want one woman, you know. And when you females get burned, the rest of us suffer for it." He took a gulp of his drink. "I poured my heart to you a while back and you never noticed. What's a guy supposed to do about that?" He asked the bartender for another round of drinks. "Just like you women, we are yearning for love too."

I know he is serious and it is time for me to be serious too. "Can you meet me at my house after we leave here?"

He jumped back. "What?"

I began to stutter. "I . . . I mean would you like to come to my house tonight? Or maybe another night? I . . . uh . . . I mean if you don't have plans. Just . . . just to have coffee or something." I know good and damn well that I don't want no damn coffee.

He seemed like the cat got his tongue. He looked up to the ceiling with a smile on his face and then faced me. "Lex, I would love to but I have so much to do tomorrow. We do have over an hour's drive from here. How about we call each other and make plans?"

I wanted to make plans tonight and he was too stupid to realize it. "I think that sounds nice. I'm sorry to burden you. I just wanted to spend some time with a special friend," I said seductively.

He opened his eyes like he had just become overwhelmed with a rush of reality. He could not believe what he had just heard. He polished off his Hennessey. "Oh . . . oh yes, we can make it for another time. What time are you girls leaving?"

"Whenever. I know they will be ready soon. Are you leaving now?"

"Soon. I think I've had enough for tonight." He held my hand and stared me straight in the eyes.

I didn't want to leave him but I had to before I said and did something humiliating. I kissed him on the cheek. "Let me look for these women. It's 4 a.m., by the time we reach home it will be almost 6 a.m." I stroked his face. "See you later," I said in that special way.

xoxoxoxoxoxoxoxoxox

I am so ready to get out of here. Where in the hell is Sidney? The last time I saw her she was letting some man grope her body like she was a single teenager. I thought I was into this party scene but I guess I'm not. All these men here trying to rub their hard dicks on your butt is nerve wracking. I mean, why can't two people just dance and not turn it into some dirty rotten porno tape.

Not one man in here has asked me to dance with their mind instead of their dicks. They don't know me from Eve. I loved to dance and I liked to come here but I guess this was not a good night for me. I could usually come out and have a good time but for some reason I just couldn't tonight. The smoke was bothering me. It's too crowded and hot. All the men in here lacked the ability to capture my attention. Except for that fine man Sidney had run off with. He was fine. Even I had to admit that.

I would be elated when Alexis and Sidney are ready. It is after four in the morning. I had to get some rest before Jerome and I go to the show tomorrow. I would rest until he brings Malcolm home. This club scene has worn out its welcome. I'm sorry, Shadow, but I have had enough of you. Here come Sid and Lex now. Thank you, God, for answering my prayers.

Chapter 11

Alexis

Damn we're here already. I gathered my shoes and decided to walk to my house barefoot. "All right, Tracy and Sid, I'll talk to you later. Have fun tonight, Tracy," I shut the car door and walked from the car. They watched me get into the house and Tracy pulled off.

I was so glad to be home. I'd had a wonderful time tonight. Or should I say, last night. It had been nice to get my party on. And it had been nice to see Elijah again. Getting to my bedroom is going to be a chore since my feet were killing me. Who is ringing my doorbell? "Oh my god, Elijah what are you doing here?" I opened the door for him.

He had a smile on his face. "I just wanted some coffee." He walked right in past me. He then turned to me. "I know you are wondering what I'm doing here. It's that I couldn't think of nothing else since the club."

I did bark up this tree. I played big girl in the club and now I was scared like a virgin on prom night. I couldn't believe he came here. I was not upset, just caught off guard. "Well, I just got here. And I had not even made it upstairs yet. I thought you weren't coming. I mean, I thought you had so much work to do," I said massaging my aching feet.

He sat next to me on the loveseat. "I can't play these games with you. And I damn sure don't want you playing games with me." He sat on the floor and took over massaging my feet, "Lex, I have been longing for you for some time now and I had my chance before and I let it go. Now, seeing you at the club tonight gave me that chance again. I want to try and develop something."

"Talking about getting right to the point."

He continued to rub. "Alexis, I know I'm putting a lot on the line here but you are worth the risk. Aaron may kill me but I continue to think of you. That night we spent together has never left my mind. I was hurting for you but my heart was hoping that you would come with me and let me love you."

I had to take my feet away for this. "Elijah, I don't know what to say. I care about you deeply and that night I was devastated and confused.

I thought of that night many times myself. I never acted on it because I was getting over Aaron."

"I know that."

"Then do you know that I feel more than just friends for you?"

"No, I did not know that," he said, caught off guard.

"Well, I do. It's just that we are treading on troubled waters by dealing with each other. I loved the night we spent together. I would not change that night for anything in the world. Most importantly you never said a word to anyone and that showed me much respect."

"Well, that's why I waited until Tracy pulled off. Look, we don't have to make love or call each other every day. Let's just keep in touch a bit more often and see where it takes us. What do you think?" he said, walking toward me.

"When I asked you to come over tonight I was not playing. I counted on you saying no. Now that you are here I'm a bit nervous."

He grabbed my waist with one hand and my face with the other and kissed me like a prince would kiss a princess. "I knew what you were up to. You can't resist me." He started laughing.

I smacked his chest. "Don't flatter yourself. I thought you looked good as hell and I guess the rum and coke got to me."

"Look I better go. I'm glad that you got home safe and I wanted to tell you what I just told you. Now, whenever you are ready to go out or if you want to, I'm here. You know the numbers." He put his coat on and started for the door.

"Elijah, wait." I blocked the door. "Don't go. I mean, we didn't have coffee."

He let out that handsome smile. "I like mine black and sweet." He pinned me to the door and kissed me like no other has, rubbing my hair and giving all of his tongue.

I couldn't help but to give in. I wanted this and he did too. His hands caressing my breasts felt so good. And his chest is so firm and masculine. I am so glad that he came over here. I wanted Elijah and I wanted to try and make this work. I grabbed his face. "Elijah."

He gasped for air. "Yes, Lex? You want me to stop?"

Oh my god, this is a step that I wanted to take but was so very afraid to. "No, take me upstairs."

He lifted me up and carried me upstairs while kissing me, never letting my lips go. When we got upstairs he let me down and stood me up. "Shower with me." He led me to the bathroom in my bedroom and turned on the shower, all the while never letting my hand go. I let him undress me and I helped him undress. I had almost forgotten what his body looked like. Damn good, that's what it looked like. We stepped into the shower and let the steamy hot water douse our bodies, still kissing and enjoying each other, loving all that he was giving me. I turned so he could wash my back with some Bath and Body raspberry shower gel, washing my back while kissing my neck. I couldn't help but to reach backward and put my arm around his neck. He let me turn and wash his body while still caressing mine. I had an overwhelming urge to just jump on him, but I just let the mood we created flow.

We finished our foreplay shower and dried each other off. As I let him guide me to the room, he grabbed some body lotion off my dresser and turned on WBLS's Quiet Storm. Hearing Ready for the World's "Tonight" was perfect for this moment. He gently laid me on the bed. "Lex, you are so beautiful. Let me massage your body. I just want to touch, feel, and admire you."

I could not say a word back. Shit, it has been eight months and I am not going to deny a man who wanted to give me a body rub. He turned me over and spread the lotion all over my back, using those soft but masculine hands, and massaging my back with slow and long strokes. He made my body collapse into pure pleasure from my back to my buttocks to the heels of my feet. As he turned me over, he rubbed my shoulders, down to my breasts, and to the tips of my toes.

He came up to look me in the eyes. "Lexi, I love you. Let me show you."

I held his face and kissed his lips. "Elijah." I will not stop him from this. I was feeling so good right now, I couldn't control myself. I mean I do love Elijah, but a relationship with him will and can get so complicated. But you know what? I do not even care. I have this man that loved me, and I had not even known it, in my arms and in my bed. He had kept his distance so well that I had known nothing of his feelings. He has been the most upstanding man I have ever known, not to mention the best damn lover. "I want you too, Elijah. I want you too."

From that point on, we made passionate love until midmorning, kissing and caressing and showing one another how much we do care for each other. How we had held back what should have happened a long time ago. There is nothing like being held in the arms of a man that truly and deeply loved you, feeling his heart beating next to yours and being scared of what could happen and what may not happen. We told each other how grateful we were to have finally said how we felt. There was nothing more powerful than having multiple orgasms simultaneously, watching his handsome face crumple in ecstasy. His hands felt strong when he intertwined his fingers in mine. His breath was hot against my flesh. The look in those deep brown eyes when he asked me to look into his and the mood left in the room when our bodies collapsed from the most pleasantly exhausting sexual experience that we have ever had made me feel that though it will be noon soon, I was so excited that I could go on all day and night. But for now, I will let him rejuvenate.

Chapter 12
Simone

"Oh shit! Make it stop! Make it stop, please!" I couldn't help but scream. This act of labor is killing me and the most painful part of all was not knowing where that damn Aaron was. "Mom, did you page Aaron again? Whoa! Shit! Ouch! When is the epidural going to kick the fuck in?" These contractions are coming in less than a minute apart and the epidural had not taken affect.

"Monie, honey, you have to calm down," My mother said, trying to calm me down while wiping the beads of labor off my forehead. "The pain will ease a little if you calmed down. Now I paged Aaron and called his cell phone. I even called Elijah and he's not home either. This may have to go on without him."

"My god, this shit hurts!" I screamed with the next contraction. "Whew, whew, whew, whew, whew, whew," I panted during the contraction. I couldn't believe how much this hurts. I felt like I couldn't even recover from one contraction to the next. I knew my body was going to crack in two or explode. I didn't know how much more of this I could take. I have been in labor for nineteen hours now and I was at my wit's end. "Oh here it comes again! Aaron, I am going to kill you!"

"Girl, if you do not stop making threats you know these white folks will have the cops sitting right at the foot of the bed after you deliver. Now just breathe deeply and you will be fine. Monie, my sweet little Monie, you are doing fine. I know you don't think you are right now but when that precious baby comes out you will forget so quickly what just occurred," she said, wiping more sweat from my head and giving me ice chips.

Dr. Morehouse walked in to check my progress. She was a light brown-skinned woman and very tall. She had to be six feet tall. I have been going to her for years and felt very close to her but I hated it when she had to put practically her whole hand up my canal to check for dilation. "Simone, you are ready to push. Nurse, will you set up please? It will be almost over. It all depends on your pushing ability and how much you cooperate."

"Doctor, I am so glad to hear you say that. I am getting so tired of this! Ooh . . . ooh . . . ooh!"

My mother kissed my forehead and wrapped her arms around my shoulders. "This is it, sweetie. This is the moment that transforms a girl into a woman. Mommy is right here with you, OK?"

"OK, Simone, with the next contraction I need you to give a good and strong push," Dr. Morehouse said.

"OK!" I screamed. I could not help but grunt and bear down. I pushed and pushed and nothing was happening. "Is it over yet? Do you see the head yet?" I begged.

"You're doing great, Simone. C'mon on, baby, push! That's it, Monie, push!"

I pushed for an hour and finally I heard the tiny sounds of a little person crying. I couldn't believe my eyes when I saw this little person. "Oh my god! What is it? What is it?" I demanded.

"Look at this big boy," Dr. Morehouse answered. "Grandma, now you cut the cord."

My mother jumped at the idea of cutting the cord. "Dear Lord, thank you Jesus. Thank you. Look at him! Don't cry, baby, grandma's here. Lie on you mama." She kissed the baby and me.

I was still in shock at what was lying on my belly, crying and squirming around while the nurse dried him off. "Oh, baby, don't cry. Mommy is here. Mommy's here." I just held him with tears filling my eyes. The emotions were overwhelming. "Mom, look at him. He looks just like Aaron."

"No, you think so? I think he looks like you when you were a baby. Then again, he does look like Aaron too around the nose I guess. It doesn't matter, he is precious," she said.

I can't believe I am holding my baby, the one who has been in my belly for nine months kicking and turning. He had all his fingers and toes, and his lungs definitely worked. I hated it that the nurse had to take him away for measuring. I sent my mom in to go with him and take pictures and to make sure that he was not going to be switched. I had that fear in the back of my head. Well, Aaron missed it. He don't even know that his son had been born. I couldn't dwell on that though. I have a son, a son that will need me for the rest of his life. Here is to many nights of waking up every two hours, dirty diapers, and love. I had just given birth to Aaron McKnight Jr. I just thought of something, my mother was right, I did forget all about the pain I had just endured, the whole twenty hours of it. That is so weird; the labor of love seemed to be a thing of the past.

Shannon N. Davis

Chapter 13
Tracy

"You know the show was excellent, Jerome."

"I'm glad that you liked it. I had heard it was a good play," Jerome said while flagging down the limo he had rented for us tonight.

"I still can't believe you went and got us a limo for the play," I said as the limo driver opened the door for us to get in. "You didn't have to go through all this trouble," I said as we both climbed into the car.

Jerome began taking off his leather jacket. "Well, you know that I want to make an impression on you. Tracy, I think you are special enough for a limo. Besides, it will give us a chance to talk and not worry about all the lights and traffic of Manhattan. Are you telling me that you are not impressed?"

He knew I was and I knew he wanted to hear me say it. "I am deeply moved," I said, holding my hand to my chest. "I am glad that I didn't let your mother get this nice night."

"So you got jokes, huh?" He had moved from sitting across from me to being right next to me. "Tracy, I want to talk to you about something." He kept a sincere stare with his big coal-black eyes.

"What?" I knew where this may end up. He could never have a nice night without going there.

"I want you to know how I feel about you. I mean, I need you to know. I need you to know how much I desire you. I need to feel you in my arms every day."

"Jerome . . .," I said, feeling uneasy

"No, let me finish," he interrupted. "Let me finish. Do you know how much I want to have you in my life? To make love to you all night long? To feel your body next to mine in the morning? To see you day in and day out? Do you know these things?" He pleaded.

"I . . . sort of . . ."

He interrupted again, "No, I do not think you do. As a matter of fact, I know you don't." He leaned into me and passionately kissed my lips. "Do I need to say more?"

That was the nicest kiss I have had in a while. It had felt so nice and tender. It had felt wholesome and real. Looking into his eyes, I said, "Jerome, I don't know what to say. I . . ."

He leaned into me again, this time not letting me go. He held on to my face and neck with both hands and passionately gave me all he had in his kiss. Stroking my hair and rubbing my thighs, he stopped kissing me, and said, "Tracy, I know it has been a while but I want to show you how much I love you."

I tried to catch my breath. "Ten years."

"Things have changed in ten years," he said with a smirk. "You're beautiful and I bet tasty."

"Jerome, no we can't. You know why." I took a gulp of spit down my throat. "I want to but I . . ."

He stood in front of me on his knees. "Baby, there is nothing, and I mean nothing, to be afraid of. I love you, Tracy." He began kissing my neck and opening my dress with his hands, feeling my breasts and devouring my neck. Then he engulfed my breasts with his hot wet mouth, all the while rubbing between my legs with his fingers.

I couldn't believe how good he was making me feel. I had forgotten how good it felt. I couldn't make myself stop him. I knew Jerome was a good man and I knew he was crazy about me. I just don't know how I could get through my thoughts of how my life with Malcolm, my husband, had been. Now, that he had just slid my panties off and had begun massaging my clitoris with his tongue, I may have to try harder. I couldn't believe I was giving in to the pleasure of this. My pelvis rocked up and down to the motion of his tongue, rubbing his neatly trimmed head. I could now feel how much he loved me. "Jerome, oh, Jerome," I panted.

He never said a word, just loved from down below. Clamping down on my clitoris gently with his teeth, tightly holding my thighs apart to keep them open just right to his liking. He must have known how good he was making me feel because he was doing it better and better. My pelvis was rocking up and down much more aggressively and I'm at that point that makes a person do what they do. Oh shit, I couldn't believe my heart is beating out of chest and my eyes had just completely crossed. I felt weak and drained but content. With my head rocking from side to side in disbelief, I asked, "What . . . what just happened here?"

He came up to my eye level and kissed me gently. "I knew you would taste good."

I began to laugh. "We're here. Damn that was quick!" I closed my dress and put my panties in my pocket. "Jerome, we just crossed the line."

"Don't hate me. I thought you wanted it too."

"No, I am fine. Let's just go. Driver, please let us out."

The driver opened the door and let us out. We both walked to the door, neither one of us saying a word, both wondering what was going to happen next. I felt like I had just ruined my life. I felt like I had just lost the pureness of our relationship though it had felt so good—definitely a lot better than my vibrator.

Jerome took my keys and opened the door and let me in. He shut the door behind him and grabbed me. "Let me make love to you tonight and every night," he said looking deep into my eyes.

I broke away from his hold. "I can't! I just can't! I'm married."

"To who?" he asked. "I mean, as far as I know your husband died ten years ago. Please, Tracy, please don't do this!"

"God, why don't you take no for an answer? What is so hard for you to understand? I'm not ready to get involved!"

Jerome slapped his forehead in disbelief. "You have mourned enough! This is completely unhealthy! You know I love you. You know that!"

"You don't know what you want. I owe it to my husband to not do this. I owe it to Malcolm."

"You don't owe anything. You mourned your husband's death already. And you know I am nuts over Malcolm as if he were my own. He is more comfortable talking to me than you. Is that what you hate?"

"Who are you to judge how long I mourn the only man that I've loved? Malcolm likes that you come to show him basketball. I just can't, Jerome. I just can't."

"Are you afraid that I can love you and that you'll love me back? And by the way, Miss Know-It-All, Malcolm does not need help with basketball. He wants me around."

I began to pace back and forth. "You know what? This conversation is over! Please leave," I said with my arms folded.

"You know, Tracy, I'm so in love with you. But I am not going to beg. I am not going to beg a woman who is faithful to the dead. I give you credit, though; you remained faithful 'until death do us part,'" he said with open arms.

"Don't be so cruel! I can't help it if I love my family." I could not hold back the tears. What he said to me hurt deeply.

"I can't understand why you are being hard on me. Have you ever lost someone that you loved beyond life? Have you?"

"No, I haven't. I don't truly know your pain. I can tell you that I love you so much and I see now that I can't have you. So no, I have not loved someone and lost them. However, I do love someone who is breathing and living and she can't see past her husband's tombstone to see just how much. Do you know how that kills a man's ego? Do you?"

"No, I don't," I mumbled while sniffling.

"Well, then you can figure it out without me. I'm through here. I refuse to compete with a dead man. I just can't do it. I have done it for over two years and I am done. I am telling you this; I am putting my two weeks notice in."

I stood up. "What?"

"I can't be around you and want you the way that I do. I can't drown in that kind of misery. You've drowned and it must be killing you. It actually has because you are so worn and so out of touch with love that you can't see it. Your insides are so dead."

"We have the Vegas account and you don't have a job lined up."

"No, I don't have another job lined up. I will manage with my savings until I find one. After Vegas that's it." He buttoned his jacket and started for the door.

Crying even harder, I said, "Jerome, please don't. I'm hurting so badly. And no one seems to understand that."

He opened the door. "You are so right; I don't have a clue as to what you are feeling. And from this point on I won't have to try and decipher it. I hope that you don't smother Malc with all this pain. The boy is hurting too knowing that you are so hung up on his ghost dad. I'm sorry for you and I am sorry that I'm not strong enough to compete with the dead. Happy marriage." And he slammed the door.

Why did I do that? God, what is wrong with me? We had just shared an intimate moment and I screwed it up completely. I don't blame him for leaving me. I am so mixed up and confused. I can't help that I loved my husband so much that I can't move on. If I love again I will make the same mistake I did when Malcolm was alive. I know what I have to do and I just have to get enough courage to do it.

Shannon N. Davis

Chapter 14
Sidney

"Hello, this is Sidney. Maleek, how are you?" I was calling on my cell phone.

"Oh yeah, what's up, girl? I didn't think I was going to hear from you again," he said excitedly.

"Well, I'm not sure if I should be calling you or not. I mean, you know my situation," I explained.

He cleared his throat as if he were just waking up. "Yeah, I'm all too familiar with women and their situations. So what made you call?" he asked.

Truthfully, I'm not sure why I called. It is very exciting to have someone interested in me, and that I was interested in someone other than Marcus. I have thought of this long and hard since the other night and I am definitely attracted to Maleek and I would like to step out of my character for a while. Everyone does and now it is my turn, "Well, I loved our conversation at the club the other night and I thought maybe we could get together sometime or another."

"You did, huh? Well, that is cool with me. I'm going to be upfront with you before we start this . . . this . . . thing that you think you want to start. I don't want any part of your drama. I mean, if you are going to hang, then hang. Not ever do I want to see you crying and upset, telling me all about your sad marital stories." He cleared his throat again. "Now, I'm not coming off strong, but as you also know of my situation, I am thirty-seven years old and I have no children. I want a woman that wants the same thing I want. Now, I know I cannot have that with you. But I don't mind having you as a friend and I will let you drive the course of this relationship. After all, you are the one with most at stake."

Damn he is right to the point and held back no punches. "Talking about being upfront. Well, I have no problem being a friend. That is all I can be to you anyway, you know, with a husband and children and all. You don't have to school me."

He chuckled. "Cut it out. I am not giving you Maleek 101. I think you're cool. Let's catch a movie tomorrow night."

Here it is and I have the chance to back out and stay faithful. "How about 8:30 or so? To keep it friendly, I will pay for the popcorn." We both laughed

"Hey, I'm not a man that is too macho to let a woman pay for something. I going to super-size it on your liberal behind!" he claimed. "Look, I have to get going I have a photo shoot in two hours."

"Oh yes, we can't keep the little models waiting now can we, Mr. Photographer?" I teased.

"Hey, someone has to do it! So tomorrow night, and call if there will be a change in plans. All right, I will talk to you soon." He hung up the phone.

Sidney, what the hell are you doing? You are a married woman. This is something I have to do. I need to see if I have those womanly qualities that a man would want. I am tired of being "Sidney, the good wife." Or "Sidney the great mother." Or "Sidney the great friend." Sidney this Sidney that. I want to be "Sidney the free." I am glad this whole thing with Marcus and his other daughter came up. This really made me reevaluate my life. I mean I never dated. I never broke a man's heart. I never had the freedom to just get up and go. I have always had Marcus, my first boyfriend and now husband. I had children right away and never had time to even consider if I wanted higher education and a career. Even my twin has her CPA and Tracy has the advertising business that may take off really big if she gets the Vegas account. And Alexis is a big time head nurse at the women's clinic. And all I have are three kids and a husband that has four kids. At least he owns two restaurants. I have nothing.

I love my kids and Marcus too but I want to become "Sidney the woman." I have no experience with nothing but breastfeeding and lovemaking. I know some women would be content with that but I think I am not anymore. After a while you need something more. Yes, I do go out with my best friends every so often, but that is not enough. I've watched them date and have fun. I've listened to stories of old boyfriends or friends that had not made the cut to become boyfriends. All the time Alexis would tell me how blessed I am to have had only one man all these years and I wanted to tell her that it is not all that it is cracked up to be, definitely not all that. I am not saying I want to sleep with Maleek but I damn sure want to live dangerously for a while. Marcus will just have to understand. It is time for Sidney to be there for Sidney. For Sidney to discover who she is. Here's to my coming out party!

Chapter 15
Alexis

Oh this is really nice, waking up next to someone in the morning. Since Elijah and I got together it has been nothing but bliss and good love. The physical is great but the pure intimacy we share is a completely different thing. He calls in the morning and sends roses to the clinic and he signs the card with a smiling heart drawn after his name. I have no idea how Shelley let him go. She is nuts. I get excited all over when he calls or comes over, like I'm sixteen again. But we can't lie in bed all day; I have to get to the clinic and he has to get to the office. "EJ, are you going to sleep through the afternoon?"

He rolled over and wrapped his arm around my waist. "I would if you would too."

"Oh no, buster, get up. You are going to drain me dry if I lie in bed with you another minute." I pushed him toward the edge of the bed.

"C'mon, Lex, Aaron is not going to be there today. He is playin' daddy now. That man is a mess," he said while getting out of bed.

"You said it right, 'playin' daddy.' Little twit was nowhere to be found when Simone had his son. He ought to be shot," I said in disgust.

"Well, we all know how Aaron is. And the sad part is that he is getting worse. He blames it on not being able to have you anymore. I know that's a crock and so does he."

"Me!" I hopped out of bed and went into the master bathroom. "What are you talking about? I have not a thing to do with Aaron and his string of women."

He began brushing his teeth. "Look, that is what he told me." He gargled. "Like I said, that is a crock and we all know it. He is proud to be a daddy though."

I sat on the toilet. I'm not sure what I am feeling right now but it is still strange to me that he'd had a baby by my best friend. "Sidney said he looks like him but cute. Simone's labor was a little rough I heard. Tracy and Simone went to the hospital to see her. When they got there Aaron had been there already."

He turned to look at me. "Are you OK with this?"

"Oh yes, I'm fine. It bothered me at first because it's really real now. Not saying that it was not real before, just now this innocent baby just made it official," I said with my head down.

He grabbed my hand and made me stand up. He then proceeded to give me the tightest and most affectionate hug, "Hey, I know it's rough; what can I do to help you feel better?"

I held him tighter. "Exactly what you are doing. Your just being here is exactly what I need." I broke the hold he had on me. "I better shower. I have to get dress and so do you." I began to run the shower and tie up my hair.

He leaned against the sink. "I'm going to tell Aaron about us."

I had known this was coming. "Do you want me with you when you do?"

"You could but I don't need you to. We are *grown* men and we *should* be able to handle it. I do not want to wait until we are seen together. To me, that is more awkward. I think telling him man to man is the best thing for the man with the biggest ego I have ever seen. I love him like a brother and I owe it to him to tell him face to face."

I got in the shower. "Well, you are a brave soul, Elijah. It won't be pretty. He can't handle the truth!" I said, imitating Jack Nicholson from his role in A Few Good Men.

He laughed. "OK, Jack, make room for me because I am coming in. I mean, literally *coming* in." He jumped in the shower and we made it as pleasant as a shower could be.

Now, I do not have a problem with Aaron knowing about Elijah and I, but I do have a problem with the chance of their friendship being ruined. They have more to lose than I do. I'd already lost my best friend. I guess it will be his turn. Fortunately for me, I had two other best friends to run to.

Chapter 16
Simone

I knew that having children was hard work but not like this. This little guy wakes every less than two hours. I have not slept for more than two hours at a time since the day before I had him. Aaron thought he was taking care of the baby when he'd wake me up every five minutes asking me what to do while I tried to catch up on some sleep. Then conveniently his cell phone would ring and he'd have something unexpected to do and I wouldn't see him until the next day. Now he is here, telling Li'l Aaron what a strong boy he was and how he was the king of the world. This whole scene is making me more nauseous than when I was two months pregnant. "Aaron, what are you doing here?"

"What kind of stupid question is that? I'm here seeing my son," he said holding the baby in the air.

"Well, you were not there when he was born so why play big daddy now?"

He put the baby in the bassinette. "I am not going to fight with you, Simone. I explained that whole thing."

"No you lied about that whole thing! You were with Nicole and you had your cell off!"

"It ain't like you don't know about Nicole. I got here as soon as I heard the message your mom left. I told Nicole that I had to go to the hospital. The both of you know the deal. Damn, you women get on my nerves!"

No, he had not said that. "Well, what is wrong with you, Aaron, is that you don't know what to do with your life. And this is not the life I want to be a part of. And it's definitely not for my son."

"He is not just your son, he's mine too. Look, I moved out like you wanted me to and now you are still beefing! What do you want, Simone?"

"Nothing from you that's for sure. Look, this is not going to work. We have to schedule a time when you see Aaron and that will lessen the time we will have together because you make me so sick."

"Hey, it is no picnic being around you either, missy! And why in the hell didn't you give him a middle name?" he screamed.

"Well, if you had been there maybe you could have contributed, but since you were not, you just have to deal with it." I knew that would sting.

"You just won't leave it alone will you? You asked for this. You wanted to keep the baby and now you want to complain because things ain't going your way. Now, we are going to have come up with some solution to this mess that was created." He walked toward the bassinette. "I love this little boy and I am going to be his father. I am going to continue to treat you like the mother of my child. You need me I'm here. I'm not going to let you run me out of this kid's life."

"I was not trying to. I want you to be in his life. I've moved on from the traditional family mode. I want you to just be there for him. I only ask is that you don't disrespect him for some bitch that you do not plan on staying with for more than the time you spend with her in bed."

He started putting his coat on. "Don't worry about that. He will only see me with a woman that I plan to be with." He opened the door. "I guess little Aaron will never see me with another woman. I will talk to you later."

That man is going to end up on a lonely road one day. He has a son and will most likely do good by him, but he is a horrible individual. He will hurt woman after woman until someone stops him dead in his tracks. Thank god I've stopped longing for him. I now have a new man in my life and that is my baby boy. Just look at him so cute and cuddly, those chubby cheeks and fat ham-hock legs. I want to just eat him up.

As for Daddy, we can only pray for him. I hope he finds what he wants to do with his life. I was thinking I may have just done Alexis a favor. She had gotten rid of him before she got trapped. She does not have to deal with him ever again. Unfortunately, I have to deal with him for the rest of my life. I guess I've made my bed and now I'm lying in it.

Chapter 17
Sidney

Marcus is sitting there in a daze, wondering what he is going to say to me. "Baby, I don't know what to say. This is going to be rough but I know we can get through it."

"Marcus, it is confirmed that this child is yours. The proof is right there in your hands! Oh god, why? Why?" I screamed. "I was hoping in the back of my mind that this was a stunt played by Taniesha. But it is true! It's true that you are a father to another child."

"Baby, I know, I know. Please, let's calm down before the children get home. I don't want them to find out this way. Sidney, please try and calm down. You know the last thing I want to do is hurt you. I know I hurt you all those years ago but I had no control over what Taniesha did with her body. I have always been there for you and the kids and that will not change with Robin. Remember she doesn't even know I exist. Now, you didn't go with me to get tested but you are going to be there for the court date, right?"

I walked to the window and he followed and stood right behind me. "Marcus, I don't think I will be. I don't think I will. Not to the court date, not anything."

"What are you saying?" he said sounding completely puzzled.

"I'm saying that I think I want out of this marriage." I turned to look him in his face. "I want to separate for a while to see if this is what I want."

He looked devastated at what I was saying. "Sidney, you are not thinking straight!"

"Yes, I am. I need to see what the true meaning of my life is. I no longer want to be the dedicated housewife and mother. I want to get a career. I want to explore life."

"You want to date other men, right?" he asked.

He knows me so well. I knew I could not pussyfoot around this. "Yes, I do."

He backed away and held his head in his hand pacing back and forth. "Oh no . . . no . . . no . . . no! You are a married woman! A married woman, Sidney! Do you even know what you are saying?"

"Yes, I do! I want to see what life is like outside this house. I don't know what's out there, Marcus."

"I do liars, cheaters, beaters, drugs, alcohol, and AIDS, herpes, homosexuality! Take your pick!" He threw his hands in the air. "You are so wrong about this. I'm not letting you go, Sidney. I won't! I worked too damn hard to make you happy. I gave you all that a woman could ask for and more. If you wanted to work at a career you should have said something. Instead, you faked the funk and made me think I'm making you happy!"

"You did make me happy but now it is not enough. I want something different and you can't give it to me. Marcus, please understand what I'm going through."

"I understand perfectly well. You want a career right?"

"Yes."

"You want to explore life right?"

"Yes."

"And you want to fuck other men right?"

"Yes . . . no . . . it's not like that!" I was beginning to lose ground here. "I have been with you all my life and I want to see what life has to offer; you did."

He yelled to the top of his lungs, "I was not married to you then! How stupid can you be?"

"Stupid? You've never called me names before, don't start now," I demanded.

His tone changed a little. "You've never wanted out of our marriage before either. I can't let you do this. Sidney, I love you so much, baby, I couldn't bear to see you with another man. I'm begging you to let this marriage work."

He can always bring out the emotions in me, and just when I was holding a firm stand the tears began to fall. "Marcus, just let me go. I'm so sorry that I'm doing this. I'm not leaving the kids, just this marriage. I don't want a divorce, let's just separate for a while."

"Oh yeah right, I'm supposed to say 'OK, Sidney, got out there and fuck all the men you see and if they are better then stay. And if you're not happy come back.' Girl, you must have lost your goddamn mind! Never is that going to happen. Once you leave, Sidney, you're not coming back. You are not staying in my home either!"

"You're home?"

"Yes, my home. You've had no job or career, right? Therefore, you didn't have a penny to contribute to this home. Which means this is my home."

"You wouldn't dare!"

"The choice is yours, cupcakes!" he said arrogantly.

Now I'm pissed. "Who will take care of my kids? You're trying to trap me here! Fuck you, Marcus! You know I'm not leaving my kids!"

He walked to me with a look on his face that I have never seen. "And you are not taking them from this house either. I mean, that with every fiber of my being. Now, if you want to go then go, but the kids stay here. Now, when you go out and sleep with this man that you're seeing and it doesn't work out, don't come crying to me."

"Marcus, please stop this."

"No, I'm serious—so serious that I could scream. I love you so much that I can't stand myself. Everyone knows how good you have it. Simone spent her whole life sleeping with other people's men to find love. She slept with her best friend's man and got pregnant by him. Tracy found love with the dead and Alexis is still searching after being dumped at the altar. They have always told you how blessed you are and you took me for granted."

"I don't think that letting this go on just because you owed it to me is a good idea. I'm not sure if I was ever happy in this marriage."

"Sid, how could you say that? Do you regret being with me? Our life together?" A tearful pitch in his voice shattered my heart.

"I'm not sure, Marcus. I am just not sure." I sat on the couch.

He turned away to try and hide the pain I'm causing. He leaned against the wall looking up at the ceiling with tears streaming down his face. "I have never hurt so badly. I would love to support you on this. I love the fact that you want to establish a career and I will stand behind you on that. I just can't take you back after you've had an affair. I know you are upset about what happened back in high school. I wasn't married to you then. Everyone said we would not last getting married so young. I thought we beat the odds. Now, I see they were right all along." He looked my way. "Don't let this linger on. Tell the kids you are leaving. I don't expect to see you here when I get back. I'm going to the restaurant to finish payroll."

"I'm so sorry, Marcus. I have to do this. Please don't leave. I want to talk this out," I said between the uncontrollable tears.

"Don't leave? Isn't that what you're doing? Thanks for nothing." And he walked out of the door, never looking me in the face.

Chapter 18
Sidney

"Mom, I don't know why we have to have this . . . this . . . joke of a meeting! Alexis is not going to go for it at all!" Simone pleaded while sitting in the front seat of our mother's car.

"Girl, please! You slept with your best friend's man. Or should I say, former best friend?" she teased. "Monie, you girls need to talk. Even if you two decide to never speak again, you need to at least say so. You girls shared your whole life together and now you let some male part get between you. And I mean that literally!"

I had to step in. "Mom, you need to understand that that is something they have to work out on their own time. I hate what this is doing to all of us but Alexis is not going to have it. Speaking of Alexis, does she know about this little meeting today?"

"No, Sidney, the mothers have decided that the four of you need to talk. And like I said, if that means it is just to end a friendship of a lifetime that means just that. Simone and Alexis have not spoken to each other since the wedding," she explained. "None of you were going to know about this meeting until we were driving you to Tracy's mother's house. So Alexis doesn't know either. Because I was blessed with twins, I have two daughters to bring to the table."

"I have Li'l Aaron to care for and I don't want him to hear all the yelling and screaming going on," Simone said trying to get out of it.

"Not gettin' out of this one, sweetie!" Mom laughed. "I'm taking my grand baby and he will be out the way of all the hair pullin' and scratchin' that will be takin' place. Simone, my dear, I want this for all of you. We sincerely think that you girls could patch things up. And no, it will never be the way it was in the past."

I just know that this is going to be the death of someone. I do not know how this will end up but I do know it will not be pretty. I leaned between the two seats. "This is a bad idea. I love you, Mom, but this is Simone's problem. She did the deed and now we have to have this meeting because of it. Did anyone give Alexis any thought? I mean, how do you think she is going to feel when she walks into an ambush? She never mentions Simone's name in any conversation that we ever have. This is like pouring salt on the wound!"

Simone turned to Mom. "She's right, Mom. Enough is enough. I made a mistake and no one is paying for it more than me. If I could take it all back I would, but I can't. So there you have it. Meeting adjourned."

Mom started parking the car. "No, angel face, the meeting is not adjourned until I say so. You never told her what you told us this very minute. If my memory serves me correctly, you were a nasty little bitch! You slept with her man and let it come out on her wedding day and then had an attitude like she was just supposed to get over it! Do you think you were going to get off that easily? No. As a friend you need to let her hear what you were feeling and why you felt the way you felt. All of you have some issues and all of you need to come to some sort of mutual ground. So, dear, meeting is adjourned when this is over. Now get out of my car and march your two-timing behind up there to the front door. Alexis is here."

We all walked up the driveway and I can see the look on Simone's face that she got when she felt the most uncomfortable. If I were in her shoes, I would feel the same way. However, I do agree with what my mother said, we all need to discuss this. And this is going to be a discussion of a lifetime.

xoxoxoxoxoxo

Alexis

"Alexis, you are not leaving this house! I am your mother and you've never disrespected me before, so do not start now!" my mother shouted.

"How could you guys do this? Tracy, did you know about this?"

"No, I just found out when you walked through the door. I think it is a hideous thing to do. If anything I shouldn't be here."

"Well, I shouldn't either."

"Baby, listen to me." She walked over to the bar where I was standing fixing myself a drink. "You and Simone have been friends all your lives, that should count for something. The two of you have never ever discussed this since the wedding. At least hear her out. Please, baby, the mothers are so hurt by the fact that our girls have separated from one another. We were going to have many generations of friendships and you guys just killed it."

Tracy's mom looked out the window. "Funny you chose the word 'kill,' here come Sidney and Simone."

My throat is clogged and I feel like my air supply is getting cut short. What am I supposed to say to Simone? I said what I had to say to her on my dreadful wedding day. Now, I have to rehash this mess. Look at her walking in the door, holding the baby made by my ex-fiancé. I wanted to scream. I never even saw a picture of the baby before and now I have to meet him face to face. Today is not a good day.

"Hello, everyone," Simone said solemnly.

Tracy's mom reached for the baby. "Hey there, handsome, we are going to leave the room. This is no place for a baby. What do you think?" She left the room speaking to the baby in baby talk.

I downed my drink. "I can't do this! I'm outta here!"

Simone's mom blocked the door. "Oh no, you don't! Now you girls have something to discuss and if it kills me, you girls will talk! You deserve at least that much. The birth of the baby is the birth of a new beginning. Now, whether that means the friendship you had is no longer or you're starting a new kind of a friendship, I want this to be done today. Leslie, bring the baby out so we can leave these women alone and let them do what they have to do!"

"Aunt Sharon, I know you mean well but I have nothing to say to your daughter. So please move," I said in the most demanding voice I could use to my auntie.

"Dottie, come get your child," Sharon said with an attitude.

My mother came toward me. "Baby, don't be like that. Now we are leaving and we are leaving the four of you here and you are not to leave! None of you!" She pointed to all of us. She kissed me and opened the door. "Leslie, let's go!" The three of them walked out with devious smiles on their faces.

Shannon N. Davis

Chapter 19
Alexis

The room had been silent for almost an hour. No one dared to say a word. I guess everyone is waiting for either Simone or me to talk first. I know I will not say one word to that woman. Simone had destroyed that. She ruined that the day she slept with my boyfriend. I think this is the dumbest idea I have ever heard. Why in the world are we here?

Tracy walked to the bar and poured herself a glass of seltzer water. "Well, ladies, what do we have to do to get out of here?"

"Just walk out of the door," Simone said.

"That's funny, Monie, but we should talk about something," Sidney added.

"Look, I don't want to be here, especially if we are not going to talk about anything."

I couldn't resist saying something to her. "Hmmm, you are the reason we are here in the first place. So you want to talk, so talk."

Simone put her head in her hands. "Well, for starters, I'm sorry, Alexis."

For some reason, I couldn't hold back the frustration that I've had hiding inside me. "Sorry? Oh, you're sorry now? For what, about the fact that you slept with Aaron? Or is it the fact that you got caught doing so?"

Simone stood up. "That, among other things. You have no idea how I wish I could take all of that back. I realized a long time ago that I made a huge mistake."

"At least we are talking," Tracy said.

I stood a few feet away from Simone. "I thought I didn't have a word to say to you but I see that I do. Why, Simone, why?"

She tried to clear her throat. "I ask myself that every day. I think I fell into something that was worse than a snake pit. Aaron was so charming . . ."

"You got turned on by charm?" I questioned.

"No, it was not like that! I began falling for his flirtatious ways by flirting back. And then one thing led to another. I'm not placing the blame on Aaron alone because I'm also to blame. His flirting ways became sweet and kind and I loved it."

I hated hearing this but I would not tell her to shut up. "So he came on to you first?"

She sat down. "In the beginning he was, and then when he opened doors that only I had to close, I just could not see myself closing them."

"That sounds good but I was your friend, Monie, and you were not flirting with some man that was married to a woman you didn't know. You knew about Aaron from the moment we met. You slept with him knowing that I was sleeping with him as well and let it carry on for months!" I said getting angry again.

"I know . . . I know I was so wrong! Don't you think I know that? We discussed that and I wanted to stop after the first time we were together."

"So what happened?"

"We decided not to. We wanted to end it, seriously, but it never happened. The sex was incredible and that is what held us together. I began to love him and I thought he was in love with me in return. After we left the bedroom, there was nothing else. We never went out on dates locally. Everything had to be done out of town."

"That's what happens when you are the other woman," I said arrogantly.

Tracy jumped in. "Alexis, she is trying to speak her piece."

"I let my feelings about great sex get confused with love. Deep down I knew that he didn't love me, not like he loved you, anyway. I had it bad. I hated to see you two together. He was so endearing to you and I only prayed that I would be treated like that as well. I never wanted to hurt you or break up your wedding but I tried to fight the urges that I was feeling."

Tears began to fall from my eyes. I can see that she is hurting and I know that I'm hurting just hearing that they had made love repeatedly and had gone on numerous out-of-town dates. I couldn't even imagine when because I had thought I knew where he was every moment of our lives. Now, hearing all of this made me realize that he had lied to me numerous times. The funny part of it all is that I couldn't even begin to know where the lies started and ended. I wiped the tears from my eyes.

"You know I watched you sleep with other women's men before and I had never seen what I see in your eyes when you talk about him. I'm not sure if it is because I never paid attention to what you two were doing or if I had not wanted to see it."

"You are not to blame. I did love him so much." She walked toward me and touched my shoulder. "I want to change the past I really do. I saw how happy he made you. I know how happy he made me. Yeah, I slept with other men that did not belong to me but this was different. I let my relationships with these men be what they were and got out of them what I could. Aaron was a whole other story and I couldn't control it. I needed to have him more and more. At one point he was like that as well. He called more and in turn made me feel more. He began to open up and next thing you know I was pregnant and it fell apart."

Sidney went to the bar and made a drink for her and Simone. "Alexis, do you want a drink?"

"No thanks, Sid. Finish the story, Simone," I said.

"Once I told him that I was pregnant he changed and we were never the same again." She wiped the tears from her eyes.

"Did he ever say anything about ending his relationship with Alexis?" Tracy asked.

"At first yes, but that was only for a short while. Then he never mentioned it and neither did I."

Here comes that anger-filled volcano. They never discussed ending my relationship? Now, I guess that's why he had done it so disrespect-fully, he'd had no practice. "I can't believe you! Simone, were you just going to let him keep dealing with this? We did have a wedding coming up. You were at the table a month before the wedding when we were having a disagreement on the wedding song! How did that make you feel? And if memory serves me correctly, you were pregnant at the time, weren't you?"

"Yes," she admitted. She walked toward me and pleaded, "Lex, you have to understand that I wanted to change what happened but then I let my feelings get out of control. I love you like a sister and I was hurt knowing that I was going to hurt you."

I could not control myself so I smacked her as hard as I could. "How dare you tell me you loved me like a sister? The nerve! A sister would never do that to another sister! You are such a liar!"

She held her face and smacked me back. "Fuck that! You hit me once and I let you get away with it but not this time!"

Before I knew it we were grabbing hair and clothes, and kicking and screaming. I had two fistfuls of her hair and she had two fistfuls of mine, yelling at each other telling one another to let go. I could hear Sidney and Tracy screaming and telling us to stop. I was not letting go unless I was going to punch her in the face. My only thought was that she is no longer pregnant. Here is my chance to stomp a mud hole into her behind. How dare she tell me how much she loved Aaron? And I know she would not be as sorry if he had not dumped her ass.

Tracy pulled Simone away from me. "This is bullshit and childish! What in the hell is wrong with you people?"

Struggling to get Tracy off her, Simone said, "She hit me! I never touched her! Fuck you, bitch! I was trying to tell you the real deal and you can't handle it! Stupid bitch!"

"Stupid? Look who is stupid!" I said trying to get away from Sidney's grip. "I am not the one that slept with my best friend's man then got knocked up by him and then got dumped! Hmmph, did you really think that he was going to leave me and marry you? I think not! Now, who is the stupid bitch? Alone and with a baby from a man that never gives you the time of day!"

Next thing you know we broke free from Sidney's and Tracy's grips and went for each other's throats, knocking over the lamp on the end table and smacking and punching one another. The punches felt like they'd had months to build up in strength. She was frustrated because I had told her the truth and I was pissed off because I had heard the truth. I can't believe that I'm fighting my lifelong friend like she just had taken my purse.

Finally, we were broken up again. I yelled at the top of my lungs, "You were my friend! My friend! The loyalty should have stayed with me!" I couldn't help but sob. I'm so hurt right now. I have never had a fight in my entire life, and when I do, it is over a man—something I said I would never do.

Simone fell to the floor crying uncontrollably with her head in her hands. "Alexis, I know. I know. No one will ever know how bad I feel. None of you! All of you have been loved at one point in your lives. I have never ever experienced it!" She tried to regain composure. "And the one time that I do it was with my best friend's man. He was kind and shared with me. We had long talks and shared what I thought was love. How could I have passed that up? I just felt so good. I knew I was going to ruin my relationship with you, with all of you, but I needed to be loved and for a brief second I had that. It never crossed my mind that it would not work out."

My tears consumed my eyes and my hurt lodged in my throat. "What is it that you want from me, Simone? I can't express any more how I feel." I wiped tears from my face. "I was hurt that he cheated but I was devastated that it was with you. Out of all of us, we were the closest. I think of you more than I do of him. How ironic is that?"

Tracy wiped the tears from her face. "That is ironic. Girls, we have to look at what just happened here. We are over thirty years old and fighting. If anything, that is ironic. Simone, you and everyone in this room know what the two of you did was downright disgusting. I don't know how you can live with yourself."

"That's the truth," Sidney agreed. Sidney walked over to her sister and lifted her up and wiped her face. "Monie, my dear sister, I don't know what on earth you were thinking but what happened is old news and we now have to try and face what is going on now. You two just fought like you were in the tenth grade and your boyfriend cheated. Now, I know that you two are hurting but this is ridiculous. There has got to be a better way of expressing your feelings."

Simone pushed off Sidney. "Sidney, do you think I do not know that? Shit, do you think if I had what you had I would have done what I did? Or lived my life like I have in the past?"

Shannon N. Davis

Chapter 20
Simone

I know these bitches are not going to gang up on me with this shit. I had to pour myself a drink for this. "Now, I did wrong and I know that. I have paid the price but I'm not going to let the three of you dog me out when you all have your own issues!"

"What issues do we have?" Tracy and Sidney said at the same time.

"Yeah, what issues, Simone?" Alexis asked with an attitude.

"For starters, Sid, you left your husband and family for a man that you met at a night club. Now, what were you thinking?" I said directly in her face.

"What?" Alexis and Tracy asked in surprise.

"No, sweetie, this is not about me! I don't know why you just said that. That has nothing to do with you or anyone else. Mom opened her big mouth," Sidney said in defiance as she walked to the bar to fix a drink.

Tracy walked over to the bar and looked Sidney in the face. "You're not leaving Marcus are you?"

"Nothing is official yet," she answered.

"What happened? Why are you doing this? Marcus is the love of your life," Alexis questioned.

I'm glad that the heat has turned off me and onto Sidney. How many times are they going to beat me in the head with what happened between me and Aaron? I know I should not have, but shit, they think that they are so much better than me when their own backyards are just as filthy as mine. "Just because Marcus had a child with this other woman you have to trip. What sense does that make?"

"I don't need it to make sense to you! As long as I am fine with it, it is no business of yours, yours, or yours!" Sidney pointed to each one of us. "Like I said, nothing is official yet."

Alexis threw herself on the couch. "Girl, you are nuts! If I had a man like Marcus I would not let him go."

Sidney frowned at Alexis's statement. "Well, maybe you'll find what I had with Marcus with Elijah. You two are getting closer and closer these days."

"What?" Simone and Tracy shouted out at the same time.

Alexis stood up and walked toward Sidney. "I did not tell you that for you to tell everyone."

"No, you didn't, but since you want to judge me, I figured we should judge you as well," she answered in her defense.

"Ain't this a trip?" I said. "All this time you have been downing me for sleeping with Aaron and you are fucking *his* best friend?" I started laughing. "You, my dear, are one of the biggest hypocrites I have ever seen! What in the world makes you think you are better than me? From what I see you are no better than me."

Alexis looked at me with an evil eye. "Simone, I am better than you. I'm not sneaking behind people's backs. Not that I have to explain anything to you, we just started this and neither one of us are in a relationship. Nor, am I pregnant! Not to mention I did not break up any weddings!" Alexis exclaimed.

"Stop making me laugh! I wonder if Aaron knows of his legal partner's new love affair?" I arrogantly questioned.

Alexis walked up to me like she was ready for round four. "Not yet and he won't know until Elijah tells him. Now will he?"

I couldn't help but giggle. "First of all, step back!" I said stopping her with my hand in her face. "Second, that is none of my business. What you do is you and yours. But answer me this, is this payback?"

"No, not at all. We have always shared some sort of friendship and then one thing led to another," Alexis obediently replied. She poured herself another drink. "Let the record show, he is no longer with Shelley and I have been single since my wedding disaster. But I am quite sure you know all the sweet details on that one, don't you, *Monie love*?" she said with such malice.

Chapter 21
Tracy

How in the hell had I gotten here? These girls are here going tit-for-tat and it is nauseating me, arguing and fighting over men, no less. I had to break this shit up. "Look, you girls have been best friends all your lives. Now, I know that none of us are perfect but do not let the likes of men ruin what you had prior to their existence."

Simone, looking like she'd had a bit too much to drink, poured another drink. "If it ain't Mrs. Death-Do-We-Part! Since when do you have advice on men? Aren't you the one that is still in mourning after ten years? Things have changed in the world of love, lust, and lies since then, missy."

"It hasn't changed that much for me to know that you only sleep with someone who is not tied down to another. Especially, your best friend's man. Let's not forget why we are here in the first place."

"Don't make me laugh! There is no way in hell I could hold out that long. You give a new meaning to *dedicated*!" Simone said sarcastically.

"That's not funny, Simone," Sidney said taking away Simone's drink. "I'm quite sure losing someone is a hard way to go. You never know what you would do in that situation."

I was not going to let this woman get under my skin with her ignorance. The one thing that I didn't like about Simone was that when she drank, whatever was on her mind that minute would soon turn into the latest headline. "Let's not bring up my dead husband, OK?" I said trying to stop her snowball.

Alexis came over and sat next to me, being consoling. "Simone, don't be like that. What happened to Malcolm was not her fault. And it is definitely not for you to use to hurt her."

"Monie, you can be a true idiot sometimes! We may have the same genes but our thoughts are completely different," her twin sister added.

"This coming from a woman that has a fine *faithful* husband, three wonderful kids, and a house that you can decorate and re-decorate when the season changes! Not to mention not having to work a day in your life! Girl, you betta' sit your lucky ass down!" Simone said, reminding her of what she had and was about to throw away. "And you want to give it up for a piece of dick you found in the club? Are you crazy?"

"Stop it, Simone!" Sidney said angrily.

"Oh no, I'm just getting warmed up on your ass." Simone took a swig of her drink. "You run around here acting like you are better than me and that I am such the whore of the family, the black sheep, the misfit; the one that should have been locked in the attic when company came over for dinner. And deep down you wanted to be the whoring, misfit black sheep that should have been locked in the attic." She took another swig of her drink, this time polishing it off. "A definite case of the pot calling the kettle . . ."

"I said shut up, Simone!" Sidney repeated.

"And I said I was just getting started! Your life must be pure hell! A man that comes home and supports you in whatever boneheaded idea that you come up with. Never gives you a hard time with anything. Shit, I guess that would be pure hell, wouldn't it? Right, girls?"

The next thing you know the same two women that had shared a womb for nine months and fought to get out of it, looked like they were fighting to get back in. They pulled hair and gave punches and smacks like they had never shared a blood path. My heart ached while Alexis and I tried to break up the twins who had very different outlooks on life.

I finally grabbed hold of Simone, barely restraining her. "Stop, Simone! Stop, goddammit!"

Trying to break free, she said, "No, this bitch always dissed me over the years, always telling me how wrong I am, and when I finally tell her how fucked up she is, she wants to fight! So, bitch, bring it on!"

Alexis was trying her hardest to hold back Sidney. "Damn, Simone, just stop!"

Sidney broke free from Alexis's restraint. "You know what, you miserable wench? My life is none of your concern. I apologize for losing my composure." She tried to fix her ponytail that was now a bad version of an Angie Stone afro.

I couldn't take it anymore. I have had enough of the mud slinging and the hair pulling; we are grown women and had never once had a fight like this when we were kids. I couldn't take another word. Not to mention my mother is going to have a coronary when she sees the condition of this house.

I let Simone go. "Damn y'all! All of this for what? Huh? For what?" I surveyed the room to look for an answer and received nothing. "Simone, you were wrong for sleeping with Aaron and every other man that did not belong to you. We know that and that is the reason we are here today, not to go bald by trying to pull each other's hair out! I mean, my heart went out to you when you were confessing. I honestly felt your pain. It had to be a confusing time for you. Unfortunately, wrong decisions were made and people were hurt. Now, we can try and put it behind us. It has been a year."

Simone tried to add something, "But I—"

I put my hand in her face. "Let me finish! Alexis, with all that has happened, I know you are hurt and probably always will be. I also felt your pain, when you had to hear all that went down between Monie and Aaron. But from what I see, she is truly sorry though it came out screwed up," I said, giving Simone a dirty look. "But this is your friend. And she was trying to make amends with you tonight. Where is Aaron? He is probably screwing some girl in the backseat of his car. I'm glad you heard her out. Now, take what you heard and do something with it. Either try to reestablish a relationship or just part company. And whatever decision you make just accept it, OK, Simone?"

This time I poured a drink of straight Absolute. "Sid, what is going with you I really do not understand. What you have is probably what I would have had with Malcolm." I felt the tears build up in my eyes. "You have what I have yearned for since I buried him. You can't take having your loved one for granted. I did that one day and I lost him forever. It is always so easy for you to tease and make fun of me but none of you had to deal with what I am dealing with. None of you!"

Alexis broke the flow of my speech. "Trace, what are you talking about? Malcolm's car accident was something that just happened. Not something that you could have taken for granted."

As my tears began to fall from my exhausted face I tried to explain, "No! His death would have been avoided if I had not taken his kindness for granted. I was supposed to go to the grocery store but I deliberately didn't go, knowing that he would go instead. So when I exaggerated how tired I was, he as usual became the husband that I've loved over and over again said that he would go. And the rest is history." I sat on the chaise lounge and cried my eyes out.

All three of them came to me with tears in their eyes. Alexis, always being the one with the most compassion, spoke as she rubbed my back, "Tray, you blamed yourself for his death all these years?"

I gained composure to answer, "Yes. I never told a soul until today. After seeing the four of us humiliate ourselves, I could only think what I would do if my husband were still here. I would give anything to have that decision to make. Anything. So you see, Simone, I don't mind being *Mrs.Death-Do-Us-Part*," I said with an attitude. "I loved him that much."

Simone wiped her eyes. "I am sorry, Tracy. I am a jerk. I can't help being jealous. I must admit I am jealous of all of you. The one thing I can say is that Malcolm's accident was not your fault. You are a beautiful and successful woman. You have a great son and a man that loves you. Jerome loves you whether you admit it or not."

For the first time in the last few hours all of them agreed on something. Simone sat on her knees in front of me. "Tracy, just open your heart to something new. Malcolm is never coming back." She put her finger over my mouth. "Now, let me finish. He would have wanted you to be happy. That was his main goal in life. That is why he went to the store instead of you, to make his wife happy. Unfortunately, timing was a bit off but this was the card God gave you. The writing was already on the wall, sweetie. You sending him to the store was just a fluke."

I knew she was right and it is hard to admit it, which made my tears flow even harder. "Since then, I've made a vow to be devoted to make it up to our son. He deserves that."

Alexis held me tight. "Your son knows all about his dad. You made that possible. You have to make Tracy happy now. Ten years is a long time for anyone."

"I know. The sad thing is Jerome is gone. He tried and tried and he said he can no longer compete with a dead man." I blew my nose on the napkin Simone gave me. "After we went to the Broadway show, he did and said everything in his power to get into my heart. I mean, we had a bit of intimacy."

All of them looked like they were all too eager to get a piece of gossip. Alexis was first to ask me the dreadful question, "You two did it?"

"No! Are you crazy?" I said raising my voice. "He just tasted me that's all."

"Did you taste him?" Simone asked.

"Hell no! What do I look like?" I yelled.

Simone's sober moment quickly ended. "You look like a woman that just got her pussy ate!"

We all laughed and for that brief moment I had my lifetime friends back. I knew there was no chance in hell that I was not going to be able to tell them the whole story. "Well, we were kissing and then he wanted to make me remember what ecstasy was. He wanted to know how good I tasted. I just couldn't stop him." I began to chuckle like a schoolgirl. "It was nice."

Again we cracked up at my expense. I was cool with it. Thinking back it was nice and would do it again if given the chance. "Unfortunately, after he was done and I hit my point, I wouldn't let it go any farther. I stopped him dead in his tracks and it went downhill from there."

"So you two started a fire and then you put out the flame?" Sidney said in disbelief. "Girl, are you crazy? I would have had to take that and worry about the emotions later. And you know Jerome is a long-time deal. Not like Maleek."

Shannon N. Davis

Chapter 22
Sidney

I know these girls are going to chew me up with what I'm about to say but since my little secret is out, I might as well. "I met Maleek and I'm not too sure what I want to do with him. I mean, I want to sleep with him. I am very attracted to him. I'm not sure if I am doing this because deep down I want to or if this is just revenge on Marcus."

"How could you want to get revenge on a man that has loved you unconditionally all these years?" Alexis asked.

I stood up to try and explain. "I never got a chance to date. To see what life has to offer. I got married right after high school and then started a family. I have never dumped a man or gotten dumped. I have been faithful ole Sidney, wife, mother, sister, and friend. That's it! I never went to college. I never did anything crazy. I never went on vacation with my girls. I went from high school to family life. Nothing in between."

"You have a wonderful life, Sidney," Alexis said.

"Well, my perfect world is not so perfect. I wanted more and I still do. Simone, you said that you were jealous of us, that is so funny because I was jealous of all of you. I mean, you guys had many stories to tell about your dates and your college life. I never even had a real wedding. I went to the city hall." I broke into tears. "Don't think that I don't love Marcus and the kids because I do. It is just that, for once I want to do something out of the wonderful world of Sidney. Just once! Let Marcus be disappointed in me."

"Simone, you are talking nonsense! That man loves you to death! And to blow it all away for a man that may or may not be with you for the rest of your life is ridiculous!" Tracy said.

"That is dumb, Sid," Simone said, agreeing with Tracy.

"Marcus cheated on me with someone and I had to deal with that! Now, I have to deal with him being a father to a girl who is older than my daughter! I don't know if I can handle that. When he goes to court, I have to sit and act like the doting wife when I really want to catch the next thing smokin' out of here!"

Alexis walked toward me. "You can't be serious. You really want to leave Marcus? Is Maleek that special to give up your family for? Marcus had no idea about this child. So why would you punish him?"

"It is not a punishment. It is not because of Maleek alone. I want to be Sidney! I want to try and see if I can get a career. Hell, Lex, you are a registered nurse. Simone is a CPA and Tracy has her own advertising business that may become nationwide in a few days. And what do I have, huh? Seventeen years of marriage and three kids. You would think I didn't have a single bit of knowledge in my brain."

Tracy gave me some tissues from her box. "Do you think that Marcus won't be supportive of you finding a career?"

I wiped my tears. "I honestly don't know. He never asked what I wanted to do with myself besides give birth to his kids. He never even let me work in one of the restaurants. I have no clue how he would react. All of our kids are in school now so maybe he would be a bit understanding." I then blew my nose and wiped my eyes again. "For once, I would like to step outside of my life for one minute. Just to see what it is like, whether that is school, working, or an affair with Maleek. Even if it is just once."

"Then talk to him. And forget the affair part," Alexis said.

"I think that would be the right thing to do rather than go out and do something you know that you would regret," Tracy said while brushing my hair back. "I really don't think that Marcus would have a problem with you doing something more fulfilling with your life."

Simone poured a glass of water. "Sidney, my big sister by five minutes, why don't you have a heart-to-heart with your husband? Let him know how you feel. Don't end your marriage over this. It would be sinful."

"I hate to admit this but I agree with, Simone," Alexis hesitantly said. "Give this some more thought. Sleep on it and make a more rational decision with your husband."

"Just don't sleep with Maleek!" Simone so rudely interrupted.

Alexis continued talking, "Girl, you have what sistahs are craving for. So what if he has a daughter! Your heart will love her as if she were your own. Then again, she is practically grown and may not want to deal with another family. She had thought that her father was the man that raised her all her life. This is probably just as difficult for her."

I hate it when all three of them make sense. I walked to the bar to pour myself a glass of soda. I have had too much to drink for one night. "You girls are probably right. I just don't want to go to court with him. I hate that damn Taniesha! Screwed up everything! But now that we have had this meeting that our mothers have so insistently made us have. What have we learned?" I said that so the tension could get off of me for a minute.

The room was silent for a minute until Tracy broke the silence. "Alexis, do you think that you and Simone can ever be friends again?"

Alexis threw herself on the sofa as though she was ready to pay by the hour for what she was about to say. "Oh, Tracy, I don't know. She crossed the line."

"Don't tell me, tell Simone."

Alexis looked at Simone with deep struggle. "Girl, I can't say that I can be. Especially, not the way we were. I mean, you hurt me deeply. And to top it all off if we were going to be friends, your child would be a constant reminder of the betrayal. Now, I have nothing against an innocent baby but I am so against the way in which it was conceived."

Simone wiped her tears and for the first time in a long time I made note of the sincerity. She walked toward Alexis and sat next to her. "Do you think you would at least try? I know I went beyond the mark but I miss my friend deeply. I would be appreciative if you would just say that you would try and consider it."

"I miss my friendship with you too, Monie, but I need to seriously think about it. I mean, the trust is gone. Like I said before, losing the relationship with you was worse than getting humiliated on my wedding by my boyfriend as crazy as that may sound." Alexis wiped her eyes filled with tears of sorrow. "So let me ask you this, would you forgive me if I did this to you?

Simone stood up. "That's hard to say. I'm not in your shoes. I would want to that is for sure. If you can't forgive me, then I respect that. But I can tell you this, I love you and making myself look like a fool and begging for your forgiveness is the least I can do. I think it is all worth it. You are worth begging for."

xoxoxoxoxoxo

Just then our mothers came slowly walking through the door hoping to find all live bodies. Tracy's mother had a stroke like I had imagined. She went through the living room picking up pieces of knick-knacks, asking what in the world had gone on. Meanwhile, our mother and Alexis's mom were looking at their daughters' roughed up appearances, never saying a word and remained silent. I guess it was completely obvious what had gone down. So I do not know why Tracy's mom had such a hard time believing what she had walked into.

I couldn't help but ask them the dreadful question, "What's the matter?"

"I can't believe you heffas fought in my house!" Tracy's mom yelled.

We gathered our coats and Simone took her child and we headed for the door. After all, did they think with all the tension we were going to talk quietly over tea? I could see that Simone and Alexis wanted to say something but kept everything to themselves. We got into our cars and headed to our destinations without even saying goodbye.

Chapter 23
Tracy

Tonight's events really put our lives to the test. We all vented in some sort of way. I'm quite sure Alexis and Simone feel somewhat better now that they have said what took them a year to say to one another. I just hope Sidney reevaluates her situation. I would kill to have my husband back in my life. I know that is not going to happen. Trust me I do. I hope the cemetery keeper is not out tonight. I have to visit Malcolm's grave. It is dark and creepy, but somehow I feel safe.

I have not been here in three weeks but I don't want to stay long. So I better begin talking. "Hello Malcolm. After ten years, I still come to your grave and replace the flowers I left from my previous visit and talk to you. I guess it makes me feel like I used to feel when we talked late at night before we went to bed. Remember that? God only knows how good it felt to be next to the one I loved wholeheartedly. I can still feel you tickling me until I turned bright red. I even still giggle when I think of it. Almost as if you are here touching me.

"Our son is the most tremendous person I know aside from you. He thinks he is a man now that he will be thirteen soon. He has his whole life mapped out already. He reminds me so much of you; he has your determination and strength. I remember the way you calmed down a hostile room with your kind words. Your sense of humor was always amazing. You really would have had something to say about tonight.

"I mean, tonight, my best friends and I went at each other's throats. It was the most hurtful thing I have endured since your death. We said things to each other that we can't take back but were true. No matter how much we loved each other, we seem to have carried some secret grudges against one another. It just made me think that these women whom I love dearly take life and love for granted. If I could just have one more minute with you I would do anything."

I began to feel tears forming in my eyes. "My beloved husband, I miss you dearly. I have done everything in my power to keep your memory alive for our son and myself. I've done what I thought should be done since I think it was my fault that you are not here. I still make decisions based on what you think is right or *would* have thought is right. I guess that is why I've never been with another man. I would feel like I was having an affair. I know it may sound stupid to a lot of people but this is how strong I know our love was. Even in death you still have my heart.

"This is going to be a different kind of visit. I have to let go of this invisible life I've created. I mean, you are gone and will never return. I've always known that. It's just that I couldn't ever come to grips with it. I thought I'd let our son down and would let him down again if I tried to replace you. When you died, he was only two and he barely remembers you now. I pumped so many things into his head to try and get him to know you. I tell him how you reacted in certain situations so he can be like you. For the most part, I think it worked. He seems to be like you in many ways.

"The one thing I couldn't give him was a real-life father figure. He wants that so badly. He just recently started mentioning it. He even asked why I still wear your ring. I told him how this ring symbolized what we meant to each other. I told him things in our lives may have changed but this ring stays the same. This ring is Malcolm and Tracy forever. I made sure you wore yours so you would always have it on. Remember the night in the Poconos when we vowed to never remove it? We said that if it gets dirty we will just wash it until the finger comes off. That night was one of the best nights we spent together."

I could barely get my words to form. What I was about to say would finally bring some closure to my grieving. "Malcolm, I can't stop my tears because, baby, I have to take off the ring. This is the hardest thing I have ever had to do. I feel like I am killing you all over again. Tonight made me realize how unhappy I am. For the longest time I mourned for you and never stopped to think about what I was doing to myself and our son. He gets sad because he knows I'm not happy. I have been sad for ten years, longing for you day and night. I really thought I was doing right by him. I guess I went about it all wrong. I know now it is not enough for him to be raised by his father's spirit. Malcolm, I am so, so sorry for making this mistake. Will you ever forgive me?"

I traced his name, carved in that tombstone, with my finger. "I never thought I would be saying this but I have or had someone in my life. His name is Jerome. He is a wonderful man and Malcolm took to him deeply and so did Jerome. Malcolm wants a father figure. He wants to talk about girls and all the other things guys talk about. I even caught Jerome teaching him how to shave; that was definitely a Kodak moment. It is just that I don't want our baby hurt. I know you would never have hurt him. It has to be difficult for another man to step in. It is so funny but Jerome was never put into that predicament. It seems as though they have clicked like they've known each other before. I think you would approve of it."

I leaned on my knees with my hands clutched tightly to my chest. It felt like my heart was breaking into a million pieces. My wails of sadness could wake the dead. "Malcolm, I think I screwed up Jerome too. I let this man stay around me knowing that he wanted more than just a business and friendly relationship. I let myself believe that I didn't want him but had him around. I took him for granted and now he is out of my life. I will see him in a few days when we go to Vegas and after that he is through with me.

"Malcolm, I am in love with him. I feel safe with him. I want to be with him. I know now it is the right thing to do. So if given a second chance, I will do right by him. Let him in every aspect of my life. Let him establish a father-and-son relationship with our son. I want to finally be the woman that I am on the inside. I miss that so much. I didn't realize it at first but now I do."

I stood up wiping my tears away, holding my wedding band in my hand. Trying to get it off was as emotionally draining as physically trying to pull an elephant. As I slid the ring I had worn for thirteen years and held it in my hand, I said, "This does not mean that you will be forgotten. You could never be forgotten. It just means that I have to move on with life. I feel this is the best thing to do for everyone. Saying goodbye to you is not easy since I never said it to you. Even at your funeral I said what we have always said to each other, 'See ya later, babe.' Now, my wonderful husband, later has passed and this is goodbye." I took a long and deep breath to gain the strength for my next move, the strength that I never had before. After I let my extra-long breath go I said what I should have said a long time ago, "Goodbye, my dear husband. I will see you in the next life. I will continue to take great care of our son. I love you always and forever."

Walking away was heartbreaking. It sort of felt like I would never talk or see him again. I know I will come here on the anniversary of his death and whenever Malcolm Jr. wants to come. I know the love I had for him will live on. I have no doubt in my mind of that. Only from now on, I will have to keep it in a special place. A place where I could go and retrieve it any time I want. After all, my love was true and undying. People may have condemned me for acting the way I have but the one thing I can say to them is that none of them had the love I had. My love never died.

Chapter 24
Sidney

Oh my god this feels so good—his touch and tender caress; the mist of his breath warming my skin. I can't help but let this happen. I mean, he is so attractive and mysterious. I guess that's what is drawing me to him. He knows all about my home life and has never judged me. My guess is why would he if he is about to get some low-down, dirty, lusty sex.

He whipped out my breast from my bra, engulfing it in one quick motion. Meanwhile, unzipping my pants and using his finger to probe to find the center of my love. My body rocked with anticipation of the upcoming events. Desperately wanting this man inside me, I couldn't help but want this man inside me right now. "Give it to me, Marcus."

I could not believe what I just said. He instantly stopped and looked at me. "Did you hear what you just said?"

Damn it, Sidney! Your stupid ass can't even have an affair right. I had to think of something quick before he punched me in the face or something. "I'm sorry. It's just that . . ."

He got off me. "It's just that you don't really want to be here."

"No! I do! I can't lie and say that I have ever stepped out on my marriage before. I'm so used to saying 'Marcus' when I am in ecstasy. Please forgive me," I begged and pleaded.

He buttoned up his pants and stood up. "Go home to your husband, Sidney. That's where you want to be."

I jumped up and put my breast back in my bra. "Maleek, wait a minute! I want to be with you. Don't let this mess up our evening."

He turned to me and looked at me with something I have never seen before in his eyes. "What evening? You called me sounding like you'd had a stressful day and wanted to relieve some stress. Basically you are here on a booty call."

"No way! I admit that I had a stressful evening but I wanted to be with you from the start and I figured tonight is the night. Don't you want me?"

"Don't be stupid. You know I do but not like this." He grabbed me by the shoulders and sat me back on the couch. "Baby, I would love to sex you crazy right now but you are in love with your *husband*. Let me ask you this. Did you ever consider what I may want? Did you ever think that I may have more feelings for you, more than just hollow sex?"

Damn, he got me there. I can honestly say I never gave a damn about what he wanted. I knew he would sleep with me but I had never thought of him wanting more. Shit, I have a family to care for. I guess he is right. This is a booty call. He just made me see the light. I want him but on my terms. I don't want him calling me and asking when were we going to see each other. Or when am I leaving my husband.

I looked into his sincere dark eyes. "Oh, Maleek, I am sorry. I just figured you would be down for this."

He gave me his sexy grin which made me wet between the thighs. "Oh I would have slept with you. I had all intentions of knockin' a new hole in you! Givin' it to you the way you so desperately desired. Sidney, you are a beautiful woman. You have something that I would want in a wife."

He lifted my head up by the chin. "I want a woman. Just one. But not you. I have had a married woman before and I hated it when she had to leave and return home."

"I didn't know," I said with my head down.

"Well, you wouldn't have known unless I told you. But yes, I was the other man before. That is one of the reasons I moved from Massachusetts. I needed to get away. When I fall in love, I fall hard. So just when I got away and stopped missing her, I met yet another married woman in turmoil."

"But you were about to take me to bed?" I questioned.

"Umm hmm. I sure was. You're damn straight I was. I said I was hurt not impotent!" He gave a sexy-ass chuckle that got my juices churning. "I then would have wanted more. Despite some of the other brothers out there, I want to love and be loved. That was fine years ago—to have no love but just endless nights of sex. I'm too old for the bullshit."

"I'm so sorry to have done this to you. I am really acting like a spoiled kid acting out because my parents did not get me a new CD player." I started putting on my shoes. "I need to be slapped. I mean, I was about to ruin my life and get you all tangled up in it! Maleek, I can't begin to start apologizing."

"Sidney, what you have is what anyone decent would want, not just women, you know. I would love to have someone like you in my life. Not the lusting part!" he chuckled. "We can always be friends. I would love to see you work through this and live happily ever after."

"Me too." I sighed.

He sat next to me on the couch and gave me a big brotherly type hug. "Baby girl, go home and work things out. How bad can they be? You've never creeped before in eighteen years. It sounds like you have a good man."

He is so right. Marcus is a wonderful man. I could not ask for any better. I just don't know how to handle his other family obligations. "My husband has been summoned to court in a custody battle with another woman."

He leaned away to see if I'm lying. "Stop playin'."

"No seriously. I mean, it happened back when we were seniors in high school. She kept it from Marcus all this time. Now that she is getting a divorce from her husband, she wants to drop the bomb that he is not that child's father. She wants Marcus to contest to custody and adoption." I could not help but begin to sob.

He rubbed my back trying to console me. "What does your husband say?"

Wiping my nose on my sleeve, I said, "Well, he really doesn't know what to say. He said he wants to get to know her. He also said that he will leave it up to her. After all, she is seventeen years old. I don't want to deal with it. My daughter will be sixteen. I just feel like our family will forever be tarnished! And the worst part of it all is that it is by a girl that I hate. He slept with her once after she kept throwing herself at him. He then begged me for forgiveness and said that he would marry me and give me a lifetime of happiness."

"Were you happy?"

"Yes."

"Then he kept up his end of the bargain."

I got up, getting very annoyed at his playing devil's advocate. "It just makes me mad that she has had one on me all these years!"

He followed me to the window where I was standing watching a couple give each other good-bye kisses at the car. "So is that what the real problem is? You are pissed because he cheated and he married you but she in turn was pregnant, and in your mind she had the last laugh just when all these years you thought you had one on her? Women!"

Showing my anger, I said, "You're damn right! How in the hell can this be? She knew she was pregnant when it was out that we got married! Why didn't she say something then?"

"I don't know. I guess it goes back to my previous statement. Women!" He threw his muscular arms in the air. "You women use these babies as tools to get something out of men. And it is sickening. So, are you saying that if you knew she was pregnant, you would not have gotten married?"

This man is pissing me off with his questions. "I don't know, Maleek! I don't think so. I loved him then and I love him now. I can't say what I would have done back then."

"My answer is no," he so arrogantly said. "Now, you can look at it two ways. One, if you had known you would not have gotten married, which means you may have possibly married just to spite her . . ."

"No . . . that's . . .," I tried to interrupt.

"Wait a minute now the ball is still in my court!" He put up two fingers in front of my face. "Or two, her keeping it a secret allowed you to love your soul mate and have children together. Drama free," he said sounding like Bob Barker. "I would choose option two if I were you." He threw himself on the couch like he had just proven a point.

I went to sit on the couch. "No, Colombo! That is not it all!" I started to laugh, giving away the fact that I know he was right. "You are right. I like option two. I love my husband and family. I'll find a way to figure this out. I have to stand by my man," I said sounding like a country singer.

He looked at me with those sexy brown eyes deeply sincere. "Sidney, go home. You have something worth fighting for. If you leave now then he was really just a pawn in your high school game. It would seem like he was only your husband when everything was perfect. I'm quite sure there are thousands, possibly billions, of women that would love to have your husband instead of theirs." He kissed me so softly on the lips. "You do not belong here."

We stood up together and I embraced him. "Thank you. Thank you for being a friend and telling me what I should have heard a long time ago."

"Any time. Call me sometime. Definitely call with the results of your soap opera." He gently pinched my arm.

As I started for the door, I turned around. "Oh, and thank you for not 'knocking a new hole in me.'"

He blew on his fingers and polished them on his extremely broad chest. "I am a gentleman."

"Good night." I shut the door feeling thankful that I had not completely desecrated my marriage. I would have thrown my whole life away for nothing.

I guess you could say I did step out of the perfect world of Sidney because Marcus would never know that I let another man touch me. That I even enjoyed it a little too much even. However, I will let him know that I have been a complete ass and I deserve whatever lecture he will give. I will tell him that I never again want to leave. I want our family. I can even make room for his daughter, my new stepdaughter. I will also tell him that when I figure it out, I'm getting a career. I am retiring from the housewife profession.

Shannon N. Davis

Chapter 25
Alexis

What a night! I can't believe how we had acted tonight. All of us fighting and name calling was pretty damn juvenile. I have been frustrated at the fact that Simone and Aaron had an affair but I never wanted to fistfight Simone over it. I should be kicking his ass as well. That is what's wrong with us mixed up women, when our man cheats with another woman we seem to always go after her. Nine times out of ten she also thought she was the only one. But the other percentage of women who know about the "main girl" should get her ass kicked.

Right now, I'm going to go up here and relax with EJ and forget about this whole thing for now. I want to curl up beside him and let him hold me all night. It seems like I can't get to his apartment quickly enough with this slow-ass elevator. I forgot to tell him I was coming since I left my cell phone at Tracy's mom's house.

Finally, I'm here waiting for my dark and handsome lover to answer the door. To my surprise the door was unlocked, "Ely, baby, you there?"

He came walking from the kitchen with his fine behind. He has on a pair of sweats with a T-shirt that accented his bulging chest. "Hey, what are you doing here, Alexis? I didn't know you were stopping by."

I damn sure didn't like his tone. I'm hoping and praying to God that he was not into something that would destroy us. "I know, uh, I had a terrible night tonight. I left my cell at Tracy's mom's and I just wanted to get here." I put my arms around him but he did not reciprocate. "Baby, I just want you to hold me and make love to me all night."

He broke free of my grip. "Alexis, I wish . . ."

Just then another voice came from out of nowhere, "I wish I was not seeing what the fuck I'm seeing and hearing right now!"

It was Aaron! Oh my god! Please not tonight. If looks could kill, we would all have been dead yesterday. He came toward Elijah and me.

"Aaron, what are you doing here?" I said nervously.

"No, you trick, the question is what are *you* doing here?" he stepped back to get a full view of the picture. Looking at us in complete disbelief, he said, "Oh *hell no*! EJ, not you and her?"

Elijah moved me to the side and tried to explain, "Yo, Aaron, this is what I wanted you to come over for."

"To see this shit?" he said pointing at us in disgust.

"No, to talk about it. She came over without me knowing. I wanted to talk to you man to man," he said in his defense.

Aaron repeated, "Hell, no! No! You are my brother! What is this, Lex, some sort of payback for sleeping with your lonely-ass friend? Huh?"

I can see this was about to get real ugly and I had no clue what to say. I was not expecting this tonight, not at all. "No, this is not payback. Why don't you let Elijah explain?"

He gave a long sinister laugh that electrocuted my spine. He backed up even farther, looking like a bull getting ready to charge at the red flag. "How long?" Neither one of us answered, which made him scream, "How long?"

Elijah walked toward Aaron. "Not too long. We sort of just started. Let me explain this whole thing but you have to calm down. No one can talk to you when your head is hot."

Aaron shrugged his shoulders looking like he was waiting for the next round in a championship fight. "I'm listening. Shit!"

EJ began to explain, "You knew from way back then that I had special feelings for Alexis. It was not until recently that we decided to act on it. It was not an easy decision to make, especially not for me. We didn't want to be sneaking around like two adulterers and that is why I wanted to tell you right away."

Aaron turned as red as a dark man could turn. "You knew! You knew I wanted to get back with her. All the while, you were fucking her! C'mon, E, you really want me to be understanding?"

"As much as you can be."

I never saw it coming but Aaron's fist hit Elijah's face so quickly that Elijah never had time to stop it. The two men who had once been brothers were fighting as if their lives depended on it. Elijah was begging Aaron to calm down while Aaron was saying all types of accusations of betrayal.

I began screaming, "Stop! Stop it now! Elijah and Aaron, stop!"

Neither one of them heard my cries. I tried to get between them but got pushed away by the strength of both of them. They fell and Aaron landed on top with hands around Elijah's neck.

"I could kill you! You were my boy, my best friend and partner! How could you fuck my girl?"

Elijah struggled for breath. "I love her. I always have." He was then able to free himself from Aaron's grip of death. "Yo, just stop! Damn, this is hard enough as it is! You know I love you like a brother and this was something that took long and hard thought." He got off from being on top of Aaron. "I have known for a long time that I was in love with Alexis. I even told you when you brought her to me in the club that night we first met her. However, I never let anything happen between us because she chose you."

"Oh so now that she is free, you can have her?" Aaron said as he picked himself up from the floor.

"You guys are talking about me like I am not even here!" I shouted.

They never even commented on my statement. Elijah kept talking, "No, it wasn't like that. I saw her a little while ago at the club and she was radiant. I was happy to see her since we had not seen each other since your wedding day. We made plans to get together and we did. Now, this is the outcome." Elijah held his head with both hands. "I knew this would possibly end our relationship but I couldn't stop what was happening between us."

Aaron was still trying to catch his breath. "Why didn't you tell me? I thought you were patching things up with Shelly. And what about that other chick you let be nameless?" Just as that moment, something clicked in his head. He looked at me with pain in his eyes. "I guess this is the face of the nameless woman. Damn! Alexis, I love you and I still do. Please don't do this. I was giving you time to heal. As per *his* instructions," he said pointing and rolling his eyes at Elijah. "Baby, let me make it up to you. Let me show you how sorry I am. He can't love you like I do. Baby, please! Just come with me," Aaron pleaded.

I could not believe this guy. He has cheated on me with my best friend, with who knows how many other women. There is no way I could go back to him. Not now, not ever. I tried to get his hand off mine. "Aaron, stop it please. You know what we had is gone. What you did killed that a long time ago."

He looked at me with those deep brown eyes and I saw a little of the things that I had fallen in love with a long time ago. I remembered the passion and the love, the commitment that I gave him. How sweet he was to me. Anything my heart desired I got. He made sure I was happy. We won't even mention the countless days and nights of exquisite lovemaking we shared.

Then I remembered that those were the same deep brown eyes that told me at the altar that he had my best friend pregnant, and that he shared those same eyes with his son. "Stop it, please. There can never be an *us* again. We never meant to hurt you. This is not some revenge tactic to get back at you though it may seem that way. This would not have gone down if you had been faithful. I have no idea if that was the first time or not. I just know that you and Simone devastated me, humiliated the shit out of me! Elijah and I hooked up way after. He was with no one and I have not been with anyone since you."

He didn't need to know Elijah and I slept together on our alleged wedding night. I know Elijah won't bring it up either. "This is a friendship that evolved into something nice and we would like to see where it is heading."

EJ walked toward us. "Yo, A, I am so sorry that you . . ."

Aaron cut him off, "EJ, stay away from me! How did you feel when I was telling you how much I loved Alexis and that she was the only one for me?"

"I felt terrible. That's why I wanted to put this out but I wanted to do it in a way that would not have been so traumatic."

Aaron started with that sinister laugh again. "Traumatic? Please! I knew you always liked her. I just never thought that you would get with her. I guess you took great pleasure when I got busted, huh?"

"Naw, man, c'mon, Aaron. When you first started messing with Simone I told you it was a bad idea. I told you that you had someone special and that you were getting married. I told you things you already knew but *you* took all that for granted."

"I guess you're happy that she does not want me back?" he questioned.

Elijah walked toward Aaron slowly and touched his shoulder. "Nope. I was hurt that the two of you could not work it out. I saw how bad you wanted her back."

Aaron begged for an answer that he wanted to hear, "Then why?

She was my girl. I told you no matter who she was seeing that it would come to an end when I came back the way she wanted me to."

How arrogant is he? Even if it were not EJ I was with, he thinks he could come back to me. "I have not been your girl since you cheated. Aaron, it would not have worked like that even if it were anyone else, just like I wouldn't have gotten back with you if you had cheated on me with a total stranger. When are you going to realize that? Not everyone can be your personal whore. Women have feelings other than just wanting your dick."

His once sexy brown eyes turned dark as coal when he looked at me. I almost became frightened. He kept his stare at me while talking to Elijah, "Tell me, EJ, does she like it when you sex her? Did you hit her spot yet?"

"C'mon now," Elijah said with a deep breath.

Still staring at me, he said, "No! She wanted to sleep with two best friends. Doesn't she know we talk about the women we fuck? Does her eyes still pop out when she cums?"

Elijah came quickly to my side. "Stop this shit right now!"

Still staring at me, he said, "When she sucks it, does she still slither her sweet tongue from the base to the head? Remember how you used to do that to me, sweet Lex?"

Tears fell from my face while he was publicizing our intimate moments. This man is plain cruel. Why would he stoop to such levels? "Why are you doing this? You fucked up! Not me! All I did was love you. I cherished you. I told you then and now that I can't be with you. Not then, not ever. Now you want to put our intimacies in the street?" I wiped my tears. "I'm glad I left your ass! Just get away from me! You're not even worth fighting with. My relationship is not cheap and tawdry. We have something that is worth risking everything for. You could not say the same, could you?"

Elijah noticed my misery and pushed him away from me. "Get away from her!"

Aaron finally broke his foul stare. "You bitch!"

Elijah went toward him and jacked him up to the wall. "Didn't I tell you to leave her out of it? Now, there will be no more disrespecting my woman like that. This is some shit you do to your women but not my woman! Not Alexis! Now or ever!"

Aaron broke free. "Oh what, you all pussy whipped now? Fuck you and her! I don't need either one of your asses. This is bullshit. You walk around like you always got your head on straight and you are no better than me!" He started beating his chest with his fist. "Man, you were my brother! How am I supposed to deal with this? I love her!" And for the first time he began to cry. "I love you too, man."

Elijah walked to him looking emotionally drained. "I love you too, man. That is why this is so hard. But I can't stop loving Alexis either." "We had a lifetime friendship. We had childhood. We had college. We had law school. We had a law firm," he said, counting out each item on his fingers.

"We will just have to work through this. We will give you all the space you need to come to grips with it," Elijah pleaded.

Aaron looked at him in surprise. "Come to grips with it? Uh-uh! No way in hell will I be able to ever deal with this or you. Ever! It is all over! All of it!"

"What are you talking about?" Elijah said looking confused.

"It's done! Everything. Friendship and business. I hate you both with all my heart. Everything I am and have, I hate you both!"

I literally saw Elijah's heart break. He looked liked his last breath had been taken from him. As if he had just been killed in a movie. "You don't mean that. Let's just talk and come to an understanding. We worked too hard for what we have established."

"Oh, I know all about *your* working hard. I know you worked long and hard to hold out until your time was clear to go after her. I know you worked long and hard to get her into your bed too. I know her so I know how hard you had to work to please her."

That bastard. He is relentless about trashing me. It is sad when you leave someone and they want to put your business out there like a child would. I did feel sorry for him but now he can rot in hell for all I care. "You are so childish, Aaron. I know you are hurt but do it in a more mature fashion."

Again with his Flash Gordon impression, he came to me and slapped the shit out of me. The impact was such that I flew across the room. "Dumb bitch! Now that is for sleeping with *my* best friend!"

Next thing you know, they were fighting again. This time Elijah was showing no mercy, none whatsoever and went after that ass. They fought like one of them had stolen something from the other— punching and holding each other in headlocks, screaming at each other. I could barely see due to the Ike Turner hit I had just received. Right now I couldn't care less if they killed each other. But damn, I have literally fallen and couldn't get up. Ain't this a bitch?

"Man, I tried but you have to go! You want to end the business, then fine! Just get out of my house!" Elijah pushed Aaron to the door and opened it. People were in the hallway looking at the fiasco. EJ was able to get him out. "Fuck this! We're through here!"

Aaron yelled from in the hallway, "Naw, mother fucker, I'm through! Don't let me see your ass again! Nothing good is going to come to you two. Nothing! Tell that trick bitch in there that I had better. Simone was better anyway!"

At that point I ran to the door, and stooping to his childish tactics, I said, "And Elijah here has the bigger dick!"

Elijah quickly shut the door before Aaron could repeat his Ike Turner performance. "Bye, Aaron!" he turned to me in amazement. "No, you didn't just say that!"

I pouted like a schoolgirl. "Well, he smacked me! And to top it all off, he made me sound like a two-bit whore." I couldn't help but cry. That had been painful to see and hear. He had once been the man I was going to spend the rest of my life with. Now, I'm sleeping with his best friend. What a turn of events!

Tears fell from Elijah's eyes. "I just didn't want it to go down like this. I knew it would be rough but damn!" He walked away from me and began to survey the apartment.

I walked to him and rubbed his back. "Look at this place. Baby, I'm so sorry this had to happen."

He gave me a cold look. "You should go now."

"What's wrong with this picture? What in the hell is going on here?" I asked, surprised.

He again pulled away from me. "I just can't deal with you right now."

I tried to speak over the lump in my throat. "Elijah, please. We should be together right now. Baby, don't do this."

I went to him and he backed away again. "No one told you to come here tonight. Why didn't you call first? You always do."

Now, I'm hurt. "I already told you. I didn't know that he was going to be here. Honest."

He started picking up broken pieces of glass, never giving me a second glance. He acted as though I had wanted this to happen. He had pursued me with this. I stood there in complete shock. I couldn't move my feet and leave, instead I watched him pick up glass and other debris from the floor.

He finally spoke, "Did you hear what I said?"

I sighed in disbelief and quickly went for the door. And if I couldn't make myself look even more stupid than I already did, I could not figure out the damn locks. I fumbled and could barely see through my tears. What had I done wrong? Why am I here? Why had he turned on me?

Finally the door unlocked, and when I opened it, he quickly shut it. "Stop, don't go," he whispered to the back of my head. He held me tight, talking to me with tears in his voice. "I'm sorry. I shouldn't have taken this out on you."

My sobbing went full steam ahead. "I'm sorry too. I should have called. I'm sorry." I held his hand to my chest. "I love you and I don't know why you want me out."

Still with his chest to my back, he whispered, "That's because I don't. I just don't want you to see me like this. Not now, not ever. I lost the one person whom I loved dearly besides my mother. I just thought I would be able to handle it. This is much harder than I imagined." He held me tighter and continued talking in a soft voice, "You know I love you and I want this to work no matter what. Stay and let me hold you tonight like you wanted. I need you here. I couldn't bear it if someone else I loved left tonight."

I turned around to look at his beautiful face. "Your night was just as rough as mine. Let's hold each other."

We kissed so passionately against the door. He picked me up and carried me off to the bedroom. Still kissing, we were able to remove our clothing leaving only undergarments on. We lay in bed wiping each other's tears, trying to comfort each other. He softly kissed the back of my neck and held me. Neither one of us said a word for the rest of the night. I know we both replayed the night's events in our heads before we drifted off to sleep, wondering what it was about tonight that we could have changed.

I know I would have changed two things. One, I would have changed the way I fought Simone. And two, I would not have left my cell phone behind. At least then, I would have spared myself one of the two altercations I endured tonight.

Shannon N. Davis

Chapter 26
Simone

I thought this baby would never go to sleep. I would sell my soul if I knew the fastest and quickest way to get a baby to sleep. I know I'm going to have to do something about this before I go back to work in a couple of weeks.

After the night I had, I want to sit in a hot bubble bath and let all of Sade's CDs shuffle in the player. They say music calms the savage beast but the beast that came out tonight was going to need more than Sade to soothe it, or at least a nice stiff one to accompany her.

Just the thought of a man lying next to me is making the spot between my legs throb. I'm thinking of letting a man make love to my entire body, not only touching and caressing my sexually deprived body, but my soul as well. I would have him talk to me in a way that no one has ever talked to me before and make me feel like the only way he could survive is through me. And he would be totally getting off on my pleasures and desires.

As I touched myself, I kept thinking and fantasizing about true love. With visions of my perfect man and the exquisite strokes of my hand, my juices poured right out of my body like warm water pouring from a pitcher. Water that is much needed after that one. Masturbation is becoming my nightly ritual. I should start keeping a glass of water at the bedside. Maybe two glasses, because a woman never knows when she will be ready for round two.

While I sip my glass of water, the doorbell rang. I walked to the door and saw Aaron standing there. I would hate to tell him that I'd just hit myself off and his services are no longer needed here. "Aaron, what are you doing here?" I said through the door cracked.

He looked a mess. I could smell through the door that he had been drinking excessively. I don't want no bullshit in here tonight. I'm not dealing with him that way. I have to tell myself that. I don't care how much he begs and how good he looks. I just can't.

"Yo, Simone, stop playing and open the door."

Against my better judgment, I opened the door. "It's late. Wait right here so I can get a robe," I said as I walked to my bedroom. From the corner of my eye I saw him peek inside the baby's room.

I went back to the living room and turned the sweet, sultry sounds of Sade down. "What's up? You look like you had a bad day."

He sat on the couch and gave me a look that I could not quite determine. "Why did you go and get a robe on? I know what you got."

"Whatever, Aaron. Do you know what time it is?" I said, tightening my robe.

"Did you know that Alexis is fucking EJ?" he said sounding pretty pissed off.

"Yes."

"So what, I was the last to know? This is some bullshit!"

I didn't know how he found out and I didn't want to make him feel worse than he did. "I just found out tonight. I guess you are not thrilled, huh?"

He stood up and came close to me. I could smell the alcohol but he was still a handsome man that I am very much still attracted to. He started undoing my robe. "Take this off."

I have to be strong and just say no. "Stop it. We can no longer do this. I'm done."

"Stop playin', Monie, you know you want to. We have not been together in a while." He tugged on my ear with his warm full lips, lightly kissing my neck and rubbing my now erect breast.

"No, Aaron! This is not happening between us anymore. You have to leave. The baby is sleep, so you are not here to see him."

He looked at me in shock. "Girl, you serious?"

"Yes," I said, moving back and trying to remain firm. "No more. You are not my man. You have no love for me and I no longer want to give my body to a man that does not appreciate me as a woman."

"Again, stop playin', girl. Just give me some and I will leave."

"Please just go."

"Then suck it then," he said unbuckling his pants.

"Hell no! Get out!" I demanded. What's wrong with this guy?

He started laughing like I had just told him a funny joke. "OK, OK! The strong-girl act you have achieved, now meet me in the bedroom."

He started toward my room. "Let's go."

I went to the door and opened it. "Goodbye, Aaron."

He quickly came and slammed the door shut. "What in the hell is your problem? Now, you want to play self-righteous?"

I didn't like where this was going. I was backed in a corner and did not appreciate the look in his eyes. "Please leave. I don't want to have sex with you ever again."

"Bitch, please! You are easy pussy and no one is ever going to believe that you are a changed woman."

I could not believe he just said that. "And you saying this is supposed to make me give it up? Yeah right. Just go home and sober up."

"What's the matter, huh? Is it that I am not longer attached and you don't know how to deal with a man without a woman? You ain't shit, Simone. Never have and never will be. I can't believe you."

Here he goes degrading me and pushing all my buttons. "Look, I'm changing my life around—my whole life. The only thing from my old life that is staying is my son. You know, the one that I have been responsible for from day one. Unlike yourself, barely keeping the boy an hour out of your day. So you are pissed off that your precious Alexis is screwing your best friend. So what?"

"You want to talk responsible? Look who got knocked up on purpose to keep me? I never loved you. I wanted some easy pussy and I got it. I will always take care of my son. Always! As far as you are concerned, who cares? I wouldn't have had to go there but you want to hold out on a brotha!"

Tears rolled from my eyes. I love this man enough to think that we could have had something. Now he wants to throw it in my face. I had spent days and nights trying to change what had happened between us. I lost my best friend and now have to raise a child alone. How could he be so cruel?

Part of me wanted to put my fists through his face, but I've fought enough tonight. "I hate you! I don't care what I did in the past! This is the present, and if you do not leave, I will call the police! The choice is yours."

"Go ahead and call the mother fuckers! I am quite sure you fucked them all anyway!" He turned his back to me.

"Get out!" I hollered.

Aaron charged me like a bull. Pushing me against the wall, slamming my head against it. "Don't you ever yell at me! Do you hear me? Do you?" He kept slamming my shoulders against the wall repeatedly. I could tell this was not a sane man. He was taking out his anger at being rejected on me.

He dragged me from the wall to the couch. I screamed for him to get off me. He was unbelievably strong. He became a madman and tried to force himself on me, which was not hard considering what pleasures I had given myself prior to this. I had no panties on.

We fought on the couch and he struggled with me and his pants buckle and zipper. I screamed in horror because of what was coming. This man is going to rape me. He obviously has no feelings for me other than wanting to have sex with me. I was just here for his penile pleasure. That had never changed even though I had his first child. This is the lowest he has ever gone. How could I report this? Who would believe me?

With all the struggle I gave him, he managed to open his pants and I felt the erection and warmth of his penis. He was able to get both my hands together and raise them to the top of my head while he parted my legs. I cried, screamed, and begged him to stop. He never looked me in the face. I could only hear the struggle and exhaustion in his breath that was laced with alcohol.

I continued to move my pelvis away and he still was unable to catch me. I began to feel myself tire out and he began to penetrate me. It was hurtful emotionally and painful physically. He was still not situated inside me because of the fight I was putting up. "Please, no!"

I have no idea what he heard but he stopped, and for the first time he saw my face. He looked like he had seen a ghost. He withdrew himself but never got off me. I continued to cry and tremble uncontrollably. This is not the man that I loved. This is someone altogether different.

He got off me and sat on the couch and straightened up while I scrunched up in a ball on the opposite end of the couch. Even though I could barely see through my tear-filled eyes, I noticed Aaron sobbing as well. I couldn't figure out what was wrong with him. I mean, I know he is hurt and upset with Elijah and Alexis but there had to be something else going on. Why would he want to hurt me?

He looked at me in distress and came toward me. "Simone, I am so sorry. Baby, please listen to me," he pleaded.

"Stay the hell away from me," I said as I tightly closed my robe and balled up in an even tighter fetal position. "Why would you try to force yourself on me? I know you hate me but damn, Aaron!" I started sobbing uncontrollably.

He tried to console me the best way he could but his touch that had once been lethal with passion was now detrimental and painful. I loved this man until now. I don't know what I feel for him anymore. He would not let go of me. He constantly tried to hold me while we were still on the couch. "Baby, I was wrong. I know it and I couldn't be mad if you sent me to jail. Right about now, I don't even care. Just calm down. Did I physically hurt you?" He began to look over my body as though he could see if there were any bruises.

"I don't know. My wrist hurts and so do my thighs. You barely penetrated so there is no real damage. Only mental." I wiped my eyes and tried so hard to stop my heart from breaking. "Why do you treat me so bad, Aaron?"

"I don't know." He put his head in his hands and shook it back and forth. He tried to explain what was going through that head of his. He began crying and trying to explain at the same time. "I love her."

"Alexis I suppose."

"Yes. I hate myself for making the biggest mistake of my life. The biggest. I hate you for making me weak. I hate you for being fine as hell. I hate you for wanting me as well. It is just easier for me to hate someone else other than myself," he explained.

He went on to say that he had never wanted me in that way. He had led me on merely because I was carrying his child. He had wanted to sort of keep the peace. Never did he once have intentions of loving me the way a person should. I was something he wanted only when he wanted it. He even stated that he would have married Alexis with the affair in the past if I had not kept the baby.

The love I thought I felt was long gone. Long gone. Deep down I had known that I was nothing more than a *piece* to him. And now, hearing it actually come out of his mouth put it all into place. The emotional hate and now the physical hate he had for me were nothing but a red flag warning me to get as far away from him as I could.

He also tried to apologize for the way he treated me, telling me that he had never wanted any of this to happen. He said that he loved our son and would try to establish something close to a family for little Aaron's sake. As for me, as far as he was concerned we were to be friends and nothing more. Though he blamed me for what happened between us, he knew that I was not entirely to blame. He admitted that he became flirtatious because he knew I was easy. What I was getting from this whole confession was that he had just wanted to fuck me and move on. He would not have said a word if I hadn't. How is that for undying love?

I in turn told him that I did love him and so desperately wanted a relationship with him. I told him that I wanted that and I had risked everything to be with him. I had known that he cared about me but didn't love me. I did what all women would have done when they yearned for a man so badly, and that is settle.

I settled for disrespect. I settled for unworthiness. I settled for everything but love. I gave all I had to get nothing but what he wanted to give. I let myself down. I had known deep down that he was not the one. I had known that when I first started sleeping with him. How could he be mine if he was already someone else's? I do know Alexis is laughing at my ass. Here I was, hurting because I did her the sweet justice of taking her no-good man away from her. Who's laughing now?

I wished so badly that this was a nightmare, a horrible dream I can wake up from any minute now. I finally removed myself from the couch, walked toward the door, and said, "You need to get help. Like I said earlier, I will no longer be your personal whore. I'm sorry that you hate me for loving you but I did not do this by myself. I did not conceive this child alone. You decided to hate me because of what we did. Well, I hate you too. I hate you for thinking that I was always going to be there for you when you need to abuse someone. I made an awful mistake with you. I knew that then and I damn sure know that now. No more will I be of service to you. No more will you enter my home after eight at night. No more will you show up here unannounced. You will call first. When you want to see the baby, you call first. There will be no denying that. You will pay the support at an amount that we will agree on. If you can not handle these things than the judge will make you handle them."

I opened the door, watching him gather his belongings and fix himself up while I spoke. He never said a word and just listened. "I have had it with you, Aaron McKnight. Done forever." He was taking entirely too long so I became impatient. "C'mon let's go! I want to have your ass arrested for assault. Take any longer and you will be."

He reached the door. "Simone, when things cool down we will talk."

"No, when things cool down we will only talk of the things that I mentioned. No ifs, ands, or butts about it. Take a shower and get some sleep. Better yet, get some help."

I shut the door and locked it. I would not shed another tear for this man ever again. He is not worth it and never has been. Everything I'd done to relax me was ruined. My music, bath, and self-gratification went straight down the drain. I am so exhausted. I just want to go to bed and sleep forever.

Thank god that the baby did not wake up through all the commotion. I had wished to God that I could have Aaron. I wished that he would be in my life and that we would be man and woman forever. Now I wish that he would go away forever. I guess I better watch what I wish for.

Shannon N. Davis

Chapter 27
Sidney

I can't sleep tonight. I have had two cups of my mother's decaf tea and it is doing me no good. I know Marcus and the kids are sleeping and I don't want to wake anyone up. I may even just be scared of how he would react when I walked through the door. He has every right to tell me to turn around. I sit here trying to figure out if I want to go home because I really want to be there or if I am just tired of staying in my mother's guest room. It's the room where my twin and I had spent our nights as children. My mother never had a problem with us moving out. She just prayed that we never had to come back home.

She must have heard my thoughts because I thought I was pretty quiet in the kitchen. She walked in looking like she'd been in a bar room brawl. "Girl, what are you doing up at this hour? It's four in the morning." She paused and her eyes became big pieces of coal. "You slept with that guy with the funny name didn't you?"

"No! No, I could have but I didn't. And his name is Maleek, Ma. I just could not sleep. I was thinking what I was going to do with my life."

She poured a cup of tea and asked if it were decaf. She sat at the table with me and had her motherly face on. "Sidney, my dear, your place is at home. I don't know why on earth you are here anyway. When you have a problem like this, it should have been worked out at home. You should not be here."

I couldn't look her in the eye so I stared blankly in my less-than-half cup of tea. "I know, I just don't know if I am truly happy anymore."

She looked at me like I had two heads or something. My mother had a thing for piling on the sugar in her tea. She always said caffeine has her buzzing but I could never understand how the amount of sugar she used didn't have her running marathons. Finally, her tea's sweetness was at a satisfactory level. "How could you not know? Did you think the answer was going to be in bed with whatever-his-name-is?"

"Maleek," I said.

"Maleek, Swaleek, or whatever! He does not have the answer. If you had slept with him you would have caused more problems than you could handle. I mean, you would have enjoyed it because it was new to you, something different from what you are accustomed to. It may not have necessarily been better but different." She went on to have me recall when Simone and I were teens and sex was coming for us, though it had already come for Simone. She had always said, "Sex is like food, once you eat it you feel like you need it to survive. You will always want it because you think you need it."

She was right because when I first became sexually active with Marcus, I always said, "I need some sex"—when I actually just wanted it. If I had slept with Maleek, I wouldn't have done it just once. I would have had repeated offenses and that damn sure would have caused major problems. I would have been lying to him about my whereabouts, and I wouldn't be sleeping with my husband because I had just slept with another man. How do two-timers do it?

We talked until the sun came up. I felt better and became full of energy. I wanted to fly home but something kept me from going. I'm not sure what but I went into my old bedroom and drifted off to sleep instead. I needed some loving right now. I needed to be held and caressed right now. I had never seen the logic in masturbating when I had a well-endowed husband with mega stamina for a man well into his thirties. Hopefully, when I arrive home he won't reject me.

xoxoxoxoxoxo

I did everything today but go home. I slept until three in the afternoon. I stayed around the house. My mother and William went out and she said that I should not be here when she returned. I went to the mall and shopped. Marcus is going to flip with the credit card purchases. I will wait to tell him when I feel him out.

I drove and had lunch—or dinner since it was already eight in the evening—in my car to try and regain composure. By the time I got home, it was going on ten. I could see through the living room window that the TV was on in the family room. I knew someone was up, probably one of the kids. I had not spoken to them in-depth about what was going on and I don't know how much Marcus has told them. They must feel abandoned by me.

My assumptions were correct. They were all watching television when I walked in. No one budged from the couch. I felt like their piercing eyes were shooting straight through me. Marcus just looked surprise that I was home but never said a word. I clutched my handbag and felt really sick. "Hi, guys!"

At first no one spoke. My first thought was that I shouldn't have returned. My second thought was that I wonder what Marcus told them. My sweet baby, Sasha, decided to speak first. "Mommy, are you staying home now?" Her eyes twinkled with innocence. She had the cutest dark brown skin and I always teased her about her pumpkin head. It was not big but it was shaped like a small pumpkin that would sit on a table.

I trembled. "I think so. Are you OK with that?"

Nickia, who at times, can be really nasty, rolled her eyes at me. For the first time, I felt like I'd done the ultimate transgression. I deserve this because I left my children. No matter what, a mother never leaves her children. Marquis lay against his dad and never said a word. Neither did Marcus.

Nickia turned the TV off. "Are you going to say anything else? I mean, you left us like a thief in the night."

"Yeah, Mom, how come?" Marquis said in agreement.

Since all four of them were sitting on the sofa, I sat on the ottoman. "Well, kids, your mom made a bad mistake, a poor judgment call. Your dad and I had a disagreement and I reacted poorly and left instead of working things out." I looked over at Marcus and he was looking directly at me, listening intently like one of the children.

Sasha came and sat on my lap. She began to push my hair behind my ears. "I'm getting another big sister, Mommy! Do I have to listen to her too?" she said as she rolled her eyes at Nickia.

I was stunned. I guess Marcus had no choice to tell them the real reason I left. I hoped to God that I don't show them how uneasy that topic made me feel. "Well, that depends on what she tells you what to do." I kissed her chubby cheek.

"Sasha, we don't even know if she wants to meet us. Dad said that he hasn't met her yet and that he will let her make up her mind," Nickia said reinforcing what Marcus told them.

161

Being the bratty little sister, Sasha said, "Well, she will have to tell you what to do too because she is older than you!" She stuck out her tongue as she normally does to her older siblings.

"Dad, why couldn't you have an older son? I'm stuck with three sisters now! I can't take the bickering!" Marquis said. He is such a handsome young man. He looks exactly like me but darker, just like his father. He is the only one of all our children that looks like me, but he has Marcus's personality and traits.

I talked with the kids, letting them know how sorry I was, telling them that I never stopped loving them for one second. Marcus still didn't say a word. I guess he is letting me drown here on purpose. All of the children took to the fact that their dad had another child. They handled it better than me. Nickia is not too thrilled. She is only older than her half sister by a year. Nickia just turned seventeen and Robin will be eighteen very soon. Nickia wants to meet her though. She also informed us that she is not going to struggle hard to have a relationship with Robin; either they'll have a good one or they won't. The other two were neither for or against Nickia's plan.

Marcus finally intervened and told them to go to bed. They hesitated and he reassured them that I would be here in the morning. They all gave me kisses and went to their rooms. He looked at me, still not removing himself from the couch. "I need to know, did you sleep with the ole' boy? I want the truth, not what you think I should know. And I will not elaborate on it again."

"No!"

"No?"

Tears fell from eyes. "No, I did not." He didn't need to know what could have happened. He just asked if I slept with Maleek.

He finally got up from the couch. He had lost some weight, I noticed right away. He looked tired and worn out. I watched him stretch and saw that he is still my handsome dark chocolate man, minus a few pounds. "I'm going to bed."

I was trying to wipe my tears and I still remained sitting. I stopped gazing at him and from the corner of my eyes, I noticed that he stopped. I looked at him. "Are you OK?"

"Yes, I was wondering if my wife was coming to bed." He gave me that sideways grin that I loved.

Needless to say, I followed him to our bedroom. I took a shower and it felt so good to be home. This is where I belong. I will have to adjust to the *new addition* to the family. I brushed my teeth and hair and couldn't wait to lie next to my husband.

When I walked into the bedroom, Marcus was watching the sports channel. He looked so fine lying there with no shirt on. With those dark pecs bulging at me, I immediately got wet between the thighs. He turned to me and smiled and opened the covers on my side of the bed and gestured for me to get in. "I believe you belong here."

Like the schoolgirl I have always been around him, I quickly hopped into bed. I kissed him long and strong. "Baby, I am so sorry. Please forgive me." He wiped the tears that fell from my right eye and licked it off his thumb, never losing contact with my eyes.

"You know, Siddy, I've missed you so much." He came close to me and began kissing me and holding me, smelling my hair and kissing every part of my body. My whole body shuddered with excitement and love.

We made love for hours on end, telling each other how much we meant to each other, all the while hitting the right spots. We each had multiple orgasms but never gave up on what we wanted to share with each other. Like I said before, for a man in his thirties, he could still run with the twenty-year-olds. There was no stopping him. He took his time and told me that he could because I was not going anywhere ever again. When he went down, he found other ways to keep the lovemaking going—whether it was tasting me or massaging my body with our adult massage oils or just holding me and letting our conversations on love and commitment get us heated all over again.

During one of our heated talks between lovemaking, I decided it was time to tell him what my future plans were. "Honey, I'm going to do something with my life."

Still caressing me, he asked, "What are you talking about, Sidney?"

I turned to look at him. "I want to do something with my life. I want something else other than motherhood. I mean a career."

"Are you serious?" he said as he stopped caressing me.

I got nervous and I almost wanted to end it right there. "Yes, one of the reasons I wanted out of the marriage was because for a long time I yearned for something more, more than just marriage and kids. Don't get me wrong, I love you all and would not trade you for the world. It is just that I want to do something more."

"Like what?" he questioned.

"I don't know yet. Why, do you have a problem with it?" I said getting on the defensive.

He paused and kissed me softly on the lips. "No, I don't. I do have a problem with the fact that you couldn't tell me what you were feeling. I mean, I thought I made you happy with everything. I'm sorry I let you down."

"No! You didn't let me down. I didn't have enough faith in us to think that I could come to you about this. You made me very happy. Very happy." I kissed him back.

He went on to explain to me that he was sorry for never asking what I wanted to do with my life. How he had thought taking care of everything was good enough. And that he agreed that I should have a career or something. Even if I worked one day or five days a week, he said that he would support me on whatever I chose to do. "I'm here for you 210 percent. I love you, Sid." And he began making love to me again. This time more intensely than the last four times. God, I love this man!

I guess when we finally went to sleep, we just slept. The kids never knocked on the door and we stayed locked in our room until we both figured it was time to come up for air. I love this man and he loves me. There were times when I felt I did not deserve him taking me back so easily. And he made me realize that I had acted like a complete ass. I don't care. I want to be home and I am here. And I am never leaving again. Taniesha can forget about it. I have the last laugh. And as my mother put it, "Maleek or Swaleek who?"

xoxoxoxoxoxo

I'm still basking in the afterglow of the power of our love. Marcus took the kids to his mother's for the night. He felt we needed another night to make these makeup sessions complete. I so eagerly agreed and the kids were all for it.

I prepared the most exquisite dinner for us tonight. He has no clue what seduction scene he is about to come into. I made lobster tails, T-bone steak, his favorite corn-on-the-cob, salad, and strawberry cheese-cake. All his favorites. I even went all out and made shrimp cocktail with the biggest shrimp I could find and with his Sylvia's cocktail sauce. If my dinner won't get him, nothing will.

I made the dining room into an elegant dining experience. Our finest china was in order. I draped the table and chairs with silk and sheer cloths. This called for candles and chilled wine. Neither one of us are drinkers but we happened to like Arbor Mist's Blackberry Merlot. All this with the soft soothing sounds of CD 101.9 softly whispering in the background.

My outfit is to die for. I almost matched the table cloth. I have a little full-length cream silk chemise with a tantalizing split up my thigh. The chemise's matching overcoat was sheer and had only a silk tie to hold it together. I swept my hair in a sloppy pin-up with loosely curled tendrils falling to the side of my face. He loves my hair like that. My fragrance of the evening is his absolute favorite, Red Door by Elizabeth Arden. It turns him completely on.

I was standing back admiring all the work I put into this evening when I heard the door slam. My prince is home. I seductively leaned on the wall between that marked the entrance of the dining room and the end of the living room. He looked a bit disheveled. I smiled at my husband. "Hey, big daddy, I've been waiting for you."

He looked at me and obviously liked what he saw, but he stood still and never came close to me. "What did you do with Maleek?"

I was caught completely off-guard. What in the hell is he talking about? Then again, why is he bringing it up now? I straightened up from my seductive position. "What . . . what are you talking about?" I stuttered.

He remained in his spot. His eyes were full of rage. I had no idea what was going on. He balled up his fists and kept them at his side. "What the fuck did you do with him, Sidney?" he repeated with anger in his voice.

"Nothing, I told you! Why are you asking me this now?"

He sighed in complete disgust. "You were going to sleep with him, weren't you?"

I couldn't look him in the face but I was able to come toward him. "No . . . no . . . I mean I could have but I thought against it. I . . . I was so confused and angry. Baby, please calm down. What happened?"

He backed away from me like I had a contagious disease. "Don't. . . don't . . . don't touch me ever again!" He had tears in his bloodshot eyes. He tried hard to fight them but they surfaced.

What had this man heard? I tried again to hold him and he pushed me away. My eyes filled with tears and I don't know why. "Marcus, please! I told you all of this already. We got over it, right? Right?"

"What was the reason you didn't sleep with him?" he said with both fists tightly curled at his side.

"I told you that I didn't want to! Marcus . . ."

"The only reason you did not sleep with him was because you called out my fuckin' name!" he roared.

How in the hell had he known that? My heart bounced completely out of my chest. I was petrified for the first time in my life. My husband just somehow received word for word of my attempt at a fling. I paced back and forth to try not to just lose it completely.

"What, huh? You shocked?"

"Let's not do this, please. It was nothing. Nothing!" I yelled. "I planned this nice evening for you. Us. Our new start."

He walked in long strides over to the dining room and flipped the table over. "The hell with that shit! You made it seem like you didn't want to sleep with him because you loved me and what we have when the only reason you did not fuck the ole' boy is because you called out my name. He had you all pinned up on the couch, titties in his mouth and all! You even begged him to make love to him after you said it and he wanted to send your dumb ass home. You wanted him! You wanted him!"

I watched my table and all that had been on it hit the wall and floor. Thank god I had not lit the candles. I watched his face; it showed complete disgust. He went on to tell me that his cousin Stevie worked with Maleek. Maleek, unknowingly, talked about our night. He told Stevie everything. How Maleek had wanted me something terrible. How upset he was when he had to send me away. Stevie asked all the right questions and it had not taken a rocket scientist to know that I was the woman cheating on her husband.

Marcus knew it all. All the tears in the world would not get me out of this one. I told him how sorry I was; how it had been an act of desperation. He grabbed my shoulders and held them tightly. "I asked you if you did anything with him and you lied!"

With my arms hurting at his grip, I said, "You asked if I slept with him and I said no! I said no and that is the truth!"

He let me go and walked away from me and looked out of the window. "Answer this question with the truth. If you had not called out the wrong name, would you have slept with him?"

I slowly fell to my knees with my head in my hands sobbing. I did not want to answer that. How could I tell my husband that I had wanted to sleep with another man and expect to remain married? I didn't answer and he yelled at the top of his lungs, "Answer me! Would you have slept with him?"

"Yes!" I bellowed. I couldn't look up to face him. All that talk about me wanting him to be disappointed in me was a crock of bull. The fact that this man was hurt by something I did is unbearable.

I felt him stand over me. "One of us has to leave this house."

"No!" I stood up hugging him as tightly as I could. "Please, no! No one is leaving! Baby, please! Let me try and explain."

He broke away from me. He told me that he was hurt and humiliated; how he'd had to grin and bear it with his cousin; how a part of him had hoped that Maleek was only lying to make himself look better. But in actuality his wife had wanted this man. He went on to tell me that he had been so thrilled last night at being able to hold me again, make love to me again.

I begged and begged for him to change his mind. With all the pain I caused he wanted to leave. My heart ached when he said, "My love was never good enough for you. You told a total stranger that if I had not cheated on you in high school, you probably would not have married me. Do you have any idea how that made me feel? That right there made me realize that that was the reason you were able to leave me so easily. There was no love there in the first place."

I tried to wipe my face. "That is not true. I love you and always have."

He walked toward the closet and then punched a hole in the closet door. "Damn, Sidney! I devoted my life to you!

My god, I love you so damn much it got to be illegal! I have to go!" He trembled as he frantically walked to the door. "I have to get the fuck out of here before I go fuckin' crazy!"

I ran after him as he walked to the front door. "Stop it, please!" I began screaming and crying in horror. "God, no! Marcus, please! I love you. I love you so much. I devoted my life to you too!" I held his arm back. "Baby, don't do this!" I begged.

He grabbed my face between his hands. "I never made you happy. You desired much more than I could give. You now have the freedom to see and sleep with whoever you choose. Now, I'm the one walking out."

"What are you saying?"

"I'm leaving. No, I want a divorce."

"What?"

He opened the door and walked out and looked back. "Maybe a separation but I am definitely not going to be with you. Sidney, again, I am truly sorry for making you feel like you had to be married to me."

When he shut the door, I fell to the floor screaming his name. I prayed that he would turn around. I could not move. I had hurt the only one that I have ever loved and who loved me. I had wanted to be single and go to school and date. I had wanted something other than married life. How does the saying go? You better watch what you wish for . . .

Chapter 28
Tracy

This is one of the most important moments in my career. I've worked so hard to get this business off the ground. Advertising was something that I had always wanted to do. And when Malcolm died and I needed another avenue so as not to let myself self-destruct, I really went after it. So I worked day and night.

I thought I wanted this Vegas account, but sitting here and listening to Jerome do his piece and try to persuade these men that we could increase their marketing by 40 percent, made me realize otherwise. Jerome was so handsome and brilliantly talented. I have not spoken to him in almost two weeks. He had meant what he said I guess. I've see him at the office but he's strictly business now. Sometimes, I would get there and he would have already left for the day, told the secretary that he was ill, or taken his work home. He even left a day early so he did not have to ride the plane with me and the rest of my staff.

I tried to give him his space but it seemed that I wanted to talk to him more and more. When I tried a few days after our date, he barely spoke and answered all of questions with only either a yes or no. I even tapped in on his conversation with Malcolm Jr. He so tactfully explained to Malcolm that it was one of those situations that grown people go through and that Malcolm will go through it too when he gets older. My heart ached when I heard Malcolm say, "Just because you and Mom can't be friends, does that mean we can't either?" I just wanted to hold him and tell him that everything was going to be all right. They will continue to maintain a bond. I was glad of that. I guess they will do it and I will have to deal with that. I will not ever feel responsible for taking another man from him again.

It was my turn to do my piece. I could barely focus on what I had to present but I was able to get through it. We wrapped up the meeting, confident that we would be able to do marketing for the West Coast. I shook hands with a frail-looking man in a gray suit. His eyes were like beady coals through his thick glasses. I had focused on him during the meeting for two reasons: one, he was the head honcho; and two, he kept a smile on my face. He gave me a flashback of when I was a child and we teased my cousin dreadfully about his thick bottle-cap glasses. He told me with a voice that had a lump of phlegm in it, "We will be doing business with you in the near future, Miss Lady."

I small-talked with a few colleagues and I noticed Jerome packing up. I knew that he was leaving me and my business after this but I thought he would at least say something to me. "You did a great job. I'm proud of you, as always."

He briefly glanced at me and went back to packing up. "Thanks."

I became so nervous. He gave me such a chill. I stared at him and tried to pull something to say out of nowhere. "Would you like to go and celebrate by having a drink at the hotel restaurant?"

He picked up his briefcase from the table. "Is everyone else going?"

"Uh . . . no . . . I thought maybe . . ."

He quickly interrupted me, "I don't think so. I have a cousin here and we are going to hang out tonight before I go back in the morning."

I followed behind him like a kid begging his mom for candy in the grocery store. I just couldn't let this moment slip away. This may be the very last time I see him, or at least have the opportunity to speak my piece. I lightly grabbed his elbow. "Jerome, please. I know this is sort of strained but I would like to at least talk to you for a few minutes. We haven't eaten yet and I would like to take you out to eat. You were a lifesaver in there while I choked. I want to thank you for that."

Still unable to look me in the eyes, he turned his head to the floor. He let out one of his annoyed sighs. "Tracy, you don't have to thank me. I did my job. And you did yours. Dinner is not necessary, maybe some other time."

He was stern, not once giving a tiny sign of giving in. I took my defeat and swallowed it. I softly grabbed his hand, trying desperately not to cry. "Oh, OK. I guess . . . um . . . you should be going. I didn't mean to hold you up."

"Take care," he said as he walked down the hall and quickly walked through the main lobby.

I went back into the conference room and gathered my belongings, feeling like complete shit. I mean, I love this man and there is a part of me that feels like I should have fought harder. He had been patient with me for several years and I guess he's fed up. There was no shame in my game when the tears rolled.

I cleaned my face and I practically moped to the restaurant and was seated at a table by the window. I should have sat in the kitchen and ate where no one can see such a fool, I thought. I ordered a white wine, Caesar salad, and lasagna.

My waitress was a heavyset woman with a tight white roller set. She reminded me a little of Mrs. Garrett from *Facts of Life,* very pleasant and ready to serve. She brought my wine, salad, and some dinner rolls. She gave me a confused stare while saying, "Is everything all right, suga'? You look like you lost your best friend."

"I'm fine." I sulked.

"Well, if there is anything I can get for ya, you just let me know now, ya hear? Because no one sits in Ole Grace's section with a problem. Your food will be up shortly, sweetie."

"Thanks," I said with a huge smile, hoping that would be enough for her to shut up and get away from me. Thank god that it did.

I was eating my salad and going over thoughts in my head. I had so much on my mind: work, Malcolm Jr., Jerome, and the last night I had with my girlfriends. I had spoken with Sidney and Marcus had left her and she is now crushed. It's funny how she was so gung ho about sleeping with Maleek and how she didn't care what Marcus thought; how she had been so ready to end her marriage, but was now ready to be a wife again. She was so devastated now by his departure. Alexis and Elijah were not as happy now that Aaron knew the deal. And Simone is a bit quiet these days. I know she is unhappy about returning to work now, even though she claims to be happy to mingle with adults again, since she feels that none of us call her anymore.

My thoughts were quickly broken when I caught a faint scent of Cool Water cologne. "Is the offer for dinner still on the table?"

My heart jumped out of my chest. Jerome came back! He still had his briefcase strapped over his shoulder. I quickly responded despite my being startled and completely caught off guard, "No! I mean, yes! Have a seat, please!" I swiftly cleared a spot for him. "This is such a surprise!"

He settled in the chair and sat his briefcase beside him on the floor. "Well, I left and walked down the street with not a clue what to do. So,

I'm here." He opened a menu and looked at me and then again looked back at the menu. "What did you get besides the empty salad plate?"

I could not help but blush. I'm just going to keep in mind that I will not blow another chance with him. "I ordered lasagna."

Grace came over and took Jerome's order happily. She noticed a change in my facial expression. "That's what I like to see, a pretty lady smilin'!"

I was hoping that he would not have picked up on what she said but he did. "What was that all about?"

"Well, she noticed that I was not too happy when I first came. But it's OK now," I said flirtatiously.

He noticed my ringless finger but didn't comment on it. He became uneasy like he had something pressing to say. I could feel him tapping his foot under the table. He finally looked me in the face. "Look, Trace, I'm sorry for being cold earlier. It's just that, I can't take any more humiliation from you, with your mixed signals and all. You are drivin' me clean up the wall."

"I know and I'm sorry," I said.

He put his hand in my face to stop me. "I know you are paying for dinner but I'm running this." He gave me his playful grin and continued, "I'm going to keep my distance and to do that, you know I have to leave. I just thought it would complicate things less."

I noticed that uneasy look on his face, "It was complicated all right. But it doesn't have to be anymore."

Just when he was going to respond, Grace returned with our food. He opened up his place setting and started again, "What are you talking about?"

I tried to dig into my food but my hunger had disappeared. I watched him devour his lasagna and wait for my response. I gulped down my wine and said, "I want to be with you. I . . . I . . . I want to be with you if you will have me."

He choked. "What type of game are you playin'?"

Speak now, Tracy, I thought. "No games. I have always wanted to but I had issues that needed to be resolved."

He quickly eyed my ring less finger again. "Is that why you're no longer wearing your ring?"

"Yes." I looked at my hand. "I wanted and needed to move on. I wanted to call you and tell you that I wanted to start over but never mustered up the nerve."

I went on to tell him how much I've missed him; how badly I had wanted to call and beg for his return. He in turn explained to me that he had been down and had missed me as well and that he was going to always keep in touch with Li'l Malc. He raised his thick eyebrows and said, "Your hand looked better with the ring on it."

"I know. It took me some time to get used to it," I chuckled.

"Then let me put a ring back on it," he said looking me straight in the eye.

"What?" I questioned sounding highly confused.

He backed out of his chair and stood up. He picked up his wine glass and tapped it with his butter knife to get everyone's attention. When he noticed everyone looking, he said, "Ladies and gentlemen, my name is Jerome Williams. And I have been a fool for this woman for several years now and I am going to humiliate myself one last time in front of all of you." He came around the table toward me and I am now shaking. He got on one knee and held my hand in his. "Tracy Singletary, would you please marry me right now? I don't want an engagement. I don't want a wedding parade. You said that you were ready for me and this is what I'm ready for. I have courted your behind for four years now, and frankly, I am tired of it."

"Jerome," I said trembling with emotion.

He kept his stare on my tear-filled eyes. "I love you and you know that I love and adore your son as if he were mine. I walked away from you earlier and it killed me. I don't want to walk away from you again. We are in the capital of wedding chapels, so will you marry me?"

I listened to the whole restaurant gasp with amazement. I cried with much joy. I never really thought too much of marriage. I looked at him and tried to talk through the tears. "I can't right now." Our restaurant audience sighed with disapproval and Jerome's face fell to the floor. I was not finished yet. I lifted his head by the chin. "Let me finish," I said to him and our audience. "I can't marry you right now but I will in about two hours when I at least find a dress to become your bride in. I refuse to become Mrs. Jerome Lamont Williams in a gray business suit."

173

He came up and kissed me and we held each other and looked at our adoring fans who were cheering and clapping. We kissed again and looked into each other's eyes. I wiped the lipstick off his lip. "I'm ready. I love you, Jerome."

"I love you too."

Our Mrs. Garrett look-alike came and hugged us and told us the manager said the bill was on the house. She also informed me that her husband was a justice of the peace about three blocks down. They run a wedding chapel in their home and would love to hold our wedding for us. We happily agreed and told her we would meet her and her husband at eight o'clock.

We parted through the restaurant with plenty of well wishes and kisses from our devoted audience. I told Jerome that I had seen a wonderful boutique in the hotel and he said he was going to take care of the honeymoon extravaganza.

xoxoxoxoxoxo

Grace's house was perfect for what we wanted. It was like an antique showroom from the furniture, to the pictures on the wall. It smelled like potpourri all through the house. I fell in love with her husband. He came to meet me while I finished my last-minute touches of my dress and hair.

I managed to find a full-length cream satin gown with an A-line hem. I wore strapped cream satin shoes and I wore my hair up with tendrils coming down the right side. I was unable to put on the small pearl necklace I had gotten from the jewelry store when Grace walked in the room. "Lemme' help you with that." She put the clasp on and gave me a once-over. She made me feel like my mother was there to check me out one last time. She fluffed up my tendrils. "This is the face I want to see forever. No wonder you were lookin' like a sad case earlier today. He is a wonderful man and he adores you. A bit nervous though, out there pacin' and carryin' on. I told him to calm down and that it is too late. He done already proposed and you are waiting!" She went to the door and turned around. "Let's rock and roll!"

I walked into the dining room that I guess was meant for wedding parties. There were two floral arrangements on white pedestals at the front of the room where Mr. Hampton and Jerome stood. Jerome looked even more handsome than I had ever seen him. We must have been on the same page with the cream. His suit was cream with small faint satine squares etched in it. Grace gave him a red rose to stick into his lapel and he looked refreshed, more importantly, he looked like he was glad to see me.

I gracefully went down to meet my groom. We held hands and never took our eyes off each other while smiling. The ceremony was short and sweet. We didn't say our own vows but he did tell me right before we were to kiss, "I know that for a long time you had your heart set on not being in love or married. And I for a long time tried to break through that. There were times when I wanted to give up and get lost. But there was something in you that I knew I touched and you had to know that. I am glad that I came back to you today. I'm elated that you said 'yes' today. I want to make sure you know that from this day forward the only time I'm ever going to walk away from you is to let you get some rest. Because, baby, all my love and devotion will knock you off your feet." He had also gone to a jewelry store and got a platinum band with a two-carat diamond. Gorgeous, I thought. He slid it on my finger and we kissed like we have never kissed before, letting all of our pent-up passions go.

xoxoxoxoxoxo

This is it. And I'm just as nervous as a "real" virgin on her wedding day. I mean, it has been over ten years since I've gotten any. He has been waiting for me for over thirty minutes. I hope to God that he does not think that I'm changing my mind.

I looked in the mirror and admired my honeymoon attire. I figured I would wear white because it has been long enough for me to wear it. That was what I thought when I got it. It was a white satin chemise with a laced V-back and a sheer white overcoat to match. The edges of the coat were lace. I made sure every part of my body was touched with lotion to ensure a soft touch.

When I finally came from the bathroom, Jerome stared at me like he had seen a vision from God. "You look amazing! Come here, Mrs. Williams!" he said as he grabbed me.

"You went through all this trouble? It's wonderful!" I said, admiring the room. He had gotten us the Excalibur Honeymoon Suite and the room was laced with roses, candles, and champagne.

"I wanted to make you feel like the beautiful woman you are." He sat me on the bed gazing at me. "Are you OK?"

I was nervous but I didn't want it to show. "You don't have to ask. Everything is fine and wonderful. You have made me very happy."

He smiled and retrieved the champagne. We sipped and talked on the bed for a while like old friends. I think he was trying to make me feel comfortable. But I was ready to consummate my marriage. I leaned into him and gave him the most seductive kiss I could while rubbing his jones. He quickly gave in to my advances and lay me down on the bed guiding my head down with the palm of his hand.

This man kissed me all over and I began to feel my body dance with excitement. I sang in pure ecstasy. We touched and felt each other's bodies with passion and pleasure. He licked me from head to toe and came back up to my middle. He parted my legs, letting his tongue tiptoe around every spot but the middle, making my pelvis chase his every move. He finally let his juicy hot tongue slip into my love. With the slightest touch I released, feeling like I was completely on top of the world.

He came up to me face to face to watch me catch my breath, kissing me and whispering in my ear, "You don't know how much I love you." My body regained strength and I begged to feel him inside me. I knew he was ready by the size of his erect jones. He moved his body up and down letting the jones tickle the outside of my clit. My pelvis frantically rocked for the love. He came down to kiss me and thrust himself inside me. The warmth and firmness of it made this night so complete. It felt like this was the moment we had both been waiting for.

I panted and moaned with each movement of his well-sculpted body. I loved the passion in his eyes when he kept asking, "You OK, baby?" I could never respond because I was speechless with pleasure. There was nothing in the world that I could imagine as being better right now. I love this man to death. I was nervous because I thought I would not be able to keep up since it has been so long. But I kept up and at times I thought he was slowing down.

We made love continuously from pillow to post, position after position, never taking a break. We just loved each other and enjoyed the splendid love we were making. Just when our hearts felt as though we were not going to give up, our bodies did. It was mind-blowing that we showed how appreciated being together that we just let our love flow together. We both sang the same song of heavenly love and our bodies collapsed on each other, winded and looking for air.

I wiped the sweat from his forehead. "Oh my god! What are you doing to me, Mr. Williams?"

He kissed my dry lips. "Giving you what I promised, love and happiness beyond your wildest dreams. Did I do that?"

"Yes," I said as my body quivered again from inside out. My eyes rolled to the back of my head. When I was able to focus, I saw not only fireworks but a Rose Ball Parade and a marching band. My wedding and honeymoon were spectacular event events.

We held each other tight, telling each other how much we loved each other. I told him that Malcolm was going to faint. He caressed my face. "My li'l homie is going to love the idea. I will be around full time forever and always."

I kissed his full lips. "Forever and always." Our embrace was so tight it would have hurt a pair of pliers' feelings. I felt myself drifting off to sleep with the most serene feeling that I have not felt in a long time.

My last thought was that people go through life looking for their soul mate. I was fortunate enough to be able to find it twice and for that, I am so grateful.

Shannon N. Davis

Chapter 29
Simone

My first week back at work was terrible. I miss my little baby something awful. Even though he is right downstairs in the corporate nursery, it still feels like he is miles away. I have called about four times now and it is only one o'clock. I managed to walk to the Chinese restaurant. I didn't want to spend my lunch in the nursery and have Li'l Aaron all upset when I leave like he had been this morning.

I had just ordered my food when this beauty walked in. Oh my lord, he must have been sent from heaven. I could have sworn I saw a ray of light when he walked in. He must be at least six feet tall. He had golden honey-brown skin, eyes with a tint of gold that sparkled like brown glass held up to the sun, a wide masculine chest, and was slightly bowlegged. I'm not even going to go there with the way the man was dressed. He had on black slacks with a short-sleeved white sweater that accented his biceps and triceps. Just like the Campbell's soup commercial, he looked *"umm...umm good."*

I watched him as he ordered pepper steak with onions and a Sprite. He must have noticed me gawking at him because he turned and smiled. He showed all of his straight and naturally white teeth. I think I saw a sparkle come from the corner of his smile. He nodded his head and said, "Hello, how are you?"

Let me just chill out. I am acting like a groupie or something. I just shook my head giving the "everything is OK" grin. I took my food and practically ran out of the store. Why did this man set my soul ablaze? Knowing my luck, he is probably married with ten kids. So I quickly put the thought of his fine ass out of my head.

I figured that since it was a nice day, I would just eat my chicken fried rice and shrimp roll outside. I was tired of sitting at my desk and I have only been there for one day, or should I say less than that. I called the nursery again. Judy answered, "Grandma's Touch Day Care, Judy speaking."

"Hi, Judy, it's Simone again. How's he doing?"

She was frustrated but tried not to show it. "Mommy . . . Mommy, we are doing great. He is napping now. This is rough for you, huh?"

"Yes, can you tell? I promise I won't bother you again! You won't hear from me until five o'clock."

"Simone, he's fine! You are not the first mom to do this. We had one worse!" She chuckled but then became reassuring. "Really, call when you want but we do ask parents to limit the calls between twelve and two. That is nap time for the kids. OK, Simone?"

"Yes, thanks. Goodbye." As I was hanging up my cell phone, I noticed the vision from God standing in front of me. "Hi," I said

"Is there anyone sitting here?" he said motioning at the picnic table. I was shocked and stunned again by his attractiveness. "No."

He sat down and began taking his food out of the bag. I noticed how proper he was with the napkins and how he laid them on this lap. He looked at me with that confident I-got-it-going-on smile. "Checking on your baby?"

Right away I felt comfortable telling him about Li'l Aaron. "Yes, it's my first day back at work from maternity and I'm driving the teachers crazy down there. I just hate it."

He swallowed his food and took a sip of his Sprite. "Oh, Mom, he will be fine. You said 'he,' right?"

"Yes."

We ate in silence. I wanted to ask him so many questions but advised myself against it. I was definitely ready for the dating scene again. And a man this fine has to be married! If he wasn't there was something completely wrong with him. I can't put my finger on it with men that appear to have it going on, either they were gay or women beaters or womanizers or just plain whacked in the head.

He polished off his food and broke the silence, "Where in the building do you work?"

Wiping my mouth to maintain my womanly nature, I said, "Fifth floor. Wexler and Associates Accounting Firm. And you?"

"Second floor. I just opened the physical therapy office there. Neil is my name." He extended his firm hand across the table.

"Oh I heard that the space down there had been bought. How do you like it?" I was acting surprised when I already knew that a fine-ass black man was down there. Every sister and even some of the white girls had been talking about it. They were gave me the corporate gossip

I guess. I didn't want to appear amazed but I was. They had said he was fine but not like this.

He packed up the trash. "So far so good. I'm still in the working phase but my clientele is booming. This was the best decision I have ever made."

He went on to explain that he had been in partnership with someone else and it worked out well but he had managed to get his own practice. He went to Kean College and would not tell me the year he graduated. He talked with enthusiasm in his voice, as though he was on top of the world right now. He was not at all arrogant but he was proud about what he had accomplished.

"How old is your baby?" he asked.

"Five months. He looks a year old. Just kidding! He's my angel! I got pictures!" I said sounding like a proud momma. I showed him a few pictures and put them back in my purse. I had to ask, "Do you have any kids?"

"Oh no! Not that I don't want any it is just that I don't want to have them with any drama attached," he said.

No kids I thought. I wonder if he is married or even had a girlfriend. Instead, I just agreed, "No you don't want that! Trust me, I know." I gave him a nervous laugh.

We talked like we had known each other in a previous life. He told me that he lived in Neptune, New Jersey and liked to play pool and work out, which was highly evident. He had a sister and mother whom he adored and loved dearly. He was truly a "mama's boy." I told him where I attended school and that I had a twin sister but that we looked nothing alike. I said I too shared a great relationship with my mom but my sis and I could use some work.

He noticed the time on his Movado watch. "Girl, I'm sitting here talking to you like I do not have a business to run. By the way, I never got your name."

"Simone. And you are Neil," I said.

He cupped his well-sculpted chin with the precision-cut goatee. "Simone, would you like to go with me to Atlantic City on Saturday night? I want to see the Isley Brothers and they are going to be there."

I was stunned. My ray of light was asking me on a date. But he never told me whether he was married. "Neil, I would like to, but do you have a girl or wife?"

He gave a handsome chuckle. "No wife or girlfriend. Do you have a man?"

I wanted to say "I wish" but did not. I smiled and said, "No, not at all. And yes, I will go with you. What time?"

"The show is at eight but I will pick you up at five so we could get some dinner. Is that OK with you?" he said, sounding nervous.

"It's fine. I'll be ready." I now sounded excited.

He reached his hand out to help me up from the picnic bench. "I will be there, beautiful." I cheesed like a high schoolgirl. "Let's get back to work. Here is my card, call me if there is a problem."

"OK," I said looking into his beer bottle—colored brown eyes. We walked into the building and rode the elevator. I was glad that he seemed a bit tense like I was. Since he got off first, he turned and winked at me and said, "Later."

I was glad that I was the only one in the elevator. I wanted to melt. I let go of my breath. "Oh my god!" I was so happy to have met this man. I damn sure was not going to tell the horny vultures at work that I am going out with *their* fantasy man. Hell, I know what desperate women are capable of.

xoxoxoxoxoxo

Neil and I spent this past week talking on the phone for over an hour every night. We became really comfortable with one another. We laughed and joked like we were old friends. Even at work he comes up to the fifth floor and gets me for lunch. The vultures just stare and I love it.

One night we were in the middle of talking and he told me that he thought I was special and that he was glad to have met me. I wanted to die. I did what I used to do when I was a teenager and told him to hold on and screamed in the pillow. I have not experienced something like this in all my life. There was a certain quality about him. He was genuine and it was easily detected.

I was completely dressed and just wanted to give myself another once-over. I had on a sleeveless silver silk pantsuit I bought just for tonight. I wore my hair down since Neil told me that he loved seeing my hair down even though he had only seen it down once. I went to the salon and had gotten a roller set with a rinse. I loved it. My curls were loose and bouncy with plenty of shine.

I heard the doorbell ring and when I answered it there he was standing there with that ray of light. "Wow, don't you look handsome. I better go change." He was wearing a black suit with a white shirt and black patented leather shoes.

He smiled and for the first time he gently kissed my lips. "Naw, baby girl, don't change a thing. You look exquisite. Are you ready?"

I walked away tasting his lips on mine. "Yes, let me get my purse!" I yelled walking to my bedroom.

I walked back and he was looking at Li'l Aaron's pictures. "He is handsome. Where is he? I can't wait to meet him."

"He's with his grandmother on his father's side. She claims that she don't see him enough. So I thought tonight is the night!"

When we walked outside I could not believe this man is pushing a chromed-out Escalade. It looked like it had just rolled off the showroom floor. I looked at my Camry and felt small that it was filthy. Again, I did not want to sound impressed so I said nothing except, "Nice ride."

We drove down the Garden State Parkway talking and getting more acquainted. While driving he held my hand between the console, only letting go when he needed to pay the tolls. I felt mushy all over. There was sincerity in his voice when he talked. The humor he expressed and the fact that he found me funny was even more astounding.

I was laughing when he told me that he used to want to be a gynecologist so he could see girls all day. That was until he went with his mother to the doctor's and saw a huge old woman with warts on her face and legs. He asked his mom, "Does the doctor have to see her too?" And when she said, "Yes, the doc sees all the women that come in his office," he quickly sang a new tune. He became a therapist instead.

I laughed so hard and asked him, "Why aren't you married?"

He turned and looked at me with a straight face. "Because you have not said yes yet."

I immediately stopped laughing. I was completely caught off guard. I just cleared my throat and looked out the window and watched the passing cars. He held my hand tighter and never commented on what he had just said.

Dinner was fabulous and the Isleys were out of this world. I had no idea the Taj Mahal was so big. We had great seats and I know he had to have paid a fortune for them. All through the show he had his arm around me and when I appeared cold he gave me his suit jacket and rubbed my shoulders. It was incredible. We sang some of their oldest jams together. I couldn't control my blushing when he sang along with Ron Isley, *"Make me say it again, girl. You're all I need. Oh yes you are."* I thought, not bad. Ron or Mr. Bigg better watch his back.

During intermission we got drinks and took pictures with the setup background of champagne glasses. When we returned to our seats we laughed at all the Mr. Bigg look a likes. Neil pointed out a man that had on a pink three-quarter suit and shoes to match. "Look at that clown. Now the suit is nice but the color is all wrong. If he *needed* pink then maybe in the lapel, but not the entire suit! Boy oh boy!"

I could not help but laugh, but he was right. All that pink is way over the top. I scanned all the women, and for the most part, they were dressed really well. That was until I spotted a couple wearing a matching MCM suit. "Oh Neil, check it out! Look at those two! Who in the hell dresses alike? That is so eighty-two!" We laughed hard like we were the fashion police for the Taj Mahal.

Neil played Black Jack and won nine hundred dollars. Then he started playing some dice game and won every time I blew on the dice. Neil took that money and ran saying, "I refuse to give Donald Trump back his money." We left the casino laughing all the way to the bank.

On the drive home, he told me that he loved to dance and I was all so elated to tell him that I am a dancing queen. He figured I was lying and put me to the test. He made a proposition, "Put your money where your dancing shoes are, sweetie. We're going to Club Brokers!"

"Tonight?" I said.

"Don't be scurred!" he said like in Mistakal's "Shake It Fast" song. "Why not? It's early."

"It's one in the morning," I said letting him know the time. "But since you are the hot shot, *show me what ya workin' wit'!"* I said, bringing Mistakal's song back to the table.

We flew up the Garden State and arrived at Brokers in an hour, thanks to his speeding. We got there and danced and danced. He was absolutely right. He could dance his ass off. That man had me doing everything from the latest to the hustle. We danced smiling and trying to out-do each other, letting our bodies bump and grind against each other, never once stopping for a drink. When the last song for the night was playing, the DJ played Prince's "Adore" and the lights came on.

Neil grabbed me tight, as close as we could be with clothes on. He made me look into his eyes while he sang to me again, *"From the first moment I saw you...I knew you were the one..."* He lifted my chin and gave me the most endearing kiss I have ever had. A kiss of all kisses, the kind that had it been able to talk, would have said, "You are mine, now and always."

We left the club hand in hand, feeling like we were on cloud nine. The drive home was quiet. He insisted that I get some rest and reclined the seat back while he drove home. He continued his hand-holding while driving and let the soft sounds of 98.7 KISS FM play on the radio. It was the most comfortable I have felt around a man in my life. A long-lasting comfort, not the few hours' comfort I had experienced before.

I awoke because the car had stopped and Neil was staring at me with eyes full of emotion. "You're home, beautiful."

I got my seat up and looked around. "Oh god, I slept all that time?" I put my shoes on and got out of the car.

He escorted me to the door, holding me around my shoulder. It was now six in the morning and the yellow-orange sun was up to greet us. As tired as I was, I was on a new wave of energy. I didn't want this night to end. But I also didn't want to start something that would get out of control.

When we reached the door to my apartment and I took off Neil's suit jacket, I said, "Thank you, Neil James, for a wonderful night. I have never had more fun."

"It was my pleasure," he said and he kissed my hand.

I opened the door and stepped in. He only came into the doorway. I sat my purse down on the sofa. "Are you OK to drive home, Neil? Would you like some coffee? It is almost breakfast time."

He put his suit jacket on still in the doorway. He then proceeded to come toward me. "I have to go. I will call you later when I think you're up." He kissed me again, and this time slipped me some of his juicy tongue. "I have to go. Are you OK?"

"Never been better," I said, licking my lips. I walked him to the door while wrapping my body on his right arm. "Call me to let me know you got home."

"I live in the next town over. Plus, you will be sleep. I had a great time tonight." He kissed me again and this time he held me around the waist while I reached my arms around his neck and shoulders. I gave in to this kiss instead of letting him kiss me like he had all night. It was something that was just inevitable.

We let go of the intense embrace and smiled at each other like two kids kissing for the first time. He stepped out the door and winked and puckered up his full lips like he was kissing me again. "Night, night, beautiful."

"Night, night." I blushed. When I shut the door, I clutched my hands to my chest. I felt like the most beautiful woman in the world. I, Simone Marie Campbell, had gone on her very first *real* date.

For the first time, I had gone on a date with a man that didn't have to rush home to his wife. For the first time, I didn't have to feel bad when the date was over. For the first time, I didn't feel like I was second choice or a pity date. For the first time, I was the *one and only* focus for the man I was with. My happiness was all that mattered. There is nothing more precious.

I went to my bedroom and threw myself on the bed, smiling and screaming, "Neil James, what did you just do to me?"

Chapter 30
Alexis

I'm so glad to be home. I worked sixteen hours today and I am beat. There is nothing wrong with a little extra cash. Plus, I needed to do other things besides think about Elijah. We have been distant toward one another since the whole Aaron incident.

I turned on the television to finish my favorite show *The Golden Girls*. I was unable to focus because of my thoughts of Elijah. I mean, I really cared for this man but I don't want to be on the receiving end of heartbreak. I don't know why he turned against me. It had been his idea to tell Aaron. He thought he could handle it and now I felt like I was to blame. I know it is hard losing a best friend because I miss Simone at times.

I think that instead of having him break my heart, I would just get out first to make it easier on us both. To me, it seemed like when he is going through something it is OK to exclude me. Well, that I won't tolerate. I would probably feel better if he would just talk to me instead of avoiding me like he has been recently.

I went to turn off the TV when the bell rang. "Who is it?" I asked.

"Alexis, it's me, Elijah," he said.

I went to the door and opened it. I didn't him. "Elijah, it's after midnight."

"Can I come in?"

I gestured for him to come in without saying yes. He looked nervous and I knew what he was going to tell me. So to spare us both I started, "We're through I know. You could have just called me and told me."

He took off his coat and sat on the loveseat. He looked so handsome with his red turtleneck sweater and black jeans and boots. "Alexis, I didn't say that. I came over because I missed you and I was acting like a jerk." He came over to me and hugged me tightly. "Oh, girl, you have no idea how long I wanted to hold you like this. Please forgive me. I had to get over what was bothering me."

I broke free from him. "No matter how I felt, huh? I was hurting because you were hurting and you shut me out."

He went on to tell me that that's how he handled things. He knows he shouldn't but he does. He never wanted his vulnerability to show around any woman. The few times he had, he had been seriously taken advantage of. I recalled the relationships he'd had in the past. When I first met Aaron, he had just broken up with Diane. She had treated him like dirt, always lying and trying to get him for every dime he had. She had gotten pregnant and could not work due to extreme morning sickness. So he had paid her bills. That was until he found out she had miscarried and had just not wanted to get off her fat ass. Then there was Sonya. Sonya was the girl who had three kids, which did not bother him too much but he could not get to know her too well because she was too busy struggling with the children. She was a single parent and needed help terribly. He assisted in what he could and when she got comfortable after six months she made her kids his responsibility. So that ended.

Then there was the infamous Shelley. This woman was trouble from the start. When he met her he was head over heels for her. He could not get enough of her smelly drawers. She was an attorney as well. They had multiple things in common and he had proposed after a year. She had worn the fattest diamond I had ever seen. I teased Aaron that he needed to take notes. They moved in together and that's when it fell apart. She claimed to be confined and not ready so she moved out to her own place again. Then things went OK until she felt like she needed more *space*. Elijah was crushed. He went along with it and then realized she needed space from him only. She wanted to date other people to make sure that marriage was the right thing for her. He could not take that so he saw her when he wanted some of what she had to offer. When I once asked him how he felt, he just said, "All through high school and college, I tormented women with my lies and deceit. I played the field and broke a string of hearts. I guess the saying is true, every dog has its day."

I got back on track and tried to sympathize with him but I had my own heart to save. "Look, maybe we should take a break and see if we have what it takes to be a couple."

He looked shocked. "Alexis, wait a minute! I didn't mean to shut you out but don't do this. I want you so badly. Not just sexually but as a friend and possibly a wife."

That did it for me. No way in hell do I want to be anyone's wife. Not after the fiasco wedding I'd had. Marriage is for the weak. I had to stop him. "Whoa, wait! No marriage! We never discussed marriage!"

"Calm down. I don't mean tonight or tomorrow. It was a possibility, Alexis. That is how far I would go with you." He stood up because I was heading for the stairs. "Where are you going?"

"To take a shower. I worked double shift today. I need a shower." I went up the steps and he followed. When I got in my room, I just wanted to pass out on the bed but I didn't want to have to go through the motions with him. "Elijah, you're a nice guy but marriage is not for me right now. Dating you is fine but we need to slow down."

He looked sad and I know I caught him off guard but he remained calm. "I know that. Do you think you would ever want to get married?"

I took off my shoes and socks. "Not right now, no! Been there done that. Almost anyway." I stopped and gazed at my feet, recalling that horrible wedding day. "Are you OK with that?"

He sat next to me on the bed and wrapped his arm around me. "It's fine but I don't want to wait forever. I'm here for you, and if you feel I'm not what you want, let me know now. I have played the fool one too many times myself, you know."

"Elijah, you can't even deal with a problem! You shut me out! Let's not even talk about that night when you told me to leave!" I opened my bathroom door and started the shower. "I will have to worry that if something is bothering you then I would be mistreated again. Not this sistah!"

I went on to tell him that we can still date and hang, and if something more happened, then I was cool with that. I've put my wall back up and I was no longer interested in a committed relationship. "Let's start over and be friends."

"How in the hell can we do that? We meant a lot to each other. We shared intimacies for god's sake, Alexis!" His voice cracked with sadness.

I had to remain calm because I was hurting too. "Look, Elijah, I didn't mean it like that. Let's just hold off on marriage. That's all, OK?"

I kissed him and I saw him calm down a bit. "Now make yourself comfortable and let me take a shower."

I went and shut the door. I thought about what had transpired and I didn't like the way I behaved. I know he is a good guy and I would like to see how far we could go. I tried to hurry out and apologize and explain that I had let emotional baggage from my previous relationship get in the

way. That is something that ruins most relationships. When I came out of the shower, I called for him but did not get an answer. So I

figured he'd gone downstairs to the

kitchen. To my surprise, there was a piece of paper there and when I picked it up I felt my heart beat out of my chest.

> *Alexis,*
>
> *I had to go. I guess it was a bad idea to come over like that. I knew your heart was broken and you are being cautious but I have to protect myself too. I did not want to hang around any longer. You know my feelings for you run deep. I was wrong to shut you out like I did. I should not have done that. It was rough losing Aaron even though I knew I would. I needed sometime to adjust but I should have included you.*
>
> *I have the tendency to get my heart broken as well. I fall in love and get vulnerable and then get dissed. And tonight when you were practically say- ing that I was only going to be a friend, I felt all the dissing all over again. I can't do it again. I love you, girl. And knowing that I can't be in a relation- ship with you and there is still that chance that we will never become as one is too much to bear. I al- ways said that if the person you are dealing with is not willing to try and establish the same thing as you, then you need to get out before you begin to feel this is the way to go.*
>
> *Alexis, I didn't want to say this to you face to face. I cried and showed my soft side to a woman*

before and she practically laughed. You say you can't go through marriage again; well, I can't go through letting someone I love see me hurt and upset again. I know I took the coward's way out but this is better. From the way you were acting tonight, I think you will be OK with this.

Just know that I do love you. I have from the first time I saw you. And when you gave me the chance to be with you, I couldn't help but jump on it. You're right, a break is good. Let me simmer down my feelings. Maybe then we can be on the same page.

Elijah

I sat there feeling like a jackass. I refuse to call him back. I can't bring myself to go after a man or try and work things out with him. He left and that's what he wanted to do, then so be it. I crumpled the letter and put on a silk nightie and climbed into bed.

The scent of his cologne lingered on my comforter and that's when it hit me, "I love you too, Elijah. I'm scared to let myself love again." I let my tears get me to sleep.

Shannon N. Davis

Chapter 31
Sidney

My separation from Marcus was torture. He stayed with his mom at first and then he camped out in the basement where our guestroom is. When I saw him, he barely spoke. If the kids were present he would act like things are fine, but when we're alone, the tension in the room is so thick he could cut it with a knife.

I signed up for a class in culinary arts. I loved to cook and my specialty is desserts. I actually enjoyed it. I just made it under the wire before the new classes started. I go during the day while the kids are in school and get home before they do. As for money, I was going to work part-time at the restaurant associated with the school. I need a full-time job because I know Marcus will eventually leave, but for now this is a start. I actually felt good trying a new life and career— not that good though since I miss my husband.

I rushed out of class to make it to court with Marcus. He told me not to come but I couldn't let my husband go through this alone. When I got there and found a parking spot, I noticed a tall bronze-skinned girl standing at the vending machine. I wondered if that was Robin. I entered the room and there were people waiting for the judge to come forward. I spotted Marcus on the left side of the court room. There was no sign of Taniesha.

I sat next to him and he jumped back. "What are you doing here? I told you not to come!"

I remained firm in my stand but was afraid that he would call the bailiff. "I know you did. I'm not going to let you go through this alone. You are my husband, Marcus."

Right then that bitch came through the door and eyed us. She went to the right side of the room and never said a word. She looked the same: tall, dark skinned, and hair cut short. I think she had hair that never grew. Even in school she had short nappy hair. At least now it's permed. She sat behind a man that looked vaguely familiar and I assumed it was her soon-to-be ex-husband. I know if looks could kill she would have been dead ten times over with the look he gave her.

Marcus himself tensed up when he saw her. I rubbed his thigh with my hand for comfort. To my surprise he didn't reject me. "I know we will get through this." He didn't respond.

We all stood up when the judge entered. Much to my surprise it was a black female judge. She was maybe in her late forties but had a twenty-year-old's face. Judge Ingrid Fitzgerald was her name. She wore her hair in a French roll with no bangs. She looked like she was not in the mood for bullshit. I was glad Marcus was only there to claim fatherhood of Robin. He had never said whether or not he would contest the adoption.

Judge Fitzgerald looked over the case and asked for the two parties to come forward. Taniesha and Michael went forward and pleaded their cases. I could see that the Judge was not amused with Taniesha. For that, I was the judge's best friend. Taniesha tried to explain why she kept the secret all these years and kept pointing to Marcus and me, telling the Judge that she did what was best for *her* daughter.

The judge cleaned out the corner of her eyes. "Mrs. Stone, you slept with a man that was involved with a girl, correct?"

"Yes."

"And you were involved yourself?"

"Yes," Taniesha replied.

"And you knew that your husband was not the father of your child?"

"Not at first, no. I always had that in mind but hoped that she was my husband's."

The judge was not impressed at all. "When did you know, Mrs. Stone?"

Tears began to form in Taniesha's eyes. "The day I had her. She looked just like Marcus. I didn't know what to do. I figured to just leave well enough alone."

"Besides the divorce, what do you want in my courtroom?" the judge asked firmly.

"I want to stop Michael from trying to adopt Robin. I know she is almost eighteen but he is not her father."

Judge Fitzgerald gave a wicked grin. "You are still using this child as a pawn. When are you ladies going to get through your thick heads that babies are not game pieces? This man raised her as his own. As far as he was concerned and still is, he is her father! Now, that he wants a divorce, you want to take away his child?"

Taniesha and Michael began going back and forth about who was right and who was wrong. The same young bronze-skinned girl entered the courtroom. She was tall like Marcus and shared Marcus's eyes. She shared the same sandy brown hair as my Sasha, they even walked the same. She saw Marcus and stopped in her tracks. They looked at each other in amazement at how much they favored each other. They didn't say a word. She kept coming forward and asked, "Your Honor, may I talk to you? I'm Robin Marcia Stone."

Taniesha grabbed her arm. "Baby, this is not the time!"

Robin jerked away from her mother and spoke, "Just recently my mother rocked my world. All my life I loved this man as my dad." She said, pointing to Michael, "I love both of my parents and the divorce is killing me. But just because my mother is upset with him I have to get punished." She composed herself. "Now, I have to be forced to love a father all over again because of her secret?"

The judge showed compassion for the first time. "No one is punishing you. That's why we are here, child. You are not a baby; you are a bright and beautiful young lady. I want very much to hear what you have to say. Continue."

She looked her both her parents and then turned to Marcus. "I guess you are my father."

Marcus stood up and said, "Yes, I am." He extended his hand to her but she turned to her mother who was bawling.

She continued. "Your Honor, all my life I have been Robin Stone and I want to continue that. No offense to you, sir." She turned to Marcus. "I want the man who raised me to adopt me. If I can't be his by blood than I will be by law. My mom knew how close we were and that was the only thing that would hurt him. I hate what is happening to my life. My biggest concern right now should be what college to choose, not who's my daddy."

The judge raised her eyebrow. "I see and you are absolutely correct. But Mr. Grant will have to consent. Mr. Grant, would you please approach the bench."

Marcus squeezed my hand tightly and went up front. He and Robin looked even more alike standing side by side. The judge continued,

"Mr. Grant, I know you are just as hurt by this as Robin is."

"Yes, Your Honor, I am."

"I know you have a wife and three children of your own. How do you feel about this?" she asked.

Marcus cleared his throat. "Well, I was stunned. The whole thing put a strain on what I considered a perfect marriage. We had gotten through my being unfaithful in high school and now it has been rehashed. Since she is my daughter, I want to do what is best for her." He looked at Robin. "She's beautiful and looks just like me. I have two daughters that look like me but *she* looks like me more than the two at home."

"I have been the only child all my life and all this time I had two sisters and a brother." She looked at her mother who was still bawling. "Mom, you screwed up! Just stop crying. I want Daddy to adopt me. He's my dad." Then she turned to Michael and walked to him. "Mr. Grant . . ."

"Marcus, call me Marcus," he replied.

"Marcus, please don't contest it. He is the only father I've known. I'm not saying that I don't want to get to know you but I don't feel safe right now. My dad makes me feel safe. He always has."

"Your Honor, I will not contest. My only request is that Robin and Michael would get to know me and my family. On her terms of course," he said, looking at his daughter.

At that moment, I fell in love with my husband all over again. He was noble and always willing to do the right thing. He saw that that child was hurting and wanted to make her feel safe like a child should feel. I wanted to hug and kiss him right then and there but I was too afraid of what his reaction to that would be.

The judge wrapped up the session by telling Taniesha that she was getting what she deserved. She told her that since she had kept the secret for so long, she should have just kept it for life. Not that she agreed with that, but Taniesha had gone about this all wrong. She also told her that since Michael was the father since day one there was no need for a change. Not to mention that the girl was about to be eighteen. The judge was tired of women coming in her courtroom dangling children over the father's heads. If she had her way, she would lock up every woman that came though her courtroom with this same nonsense.

Taniesha got her divorce and gained a strained relationship with her daughter. She ran from the courtroom highly upset, which she should be. Michael got to keep his daughter. Marcus, on the other hand, let his firstborn stay with another man. He seemed pleased with the decision.

Marcus walked toward me and gave me a much-needed hug. "I can't believe this."

"I can't either but you did fine. Robin is beautiful! She reminds me of Sasha," I said, holding him tightly.

He let go and looked me in the eyes. "Thanks for coming. I needed you here."

"I had to be here. Where else would I be?" I said holding both of his hands. I noticed Michael and Robin walking our way. I warned Marcus, "Turn around."

We were all face to face. Michael had a firm grip on Robin's hand. "I want to thank you for letting me keep my daughter, your daughter."

Marcus shook his hand. "No problem. I think that's what needed to be done." He looked at her, amazed. "And you, miss, I meant what I said. I want to get to know you whenever you're ready. I would like to know . . . my . . . ."

"Daughter?" she finished his sentence. "I will but for now I would like for things to settle. Your family has to adjust and so do I. Not to mention I have to live with my mother."

"She was not pleased," Michael said.

"No, she wasn't!" I said with a grin.

I could tell Marcus wanted to touch her and when she extended her hand out for his, he happily went for it. He held her hand tightly and I knew he didn't want to let go so I rubbed his back to let him know it was all right. He looked into eyes that resembled his so much. "Please, I want to hear from you. I want you to get to know your brother and sisters. Here is my card." He wrote the house number on the back. "This is the number at my restaurant and my house number is on the back."

Michael shook Marcus's hand. "I'll make sure of it. I can't thank you enough for what you did. It had to be hard seeing her for the first time and seeing that she looks just like you. I thought she looked like her mother until I saw you." He gave a nervous laugh. "Nice meeting you both."

We exchanged goodbyes and headed our separate ways. Marcus walked me to my car. He was silent and I didn't have to ask what was on his mind. I just let him have his moment. Plus, I didn't want to push. I was skating on thin ice as it was. He did, however, ask me where I was going. I told him I had to go to work and he smiled.

Driving to work I realized that I may possibly be on the road to marriage again. That made me warm inside. I was elated at the idea. I don't feel as threatened now. I must admit I had acted pretty well with all this. It had been handled properly and the only one that was hurt was my favorite rival Taniesha. I also must admit that I feel for her. If I had lost relationships with my children—and I almost did—I would go stir crazy. I know now I will no longer take the people I love for granted.

Chapter 32
Tracy

I could barely see straight but I noticed the clock and saw that it was 11:30 a.m. I was completely exhausted. I had not been this tired in ages. I think it's from all the excitement of getting married and adjusting. Malcolm and Jerome are finishing up cleaning out Jerome's old apartment. Everything is practically out. He sold a lot of things but some he will store in the attic.

I had to get up sooner or later because Alexis and the girls are throwing me a bridal shower. I had asked Alexis if she was sure she wanted to do this at her house. I told her that it wouldn't be fair if I did not invite Simone. They'd lost their friendship but I hadn't. Alexis said that she was cool and that she was so happy for me that she could overlook the issues she had with Simone. She even called Simone to get her to do some of the work for the shower.

I heard the guys come. They were racing up the steps and burst through the door. "What is wrong with you two?" I screamed.

Malcolm was all out of breath. "He said that he could beat me and I told him that was a joke!"

Jerome put Malcolm in a head lock. "Yeah, but you can't get out of this!"

I couldn't take the noise. "Guys!"

They stopped and looked at me and laughed. Jerome came and lay next to me. "Baby, you OK? You looked a bit strange."

"I'm fine, just tired and all this noise is making me irritated," I said scratching my head.

Malcolm was at the foot of the bed watching us interact. He then stood up. "Mom and Jerome, can I ask you two something?"

"Sure," we said simultaneously.

"I'm glad that you got married. I love it even." He put his hands in his pockets, something he does when he is nervous. "Just wanted to know if I can call Jerome my dad."

I was stunned that he had asked that. I had known that he wanted a father figure but I never thought of him calling another man "Dad."

I sat straight up in the bed and looked at Jerome. I noticed he had tears forming in his eyes. "Well, Malcolm, this is something that you have obviously thought of. I guess you can if it's OK with Jerome."

Jerome came out of his trance. "Well . . . uh . . . Li'l Malc, I would be delighted." He motioned for Malcolm to come between us and we hugged and kissed him. "I just want you to know that being your dad is not always going to be fun and games. When you do well I will praise you and when you act up I will still praise you only after gettin' in yo' butt!"

Malcolm smiled and put his arm around Jerome. "I know, I know. I've wanted you to be my dad for a long time. You are the only man I can talk to. I mean, Auntie Sidney's Marcus talked to me but I need something else, Dad."

I turned on the television and we lay there watching *Soul Train* like a little family. I was touched that Malcolm had expressed his feeling the way he did. I was also touched that Jerome had been moved as well. This was a moment that I wanted to freeze in time. I never wanted this moment to end, even for my bridal shower.

xoxoxoxoxoxo

The shower was turning out great. I got great gifts and a lot of kinky items. It was hilarious! We played games and talked girl talk. The food was excellent. I must have eaten all of the deviled eggs. Something I have never eaten before.

My mother was glowing more than I was; she was so proud. She gave me a sterling silver frame with our names and wedding date on it with a pair of dice engraved on it. She said, "It symbolizes the fact that you got married in Vegas without any of us knowing! But it's all good!" Then she raised her glass and we all raised our glasses. I had ginger ale. I felt a bit sick from the eggs.

I even noticed Simone and Alexis looking somewhat normal around each other. They kept talking in secret and I wanted to be a fly on the wall to know what they were talking about. I asked Sidney, "What's up with that?"

Sidney smiled. "I don't know but I hope they don't act up. Not today!"

"You got that right!"

Sidney sat next to me. "So, Mrs. Williams, how is married life? Forget that, how is the sex?"

"Sidney! Do I look like I will kiss and tell?" I said being coy.

Just then Simone and Alexis walked over. Simone gave me some more ginger ale. "Yes, do tell! We know you turned him out after ten years!"

We laughed like old times. They were right; the sex was exquisite. "How do the kids say it today? 'It's da bomb!'" We went into a frenzy. "That man is a fuckin' stallion!"

"Praise the lord!" hailed Alexis.

Just then there was a pounding and frightful knock on the door. Everyone stopped and wondered what was going on. Alexis went to the door. "Who in the hell is this?"

When she opened the door, there were two fine black cops outside. They said they got a report that the black Nissan Pathfinder outside had been stolen. I knew that was a lie because it was mine. I got up feeling lightheaded. "Officers, the car is mine."

The tallest cop pulled out a pad and checked the license plate number. "No, miss, we have a report that this belongs to a Tracy Singletary."

I got confused. "I'm Tracy Singletary!"

The other cop took out his handcuffs and cuffed me. "No, ma'am, we have you down as Mrs. Williams and we need you to come with me."

I still didn't get it. "Where?"

Right then and there they both ripped off their pants. "To the jailhouse of love!" These fools got me two strippers. Fine as hell though!

They danced around me while I was still handcuffed and rubbed their perfectly sculpted bodies all over me. Then when I was released from their capture, I started smacking their asses. I almost forgot I was the bride. The ladies were laughing and cheering. I looked at Simone and Alexis and they were the culprits. I must admit I enjoyed them too.

They took it *all* off. Simone said she'd purchased the "Where's the Beef?" package. She said, "Girl, after all you waited, you should get ten strippers! One for each year!"

They did a nice and nasty routine giving all the ladies a chance to rub and touch. Not too mention put all their money in their G-strings.

After the two-hour performance, I offered them something to eat and gave them twenty each. They tried to refuse but took the money anyway.

After all was said and done and everyone started leaving, I gave thanks to everyone. I appreciated all their gifts. I sat on the couch and wanted to pass out. Alexis came by me while she was picking up the remainder of the cups lying around. "Are you OK?"

"Yeah, I'm fine. Just a lot for a sistah for one day," I said.

Alexis called the girls over for a conference. "Girls, come here quick!"

"Alexis, please!"

Sidney was eating a piece of fried chicken. "What's up?"

Alexis, always the nurse, said, "She don't look well. I mean, I watched her all day and she looked like she was going to pass out at times." She felt my forehead. "No fever."

Sidney sat on the other side of me. "Could you be pregnant?"

"No! Don't be insane!" I said.

"Well, you could be. You have been married to a stallion for over a month! We won't even go there with you eating the whole plate of deviled eggs!" Simone said. Leave it up to her to say something crass.

"And you don't like egg yolk!" Sidney said siding with her twin.

She could be right. I mean, we never used protection and we've been at it constantly. "Maybe, I guess. I have to get a test."

"Oh, my god! You're having a baby! You created a honeymoon baby!" Sidney said with excitement.

"Let's just give her space and time. Tracy, on your way home get a test and take it. Jerome will be thrilled. You're OK to drive or do you need us to take you?" Alexis said, still being nurse maid.

I got up to get my coat. "I'm fine. I'll stop at the Rite Aid to get a test. I will let you girls know what happens *after* I tell Jerome. Thanks for everything. And, Simone, I know the cops were your idea! I'm gonna get you, girl!"

We hugged and kissed each other and I wanted mention how proud I was about Alexis and Simone but I figured they'd forgotten their differences for now and I did not want to mention it. On the way home I was thinking constantly about being pregnant. I thanked God repeatedly for my recent blessings and a possible new one. I got the test and will see what results my future holds.

Chapter 33

It was Saturday afternoon and Aaron was at his mother's house playing with his son. Aaron enjoyed the times he shared with him. It gave him a break from the chaotic life he chose to lead. His mother, on the other, was not impressed. She kept giving him evil looks and sighing around the house.

Aaron knew that when she behaved that way she had something on her mind. He put Li'l Aaron in the playpen. "OK, shoot! What is it?"

"What's what?" she said. Aaron was the spitting image of his mother, Jezelle. She had gained weight in her age but kept appearances up like a woman should. "Sit down, baby."

Aaron sat down, whining like a little kid, "Here we go. What did I do now, Mother?"

"For starters, you can stop patronizing me! When are you going to settle down? I mean, boy, you are a grown man heading for your forties. A handsome attorney with a child out of wedlock! And you have 'bout twenty women a week!" She was standing over him like he was a little boy.

"Not exactly twenty, Mom," he said jokingly like he was being modest.

"Oh, boy, shut up! You know this child needs a father. He can't have an example of some gigolo daddy! You didn't have an example. Your father quit from day one. I want you to settle down. Live a more respectful life." She sat on the chair next to him.

"Yeah, but, Mommy, I lost the only good woman I had. I will never find another like Alexis."

"And whose fault is that? You slept with her best friend and got her pregnant!" she said scolding him.

"Well, I told her to abort it! She took away my rights! Us men never have a say so. When a woman don't want to have kids she prevents it or gets an abortion! When *we* don't want to have kids we have to deal with it. We have no rights!" he said raising his voice.

She stood up and pointed her fingers in his face. "First of all, you lower your voice in my house! Second, you men lose your rights once those little wiggly things leave your body! That was her body and her choice! I'm not saying that the decision she made was right but it was *her* decision, and yes, you were irresponsible so now you have to live with it! Like it or not!"

She went on to tell him that she was worried that some woman was going to get fed up and give him what he deserves and how she had not raised him to be a womanizer. She asked him, "How would you like it if some man treated me the way you treat women? Or if you had a daughter and she got caught up with someone like you?"

He thought about it and took what she said seriously. He had four women that he was dealing with at this moment. The one lady, Nicole, loved him and had no clue of his cheating ways. He did not love her as much as she loved him, but she was closer than the other ones. If he did want to settle down he would probably choose her. But Aaron had no intentions of being that intimate with a woman. He would rather chew off his right arm and he told his mother so.

He went to hug her. "Momma, don't get yourself so upset. I will when I find the right girl! For now, just relax. I got this under control. I am your pride and joy; would I do anything to hurt you? Besides, if you dated a man that was like me, well, let's just say you won't be dating him long." He kissed her on the cheek. "I have to go. Come here, big boy!" He picked up his son and hugged and kissed him. "You be good for grandma, OK? Take him, Mom, please."

She didn't take the baby. "How are things with you and Elijah? And the law firm?"

"Fine but we don't speak. Only if it is business. I'll talk with him though. I know he didn't plan what went down. I think I'm fine with it. I think."

She grabbed the baby. "Good. You two have been friends all your lives. Don't let a woman come between that. There is nothing like a lifetime of friendship, Aaron. And where are you going? I am not babysitting for you again!"

He was halfway out the door. "I'll be back." He winked and said, "I have a date!" and shut the door.

xoxoxoxoxoxox

Elijah was watching the sports channel when the phone rang. He hoped it was Alexis since he had not heard from her since he left the note. Many times he had wanted to call her but wanted to spare himself from more humiliation. He checked the called ID and saw that it was his mother calling.

Elijah's mother, Carol, was a small and timid-looking woman, but the look was only a front. She was just as feisty as ever. She knew how upset he had been since the separation with Aaron and the separation with Alexis. She called constantly and never took no for an answer when she told him to come for dinner.

"Hello," he said, trying to sound groggy.

"I know you ain't asleep! So cut the crap! Get out of the bed and turn off the sports channel!" she demanded.

"I'm on the couch."

"Whatever! Just get up! Did you take my advice and call Aaron?"

Elijah sighed. "Nope, I forgot."

"Yeah, right! Boy, don't have me come over there and slap you. I don't even care if I have to stand on a chair to do it! You have been friends all your lives. You were born on the same day and his mother and I are the best of friends. We managed to raise two successful boys in this society. We managed to keep you off the streets and out of jail. We got you two through college and becoming two upstanding adults. We have even so far saved you from fitting the description in some police lineup! Now, if we can save you from that, then we can save you from killing one another!"

"I will see him on Monday at the office. And before you start, I didn't call Alexis either," he said sounding annoyed.

That did not stop his mother. "I don't care if you are pissed with me, Elijah Faison. You love her, don't you?"

"Yes," he said.

She continued, "The only reason you are not together is that neither of you are being honest with each other. You are both scared of being hurt again and that is normal, but life is about taking risk sometimes. When it's worth it. Call her even if it doesn't work out. Just establish closure and maintain some sort of friendship. I love you, son, and I want you to be happy. I hate to see you so down."

"I love you too, Mom. I will call her." He switched the phone to the other ear. "What are you doing today?"

"Cleaning up and cooking. Dinner will be ready at five. I expect to see you there," she said with a firm tone.

"I will and thanks for the chat. I needed that," he said. "I love you and you will always be my favorite girl."

"I know. Don't talk to me, call Alexis. Maybe you two can come to dinner," she said.

Elijah hung up the phone and paused for a moment. He dialed Alexis's number and waited until he got the machine. His first instinct was to hang up but he knew she had caller ID. He didn't want to seem like a stalker. So he left a message. "Hey, uh, Alexis, it's me Elijah. It's Saturday afternoon. I wanted to know if we could talk later. I know I left but I need to see you. So if you could get back to me, I'll appreciate it. Thanks."

He was thinking about what he would do if she never returned his phone call. He then fantasized about them talking and patching things up over dinner. Not at his mother's but at a more intimate setting. To take his mind off it he worked out and took a long shower. He could not be late for his mother's dinner.

Chapter 34
Simone

Neil decided to show off his cooking skills and made me dinner. The house was filled with a southern aroma. He made barbeque chicken and ribs on the grill. There was also some corn on the cob and rice. He made a garden salad and chased it all down with some Blackberry Merlot. He remembered it being my favorite drink.

His house was wonderful. It was a bi-level sky-blue house with white awnings. There was a well-manicured lawn with beautiful tulips outside. Inside, the house was all decked out. The color scheme was beige and off-white. The living room set consisted of an over-stuffed sofa and loveseat with a matching chaise lounge. The kitchen was whitewashed oak and the floors were marble. His bedroom was fit for a king. It had a king-sized bed with plenty of pillows and a thirty-six inch TV.

We ate in the dining room with candles and music. It was such a romantic scene. My heart melted every time he spoke or pulled out my chair. Or even when he wiped the French dressing off my mouth. He was a true gentleman. I offered to clean up but he refused, saying, "You are my guest, so let me serve you."

After dinner, we went to the basement where he had a sixty-inch TV with surround sound and a pool table. A real bachelor pad, I thought. We talked and listened to music. The music and the sound of his voice were so soothing.

He told me how glad he was that we met. He said, "This has been the most fun I've had in a while."

"Me too," I said. "Do you play pool well?"

"I'm the shark of pool. I put the P in pool!" he said, bragging. "Why, you got skills?"

"No, not really. I wouldn't mind playing though," I said nervously.

We played and played. He let me win one game. He said he didn't show mercy even to females. I smiled when he wanted a kiss before each shot. All of a sudden he stopped playing. "Simone, what happened with you and your son's father? You only say 'It just did not work out.' What happened?"

I was nervous and I didn't want him to think less of me when I told him the truth. I put down the pool stick. "Aaron and I were lovers only. He was my best friend's fiancé." I put my head down in shame.

He walked toward me and held me. "Is that why you didn't want to tell me?"

Not looking in his eyes, I answered, "Yes. He told her at the altar. I was her maid of honor."

He stood back to see if I was lying. "Yeah right, Simone. This sounds like some Jerry Springer shit!"

"It was at the time. I hurt my best friend terribly. Or should I say, ex-best friend?" I went to sit on the couch. I thought I should just tell it all. "Aaron and I started with just flirting a few months before the wedding. Then one day it moved from harmless flirting to touching and more intimate gestures. We began talking and then one thing led to another. Next thing you know, I fell in love and he continued with his engagement."

He took a deep breath. "Whoa, that's deep. Where is she?"

"She's around. I helped her plan Tracy's bridal shower. And that was only because Tracy told her to tell me. We were civil and even had small talk. Nothing like how it used to be. A couple of months ago we all had a little meeting and we got things off our chests. We even had a fist fight."

"Stop playing! For real?" he said in disbelief.

"Yup. I truly thought what I had with him was love. I have never been in love before so I though that was it. Wanting to spend time with the person all the time, being willing to start a future with that person." My eyes began to fill with tears. "I wanted so much for him, or anyone for that matter, to love me. I have always dealt with men that were either married or had a girlfriend. Sometimes I knew and sometimes I found out later. I had countless nights of booty-calls and never was able to completely enjoy a true relationship."

He was quiet and I knew for sure that he wanted to put me out. Instead he wiped my tears. "Simone, we all make mistakes. Lord knows I did. You sound like you are truly sorry. I think she knows that. Maybe that's why you were able to plan a shower together."

"Maybe," I said trying to sound convinced.

He turned my face to his. "Simone, you are a wonderful woman. A great mother. I saw that in the Chinese restaurant that day. It's always good that you recognize your faults. You are sorry and I hope that you won't continue the same pattern. I hope and pray not just because I love you, but because I want things to grow between us. I see you more than just a booty call. If I didn't, I would have tried to get you in bed already. I never pressed the sex issue with you." He kissed me. "We've been dating for several weeks now and I have not pressed it. I've thought about it but I wanted to wait a bit."

I was shocked that he said the "L" word without reservation. I kissed him back this time with a little more passion. "Thank you. I needed that. I love you too. I'm just a bit hesitant."

"Don't be. I'm here to stay, Simone." We began kissing and caressing.

He guided me down to the couch and continued kissing and caressing me. It was different from what I was accustomed to. He was taking his time and making me feel comfortable. I moaned with ecstasy and joy. I knew what was about to go down and I was ready and willing.

I lifted off his shirt and he unbuttoned mine. Exposing my breasts from my bra, he engulfed them with his mouth. Then he magically removed my pants and his. He lifted himself up to examine my body. "Damn, you're fine!" He came back down to me and removed my panties, diving straight for the middle.

I gave out a loud sigh and tried to control my pleasure but lost complete control. This is definitely "it" right here. He would not stop until I released all I had. He was so good that I returned the favor. Making him call my name and holding my hair tightly. Just when I thought he was going give me what I'd given him, he lifted me up. "Come upstairs."

He guided me upstairs and kissed me along the way. I couldn't wait to lie on that bed. We worked that bed. We covered every inch of it. He made love to my soul, touching and feeling me, making me look into his eyes, asking me if I felt what he felt. I hit the jackpot five times straight! He always got me when I thought he was *coming* for me. He would then sink it in deep, giving me all ten inches and more. I kept checking to see if the condom was still holding up. This man was, as Tracy would put it, a stallion. Damn!

He turned me from side to side and back to front. When he was finally ready to meet me, we hollered like wolves. I couldn't believe what had just gone down. For the first time in my life, I made love. This was something altogether different from what I was used to. I tried to catch my breath. "Neil, oh my god! Am I dreaming?"

I noticed the gloating on his face. "No, my dear, this is reality. You have met your man." He started kissing me. "I make love to the woman I love. I have the feeling you have never made love before."

"Never. Never ever!" I said trying to catch my breath still.

He spooned me and held me tight. I felt safe and relaxed. I know now this is where I wanted to be for the rest of my life. However, I will take my time and not rush things. Haste makes waste; and I don't want to waste my good fortune. Before I drifted off to sleep, I whispered to him, "I thank God to have you in my life." He squeezed me tighter and kissed the back of my neck. "Same here, baby. I love you too. Now, get some rest 'cause I need an hour or two to rejuvenate."

Chapter 35

Despite all the confusion going on between Elijah and Aaron, they were still able to function as business partners. They came to an agreement and hired a secretary with real skills named Renita. They never had to answer the phone and the office was under new management, which made things a little smoother since the businessmen were at odds personally.

Renita and Aaron were discussing the Wilkins case when Elijah walked in. "Good morning, everyone," Elijah said.

"Morning," Renita and Aaron said back.

Elijah walked into his office and called for Renita to see if he had any messages. He hoped that one of them would be from Alexis since she had not called him back. When she said that he had one message and it was from a client anxiously awaiting his settlement check, he was somewhat disappointed.

He was working, barely concentrating on his new case, when Aaron tapped on the door. "Yo, can I talk to you for a second?"

Elijah motioned for him to have a seat. "What's up?"

Aaron took a seat at Elijah's desk, looking at bit uneasy. "I wanted to talk to you about this whole Alexis incident." He crossed his legs and took a deep breath. "I love you like a brother and I don't want that to end. I hate the fact that it's you that Alexis wants. I can tell you that that will take some time for me to swallow but I'm willing to do that if we could reestablish what he had."

Elijah could not believe that this self-absorbed arrogant man was apologizing. "You're kiddin', right?"

"Nope," he said with a weary grin. "I loved Alexis but not the way she deserved. I knew that then and I know that now. I was just too selfish to let go. You know as well as I do that she is incredible."

"I do. Aaron, let me ask you something. Why the sudden change of heart? I mean, we fought like two men who robbed each other. Do you *really* think that you would be cool seeing Alexis and me together?"

Aaron sat there and pictured the two holding hands and making love and possibly getting married, and his stomach turned. But he knew that they both had something genuine and that he was wrong for acting the way he had. "EJ, I can't lie and say that I'm truly happy for you. I am happy for you since you are happy. I would have been overjoyed if it were some other woman. I would have done anything to have to do it all over again with Lex. Since I can't, I will just have to live and learn. You and her have been tight since day one. There were times that I was jealous of that. I knew in my soul that that woman loved me like no other. But being who I am, I threw it all away."

Elijah thought of how innocent his feelings had been toward Alexis, how they had talked and enjoyed each other's conversations. Aaron was always too wrapped up with what he was doing. Whether he had been working late or had gotten his story mixed up and Elijah had had to cover, Alexis and Elijah had had time to talk and Elijah enjoyed their time together. He gave a big sigh. "Oh my god, these women will kill me slowly!"

Aaron was surprised at his out burst, "What's up, Counselor?"

Elijah was reluctant to tell him that he and Alexis were no more. "It's over."

"What? You and Alexis? What happened?" Aaron said, confused but with a grin.

Elijah told him how neither of them had wanted to put their feelings on the table and how it was best for them to go their separate ways. He told Aaron about the note and how she had never responded. He was waiting for a giggle or smart comment from Aaron but he actually seemed sympathetic. Elijah continued to tell him that he missed their brother-hood, how upset he had been when they fought, and how he had taken it out on Alexis and ruined their relationship.

Aaron got up from the chair and walked over to the couch in the office and lay down. "Call her. Tell her what you told me and she will listen. I know her *in and out* and she will listen. She loves you. I saw it in her eyes that night. That was what pissed me off so bad, that she can love another after me! After me, dawg!"

Elijah rolled his eyes. "Man, when are you ever going to change? I mean, we are soon to be forty and you are still chasing girls like we did in high school and college! You better find you someone. Ain't shit out there but AIDS and other STDs along with baby-mama drama."

Aaron rolled his eyes in his head, the way kids do when their parents said things they didn't want to hear. "Yes, Mother. Look, you asked when I would settle down. I guess when I'm fifty years old. It is so many women out here that want to get with a brother. I'm a black man that's a well-established attorney. I drive a phat Benz and have a fly condo. We won't even go there on how a brother looks!" He stood up and posed in the reflection of the mirror on the wall. "I maybe thirty-six but this body still looks twenty-six. Besides, I never go to war without my helmet, bro'!"

With his childish statement, Elijah thanked God that he himself had matured. He had gone through woman after woman in high school and college but he had simmered down as he got older whereas his dear friend had only gotten worse. "I'm glad that you wear the helmet but what would you do if some crazy broad tried to take other things away from you?"

"Like?"

"Seventeen percent of your checking account, your car, and your life. You know women these days like to cut off jimmies! Ask that Bobbit dude!" Elijah said trying not to laugh. "One day that seven-inch cock of yours is gonna cost you more than you could spend! That's all I am saying, Romeo."

Aaron came back to sit in front of Elijah. "Pleeease, man! I got twelve inches! I ain't gettin' no more chicks pregnant. I learned that shit with Simone's ass. If I have to wear three hats! But on the real, I'm hanging tuff with Nicole. She's the coolest chick I date right now. Got it going on in and out of the bedroom. I don't have to worry about her trappin' me and shit. She can't have kids."

"That's what she said, huh?" Elijah said not sounding convinced.

"Yes. But I still wear a condom. Look, loverboy, go get your girl. I meant what I said, I won't stand in your way. Just give me some time to get used to it. A real long time. But we cool, right?"

"Yeah, man, we cool." The two men gave each other pounds and hugged tightly. "I just worry about you, Aaron. Just think about doing the right thing."

Aaron walked toward the door. "Don't worry about me, bro'. I will be around forever. The world will come to an end if I go. Who would these women have to love?" He left the office humming Shabba Ranks's words "Girls, girls every day, from London, Canada, and the USA."

xoxoxoxoxoxox

Elijah felt good that he and Aaron had been able to patch things up. He respected Aaron for coming to him and telling him that he needed more time rather than throwing away their lifelong friendship. He had been working in his office all day trying to get ready for his new case when Renita buzzed in. "Elijah, there is a phone call for you on line two. It's a personal call."

"Thanks. I got it." He prayed that it was Alexis and told himself not to get disappointed if it was not. She could have called two days ago when he left the message. "Hello, Elijah Faison speaking."

"Hey, Elijah, it's me."

"Alexis, hey, what's up?" he said, playing it cool.

She stumbled on her words. "I was returning your phone call. How are you?"

"Fine, and yourself?" He was still trying to play it cool.

"Well, you called me. But I guess I will have to make it seem like I called you first. I want to see you. Is that possible?"

His cool tactics went clean out the window. "You miss me?"

She gave a deep sigh. "Yes. We need to talk."

"You know I love you, girl. I can come over after work. I will be done in about two hours. It's three now." He got nervous; he thought he was being too pushy. "I mean, if that's OK with you."

She gave him that warm giggle. "It's fine. I'll be waiting. Oh, and, Elijah, I love you too. Let's put the shit on the table now before you even come over. There will be no more holding back. We let what we feel flow whether it is good or bad."

He pictured her with her hands on her shapely hips and that made him smile. "OK, boss lady. On the table." He heard a loud noise and voices come from Aaron's office and wanted to see what it was. Trying not to alarm Alexis he said, "Baby, I got to go. I have another call. In two hours, and have no panties on!"

She laughed. "Yeah, right! Bye!"

214

xoxoxoxoxoxo

When Elijah and Renita reached Aaron's office they walked in on Aaron and two women. Aaron was standing behind his desk pleading with Nicole. Nicole was tall and had the purest dark skin, not a blemish on it. The other woman Elijah had never seen before was named Joan. She was short and wore a Halle Berry hair cut. She was sugar brown and had a body that was out of this world. She was no doubt one of Aaron's girls. However, she was not doing all the talking. It was Nicole who was ranting and raving about how she thought she was the only one and how he should have been honest with her.

Apparently, the two women had met after being at the same place at the same time. They were in Lucille Roberts working out when they had gotten on the subject of men while on the treadmill. They had told each other about how they thought that this man was the one. They began to see the similarities in descriptions of *their* man. When they put two and two together, they had remained cordial and kept their composure and immediately left the gym—to get *their* man, that is even after being treated like a piece of dirt. "Aaron, please. You gave me the same sad and tired story you gave her! Don't even try to play me like I ain't shit!"

Elijah tried to control the situation. He went to Nicole and Joan. "Ladies, this is a place of business. I know the two of you are upset but this is not just Aaron's business, it is mine too. Now, at least show me some respect."

Nicole got agitated. Something just did not sit right with her. She looked more mental than upset. She began pacing and shouting off things like, "All my life I was cheated on and mistreated by some damn man! I am tired of it, Aaron! I asked you if you couldn't play games with me! I asked you, mother fucker!"

Aaron's face got beet red. "Look, now, I told you what I was about. You said you could handle it! You know what? This shit is tired. Both of you get out of my office. You don't want me, fine. You came here, you made your point. Now step!" he said pointing his finger to the door.

That was the straw that broke the camel's back for Nicole. She reached into her purse and pulled out a handgun and pointed it at Aaron.

"Oh hell no! It ain't even that kind of party, brother! Sit your ass down and you are going to listen to what I have to say! So sit!"

"Bitch, you are out of your fucking mind!" Aaron yelled and started coming to her.

She cocked it back. "Don't play with me! Go sit your ass down."

Renita and Joan tried to leave the office but got stopped by the firing of the gun. "Get over here." Nicole told them that she wanted them to hear what she had to say to Aaron and that she was not there to hurt anyone. She wanted to get his attention. The kind of attention she had now. When Elijah tried to intervene she quickly told him to "shut the fuck up!"

She paced back and forth, telling Aaron how much she loved him and how she had thought he was serious when he said that he loved her too. She got tearful when she told him that she had wanted to get married and have his child. When he brought up the fact that he thought she could not have kids, she told him she had lied and how she had poked holes in the condoms hoping that she would become pregnant. She also told him that her love for him ran so deep that she had stopped taking her medication for a previous mental disorder.

That blew Aaron away but he played calm to calm her down. "Baby, Nicole, I do love you. I do. You have to believe that. I just have a problem. I was just telling EJ that today and how I wanted to get with you on a deeper level. Right, Elijah?"

Elijah was caught off guard but quickly caught on. "Oh yeah, Nicole, he really cares for you. I told him to just settle down and he agreed. Come on, sis, I know you do not want to go to jail for this fool. He ain't that fine."

"Enough, E," Aaron said, sounding annoyed.

Nicole pointed the gun at Aaron and held it with a firm grip. "Is that true, Aaron? Do you love me?"

He got up slowly and walked toward Nicole. "Yes. You know I do. You are the woman that I want to be with. Look at me, Nicole."

More tears rolled down her dark chocolate even skin . She became less tense with the gun. She told him that she was not there to hurt him and that she had only wanted him to see how hurt she was and how she was tired of playing the fool.

Aaron finally got close to her and went for the gun. "Give me that, you dumb crazy bitch!"

Aaron and Nicole struggled with the gun. Elijah went to the two to break up the struggle. Renita and Joan ran out of the office.

"Aaron, no!"

"Let me go!"

Two shots sounded inside the office.

Shannon N. Davis

Chapter 36
Alexis

I ran through Jersey Shore Medical Center's parking lot from the clinic. I couldn't believe it when Renita called me and told me that there had been a shooting and Aaron and Elijah were on their way to the hospital. She was too upset to tell me the details except that Aaron's girlfriend had gone off. When I got there the ambulance was bringing someone in on a stretcher.

It was Aaron. "Aaron! My god, what happened? Where's Elijah?" I said frantically. He was mumbling something but I couldn't understand him. "I'm right here."

Elijah was coming out of the ambulance. He was obviously not touched. I ran and hugged him and checked his body out. "Thank you, Lord! Baby, what is going on?"

He was numb and talked in riddles. "She was crazy. Aaron's lies caught up with him. I have to call Auntie Zelle."

Just then trauma doctor came out to get information. Elijah told him that Aaron got shot during a struggle between him and his girlfriend. Nicole had been arrested. His mother was the next of kin and Elijah was about to call her. Elijah went to the information desk to call Jezelle.

The doctor asked me, "Are you Alexis?"

"Yes. Is he going to be all right?" I questioned.

"I can't say but we are prepping him for surgery. He wants to see you. Could you follow me?" he said, guiding me to Aaron's cubicle.

He was lying there with IVs and an oxygen tube stuck onto him. A nurse and a resident were working on him and talking between themselves. There was blood on his face and hands. He lay completely still. From the looks of him, I thought he was dead. I called his name, "Aaron, I'm here."

His weak eyes opened immediately. He slowly tried to remove the oxygen mask. "Lex." He cleared his throat. "I want to tell you something..."

I put the mask back on his face. "You can tell me after surgery. Right now just relax." He took the mask back off. "Aaron, please keep this on. Tell me later, OK?"

"No!" He flinched in pain. Just then the surgeon came for his signature on the consent form and they started wheeling him into the operating room.

I followed them while trying to listen what he was so desperately trying to say. "Lex, I love you. I always have. I may not get another chance to say it. I love you, will you ever forgive me?"

I was so caught up with making him relax and being afraid of his condition that I didn't respond. I held his hand while he was being rapidly taken into the elevator. Inside the elevator, he started again, this time choking on the words, "Lex, please! Will you forgive me?"

I could no longer hold back my tears. We reached the fourth floor, and as weak as he was getting, he held on tightly to my hand. "I do. I do forgive you. I love you, Aaron. Now relax!"

Right before he got to the door of the OR, he whispered, "I love you too. Take care of Elijah. He loves you."

I stood there crying, his blood on my uniform. I wanted so badly to hold his hand through the surgery. I felt weak in the knees and I turned to find a chair and saw Elijah standing there. He looked worn and tired. "Come on let's sit down. Did you get in touch with Jezelle?"

"Yeah, she's with my mother in Atlantic City. She's beside herself right now." He leaned forward and put his head in his hands. "He got to pull through."

I rubbed his tense back to comfort him. "He will. That's a strong man in there. Besides, he probably has a date tonight."

We both gave weak laughs. He told me that he had called Sidney and she was going to get in touch with Simone. He felt that she needed to know what was going on. Renita and Joan came off the elevator tearful and confused.

I explained to them that he was in surgery and that we just have to wait for some news. I went back to holding Elijah and we prayed together for a quick recovery for Aaron. Minutes later Sidney and Marcus came to see what was going on.

Sidney quickly ran to my aid. "Alexis, how are you holding up? I called Simone but her cell is off. My mother said she must be with Neil but she was not home to get his number out of her phone book. I just may ride over now."

Marcus came and sat with Elijah. "Sid, I can go over Neil's. You stay here."

"No, I better tell her myself," she told him.

One hour went by. By then Tracy and Jerome had gotten to the hospital. We sat there quietly, scared and hurt. Every time someone in scrubs came out we asked about Aaron and he or she would say, "We're working on him."

Jezelle and Carol came off the elevator. Jezelle was frantic about the news of her son. She begged Elijah to tell her the story again. She questioned every sentence and demanded to talk to a doctor.

An older doctor named Charles Mobley came into the waiting room. "Are you the family for Aaron McKnight?"

"I'm his mother. How is he?" she said.

He blinked and paused. It was the kind of pause you see on the soaps when a revelation is about to be made but a commercial has to break in first. "I'm sorry but we did all we could."

Jezelle and all of us screamed in horror. Elijah and Carol went to hold Jezelle up and get her to a chair. She screamed, "Not my baby! Not my baby! Please Lord, not my baby!" over and over again.

Dr. Mobley had no control over the situation. He tried to explain to Marcus and Jerome the nature of Aaron's injuries. He had been shot twice in the abdomen. The team had been unsuccessful at stopping the internal bleeding. He'd gone into shock and then cardiac arrest. They did revive him once but they were not successful the second time.

The rest of us went to pieces. Tracy, Sidney, and I held each other tightly, crying and shaking with pain. Jerome helped Tracy sit down. Jerome said, "Baby, come on. You're pregnant, just sit."

Elijah and his mother tried to console Jezelle the best way they could. She sobbed like any grieving mother would. "I just told him two days ago to be careful with these women. Two days ago! Aaron! Aaron!"

She broke free and pleaded with the doctor to let her hold her baby one more time. Elijah and Carol went with her, holding her up on both sides. I kissed Elijah and told him to be strong and watched Aaron's family go see him for the last time.

I'm not sure what I am feeling right now but I know it's numbing me from head to toe. I did still love Aaron and I would have given anything to be able to tell him that right now. But he's gone. My two friends and I remained huddled in sorrow while listening to Jezelle and Carol whimper and sob uncontrollably. I can't imagine how Elijah is holding up.

Sidney wiped her face and stood up. "I have to get to my sister. She's the mother of his child. She should know."

Tracy agreed, "We should tell her together. We still do things together, don't we?"

I did not want to face her. I would not know what to say to her. However, in a matter like this, the four of us always got through together. "Well, we might as well do it now."

Elijah came out of the room where Aaron was. From the door being cracked open a bit, I could see Jezelle hovering over Aaron's lifeless body. Elijah obviously could not take that scene anymore and so when he came out he fell to his knees bawling.

We quickly went to him and held him tight. I did nothing but hold him and tell him how sorry I was. How much I loved him so. He held on to me for dear life. My upper body felt crushed but I didn't care. Marcus and Jerome helped us get him to the chair.

"That's my brother! How do I go on without him? How?" he sobbed. Then he looked surprised. "Simone. Has anyone called her yet?"

"No, but we were going to go tell her. Neil lives ten minutes away. But I will stay here with you. You can't deal with Jezelle and Carol by yourself."

"I'm fine. Go tell Simone. She's your friend and you can't tell her that her child's father is dead over the phone." He patted me on the thigh to let me know that it was OK.

I stood up and kissed his forehead. "Girls, let's go."

Chapter 37
Simone

Neil and I ordered pizza. We decided to have a blockbuster night tonight. We were going to watch *Panic Room*. Aaron Jr. had gone to sleep quickly and peacefully for some strange reason this evening. He was lying in the travel playpen we used for him to sleep in when we were over here.

I popped the popcorn and Neil and I tucked ourselves under the covers and cuddled on the couch. I loved this man to death. Ever since we made love we could not get enough of each other. We were always touching and feeling each other and giving each other passionate kisses and holding hands. We were like two love sick teenagers.

We were not even ten minutes into the movie when the doorbell rang. Neil went upstairs to get it and I was perplexed when I saw the girls standing there. They all had puzzled looks on their faces. I got scared.

"Damn, why do y'all look like that?"

Sidney came to me on the couch and kneeled down on both knees. "Monie, we have some bad news."

Neil came to my side and held me. I asked, "What? Is it Mom?"

She turned to Tracy and Alexis whose faces were drenched with tears. "No, Mom's fine. It's Aaron . . ."

"What about him?" I jumped in anxiously.

"He's . . . he died tonight," She said and she began to cry on my knee.

I couldn't believe what she'd just said. I sat there motionless because I just could not believe it. I saw Tracy and Alexis holding each other and crying terribly. Neil put his hand on my back and kissed my forehead. I couldn't accept this. "Siddy, stop it! This is not funny! How did this happen?" My stomach felt raw when she looked in my eyes.

Tracy blurted out, "He was shot twice in the stomach. They were unable to save him."

I felt like I had literally jumped out of my skin. "Oh my god, no! No! No! Aaron, oh my god. Aaron!" I screamed.

Neil held me tight up against the wall. "Baby, I'm so sorry. Please try and calm down for the baby's sake."

That's when it really got to me. My son does not have a father anymore. He is way too young to even remember him. Even though the way Aaron and I had gotten together was wrong, I still loved him. We had created his son together. Now Li'l Aaron is without a father. I fell to the floor and the girls came to me and we huddled on the floor together crying. Neil went upstairs and picked up some tissues from upstairs to try and do what he could.

Alexis told me that two of Aaron's girlfriends came to the office and busted him. Nicole had only been there to scare him but she had mental problems and had not been on her medications. Alexis said there'd been a struggle and the gun went off, two bullets hitting him in the stomach. I was just in shock and wanted to crawl in a hole.

We were finally able to pull ourselves together. Alexis's cell phone rang and Elijah told her to meet him at Jezelle's house. Carol was staying the night with Jezelle and he needed to drive his mother's car there and he and Alexis could ride back together.

I decided to stay here with my son. Though he was sleep, I needed his presence in the worst way. The girls left and I just lay still on the sofa. Neil gave me a cold cloth for my head. He was sweet and kind and very attentive, but speechless.

I held his hand tightly while I cried. "Neil, what am I going to do with our son?"

He positioned himself over me. "Right now you have to absorb everything. The father of your child is gone. You have to get it together for your son's sake. He will be able to pick up on your tensions."

"I know. Thank you for being here for me," I said rubbing his thigh.

He kissed my lips softly once. "You still don't understand, do you? I have nothing but love for you. I feel completely helpless right now. There is nothing that I can do to ease your pain. So let me just pamper you. I'm here for you."

I popped up quickly like a volt had gone through my body. "I need to hold my son." I leaped off the couch and ran up the stairs. "I have to hold him. I have to feel his heart against mine."

I walked in and watched him sleeping so soundly. I noticed that it had been easy to get him to sleep and that for once he was not tossing and turning or whining. I figured Aaron's spirit was comforting him tonight. I picked up his angelic body and held it tight. I lay on the guest bed and held him tight, trying not to wake him with my tears. Neil came into the room and lay behind me and held us both. It truly comforted me that for once I was not alone.

The man I once loved is gone. There had been no goodbyes or last-minute fight. I would have even taken that. I had gotten nothing. I have not seen him since he tried to attack me. I made it so that he would get the baby from his mother's house and I never saw him, not even to get child support. I told him to leave it with Jezelle. I couldn't imagine with what that woman is going through. I think there is no pain greater than that of losing a child. With that thought, I held Li'l Aaron tighter and Neil sensed my fear and held me tighter.

Shannon N. Davis

Chapter 38
Alexis

Aaron's funeral went just the way it sounded, "Aaron's funeral." Elijah recalled a conversation they'd once had about death and dying. Aaron had wanted an all-out extravaganza. The church was filled with floral arrangements from friends, family, clients, and lovers. There were so many women there crying and consoling one another, I was not sure if it was Aaron's funeral or Elvis's. I couldn't believe all the women that loved this man, myself and Simone included.

Reverend Allen Beverly gave an explosive eulogy. He spoke on the little boy named Aaron and how happy he was that he had turned out to be a successful man with a charismatic smile and a charming wit. The reverend smiled when he took notice of all the grieving women in the room. "I mean, just look at this room. His charm touched every one of us in some way or form. But a higher power needed his charm even more."

Elijah was adamant on speaking on his friend's behalf. He was torn but strong enough for handling such a task. Ever since Aaron's death Elijah had made sure that Jezelle, Aaron Jr., and the rest of us were taken care of, never really giving himself time to grieve. It was not until the night before the funeral that he broke down with me and let out his anger, frustrations, and sadness. He had screamed and yelled and thrown things across the room. He made himself crazy thinking that he should have done something more to control the situation and that he should have taken the gun from Nichole because he'd known Aaron would go about it all wrong because of his temper. I informed him that there was nothing he could have done. If he had gotten any deeper in it, there was a good chance that both of them would have died.

Elijah went to the podium and looked down on his lifelong friend. He was silent, trying to get himself together and find his voice. He started to talk, but cried instead. When he got it together, he spoke, "Everyone in this room knows that me and Aaron go way back to the hospital of our birth. We would always joke and call ourselves the 'friendly twins.' And to me that is what he was, my brother. And we may not have shared the same womb but we shared something some brothers and sisters don't nowadays. Aaron was a good man to the people that he loved: his mother, my mother, his son, and myself. Not to mention all the *women* that he loved." Everyone laughed a little and looked around the room.

"I have nothing but good things to say about a brother who went entirely too soon. We grew up together, partied, made careers, and kept our biggest secrets. We had each other's back. That's what brothers do. To see this man lying here and not telling me what a corn ball I've become or about his latest date, is unreal to me. There have been times when I wanted to smack him but this is the time when I really want to smack him and say, 'Get up fool and get your shit together.' But as usual he won't listen." He laughed at his on joke.

"I just want to express to my Auntie Zelle that I loved him dearly. There is not a day that won't go by that I won't think of him." Jezelle whimpered loudly while being consoled by Carol. Elijah's eyes filled with tears. "On his last day, he told me that he had to be around because he had places go and things to do. And that is a statement that constantly replays in my mind. I guess his thing to do now is watch over us. When I held him in my arms before the paramedics arrived, he told me to 'take care of my mother and son.' That he loved me and always has and that he was glad that we squashed our latest disagreement. I think he knew where he was going. He knew his time was up and he had things to get off his chest. Telling him to hold on was all I could do. I have never felt so powerless in my life."

He looked up to the high ceilings and continued, "My life will never be the same without him. I lost a friend, a business partner, and a brother. Thirty-six years is a long time to share with someone. There is nothing in the world like a friendship like that. Speaking to you right now, I feel like I gained some power. I have the power now to carry out my promise and take care of his mother and son. And that is what I intend to do. I mean, look at this John Gotti funeral I've arranged! I know that punk is proud wherever he is with his harem." We all laughed to break that emotional silence he'd brought to the room.

"I want to end this by saying that sometimes in life we make choices and the choice Nicole made affected us all. She took away someone that was dear to other people. Not just her. She claimed to love him but how could she when she took his life. When people react in such a violent matter, thinking that this is the only way out, it does more harm than good. Guns aren't justice. They are game pieces in the game called coward. Deep in my heart I know she didn't want to take him away because when they struggled she screamed to him to stop because her finger was caught on the trigger. I knew she was sorry when she cried over his body. But I don't forgive a person who carries a gun. You never know what could happen.

Aaron was not in this world alone. He was a son, a father, and a friend. He went to paradise and we are stuck in this hell trying to figure out how to move on." He looked down on Aaron's still body and walked to him. "Yo, man, I got your back as always. You will truly be missed and will never be forgotten. I love you. Goodbye." He leaned over and kissed his friendly twin for the last time.

Jezelle ran to the casket crying over her only child's body, holding on to Aaron for dear life, pleading to God to take her instead. I held on to my mother and father tightly. My heart went out to Jezelle. There could be no greater pain. I admired Elijah for his strength and character. He held Jezelle as tightly as he could to console her and somehow it worked. There was not a dry eye in the house. Li'l Aaron's cries rang throughout the church while Simone tried to hold him and control herself.

I hated what they did to me but I had realized a long time ago that she must have really loved him to do what she had done. I don't forgive her and I would never forget but I sympathized because I had loved him too. She has a child to raise without him. I guess now she would take it easy on Tracy when she brings up how she had felt when her husband died and she was left with a child to raise. I thought that we just never know what life has in store for us.

After the funeral we gathered at Jezelle's. The church and neighbors prepared food and we were able to get our emotions together after such a moving service. I couldn't help but pull Jezelle aside and say, "Jezelle, I want you to know how sorry I am. I don't know how to express it. I've always been fond of you."

She hugged me tightly and fought back the tears. "Alexis, my son loved you. I never saw him love any other women like he did you. He never brought anyone around except you. I just wish . . ." She began crying. "I just wish he could have treated you better. I know he was capable of it. He had to be, he loved me to death."

I let her cry on my shoulder but she broke free after a while. "No more tears, we have guests." She gave me a faint smile. "Thank you, dear." She went off into the crowd, refilling glasses and making sure everyone's plate was full.

I saw Sidney, Simone, and Tracy in the hallway and I walked over. "Hey, what's up?" Simone's face was drenched with tears.

Tracy turned to me. "Just trying to help her out. Li'l Aaron is with Nickia. She just has to get herself together."

We went into Aaron's old room. His mother had kept it the way it was since he left for college. When he came home he never changed his room. There were posters of Run-DMC, Vanity-6, and a whole lot of *Jet's* beauties of the week on the wall. His trophies from high school and college were displayed. There was even a picture of him and me when we went to Coney Island and had gone to a booth to get a picture of our first date taken. I don't even know where my copy is but it brought back such fond memories of how I felt for him on that first date.

Sidney wiped her sister's face. "Girl, you have to get it together. You have a child to raise. Aaron's too young to really know what's going on but he can sense that you are stressed. That's why he can't calm down today."

"I know," she sobbed. She stood up and faced the window, watching people in the backyard talking and laughing. "Alexis, I'm glad you got to see him last."

I was puzzled. "Why?"

She turned to me. "Because he loved you. He always told me that."

"This is not the time, Simone," I said trying to avoid this.

"I blew our friendship. Even though he's dead now, if I had to do it all over again, I wouldn't." She wiped her face. "I mean, I wouldn't have hurt you the way that I did. I wouldn't have fallen in love with him. All of it, I wouldn't have done it. I know we went through this before but do you think you could try and forgive me too?"

I truthfully didn't know how to answer that. My eyes swelled up with tears. "Simone, that's a lot to ask. That damaged me."

"But you forgave Aaron," she said.

"He was going to surgery after being shot! I wanted him to calm down. That's not fair to say, Simone," I said, recalling that night.

"Then you lied to him?"

"No!"

"So you forgive him then?"

I held my head down with grief. "Yes, I did. Simone, what happened between us shouldn't have happened from the start. Granted you are sorry, I see that, but what we had could never be the same. Just because I forgave Aaron on his death bed doesn't mean we would have gotten back together if he hadn't died."

She came to me and hugged me tight. "Lexi, I am sorry and if we can't be friends at least we can remain cordial like we have been. After all, you are dating my son's godfather. I love you dearly and I know you are hurting too. I can only ask you to think about what I said."

I let her go and looked at her sorrow-filled eyes. I missed her too and I never denied that. I just can't get pass the hurt. I reached out for the other two girls and we gave each other our usual girl hug, "I love you all. Simone, let me chew on that for a minute, OK?"

We gained composure and walked into the festivities. I sat with Elijah and we talked and ate. Tracy and Jerome were across us. He was being very attentive, making sure she and the baby were fine. Sidney and Marcus looked as perfect together as they always did, gazing at each other, giving little touches of affection. What moved me more was when Neil came to the door. He felt he shouldn't attend the services so he'd come to Jezelle's house with a pan of barbequed chicken and a sympathy card for Simone and Jezelle. Simone's whole demeanor changed when he entered the room. I have never seen her glow so much. I was glad that my friend had finally found the love that she deserves and so desperately desired.

Shannon N. Davis

Epilogue
(Eighteen months later)

It's been over a year since Aaron's death. A lot of things have changed in all of our lives. But for starters, Nutty Nicole was charged with manslaughter with Elijah testifying that she had not been there to kill but to make Aaron see her point. He also mentioned how she tried to the struggle before the gun went off. She was sentenced to five years in a psychiatric facility. She is currently being treated for bipolar disorder and schizophrenia.

It's Thanksgiving Day and Elijah and I decided to have dinner at our house. He has moved in and we wanted to celebrate our wedding with family and friends only. We got married yesterday at the justice of the peace. I didn't want a big wedding and neither did he. Plus, we wanted to get married before the baby came. Yes, I'm eight and a half months pregnant! It's a little girl and I decided to name her Dorothy Corrine after my mother and favorite Aunt Connie who passed away a few years ago. I'm big as a house and I keep feeling little kicks like the baby wants to come out. She's due December 14, on my father's birthday.

Everyone came for Thanksgiving dinner and a wedding reception—my parents and friends and their families. I decorated the house with a mixture of fall arrangements and wedding flowers. Instead of pumpkin pie, we had pumpkin-flavored wedding cake. It was actually good. Sidney made it for me since she is now the official owner of her own catering business.

She finished culinary school at the top of her class. She became one with the kitchen. She and Marcus have gone through counseling and have made it through their problems. Marcus has established a relationship with his newfound daughter. Robin and Michael came to dinner with us. Robin and Nickia have become the best of friends, and most of all, sisters. Sidney has gotten used to the idea and has become close to Robin. Taniesha never interfered with Robin's relationship with her new family. Marcus supported Sidney with the business venture, and her business, "Simply Sid's," was taking off. She'd named it after herself since she'd put her mind to it and loved what she'd done. She and Marcus had gone on their first honeymoon to Hawaii for ten days. They have been married for twenty years and had wanted to renew their vows in Hawaii. Just them and the kids.

Tracy and Jerome are the proud parents of twins, a boy named Justin and a girl named Janelle. They are a year old now and as cute as ever. Janelle looks like Jerome and Justin looks like Tracy. Malcolm Jr. is growing up to be a little man. He adores his new life and family. With Jerome's help, he has become the starter for his high school varsity basketball team. He took the team to the state championship. He tells everyone that he is the next Michael Jordan. Since Tracy had spent the last trimester on strict bed rest, Jerome kept busy with the advertising firm, traveling back and forth to Las Vegas. They managed to earn almost half a million dollars with their new account. They were happy and truly blessed for everything they worked hard for.

Simone and Neil are married now. They now have a daughter named Zarah Princess James who is one month old. She looks like a seven-pound Simone. She is gorgeous. Simone and Neil got married four months after Aaron's death. She had a small wedding at their house and went to Cancun for two weeks. Jezelle kept Li'l Aaron who is just as handsome as his father was. He'll be three but he looks four, maybe five. He is definitely his father's son. Neil offered to adopt him but Simone refused, saying that she didn't want to take his father completely away from him. She wanted Neil to be a father for him just the way he was. She invited me to the wedding and I did show up. I felt like I should put away some of the anger I'd had for her. Life is too short. Simone was the happiest I have ever seen her.

Our friendship never got back to what it used to be but we do call each other from time to time. We are in the same circle of friends and it is hard for us to not have some sort of relationship. Besides, Elijah picks Li'l Aaron up on weekends and keeps him overnight. There was no way to get away from her. Then we were pregnant partly together. Our daughters will probably end up being friends.

Jezelle attended with Carol and she even helped cooked the food. She'd said that I would go into labor with all that running around and cooking. Because I was so big, she and everyone else questioned the doctor's estimated delivery date. She coped with Aaron's death well. She believes that "God made sure that Aaron Jr. was born because the writing was already on the wall. God knew that I would go completely insane if it were not for that little boy. But for the life of me, I will never understand why it happened the way that it had. But no one can question God."

We sat around my huge dining room table that seated twelve. We made tables for the children and stood around the table for what we were all thankful for. Elijah started off by saying, "I'm grateful to have a beautiful wife and a daughter on the way." He rubbed my belly. "May she be just as beautiful as her mother." Carol cleared her throat jokingly. "And my mother," he added swiftly.

He prayed for the table, giving thanks to all our blessings of marriage, children, and families, and that the closeness of our friendship was a true blessing. "There is nothing like friends and true friendships." We said, "Amen" in unison, and dug in.

After eating, talking, and laughing and just enjoying each other's company, I felt that kick again. This time it lasted a while. I knew this was it. I tapped Elijah, who was eating his third sitting, on the leg. "Baby, I think we have another guest coming for dinner!" I squeezed his leg with all my strength. "Aw!" He dropped his forked and panicked, running around trying to get his coat and my bag.

My mother and father came to my aid. The girls screamed for joy and tried to control the situation. My main focus was on this pain. I was whisked off to the hospital. My dad drove with my mom in the front and Elijah and I were in the back, practicing Lamaze breathing. That shit did not work! He was comforting but nervous. The girls, Carol, and Jezelle followed in one car. They left the men there with the kids.

I was spared and had five hours of grueling labor. I was able to push out a six-pound-nine-ounce girl. She was beautiful! Dorothy Corrine Faison was born on Thanksgiving Day. So much for Elijah's dream of her looking like me because she looked just like him just a bit wrinkled.

Elijah, the proud dad, kissed and hugged me and held his little girl, shedding tears of joy. His mother was happy to have her first grandchild and was making plans for spoiling her. She was no doubt ready for it. My parents had their plans ready also for their first grandchild's spoiling as well. We were in trouble. Elijah took his mother and Jezelle home and my parents left. I was pooped.

Right when the nurse took the baby to the nursery, my door opened again. It was my girls. They were happy for me and came and sat on the bed. "I thought you guys went home."

Tracy rubbed my leg. "Naw, we gave you and Elijah time to get acquainted with Miss Thanksgiving."

"I know . . . she had too much to eat I guess," I said with a smile.

Sidney came and sat close to me. "Look, you girls are too damn old to be having babies. You see mine are grown! Almost ready to leave the house." She reviewed the pictures from her digital camera. "But seriously, Lex, she is out of this world. I'm so proud of you. Look at her!"

As I reached to hug her, I said, "Thanks, girlfriend."

Simone stood up from the foot of the bed. "So when's the other coming? Sidney, Tracy and I have two or more. You must keep up the trend!"

"When you do! This is it for me. My body can't handle this again!" I said laughing. "Shoot, I will be forty in a few years and so will the rest of you!"

We sat there talking about how our lives have changed since the beginning of this four-woman group. I loved my life with them in it. I couldn't even picture life without them. We did our usual huddle-and-cry-tears-of-joy when one someone had a baby or major event. The power of friendship is truly amazing. I agree with Elijah, there is nothing like friends—true friends.

The End